EVERYMAN, I will go with thee,

and be thy guide,

In thy most need to go by thy side

LAURENCE STERNE

Born at Clonmel in 1713. Was ordained and
became prebendary of York in 1741. Welcomed
into London society, and received perpetual
curacy of Coxwold, 1760. Travelled on the
Continent for much of the next six years and
died in London on 18th March 1768.

LAURENCE STERNE

A Sentimental Journey
The Journal to Eliza

INTRODUCTION BY
DANIEL GEORGE

DENT: LONDON
EVERYMAN'S LIBRARY
DUTTON: NEW YORK

© Introduction, J. M. Dent & Sons Ltd, 1960
All rights reserved
Made in Great Britain
at the
Aldine Press · Letchworth · Herts
for
J. M. DENT & SONS LTD
Aldine House · Bedford Street · London
First included in Everyman's Library 1927
Last reprinted 1969

NO. 796

SBN: 460 00796 3

INTRODUCTION

READERS for whom *Tristram Shandy* has proved too much, or those who have been put off Sterne altogether by the excess of praise and censure that has accreted round his reputation, need have no misgivings about *A Sentimental Journey*—his 'Work of Redemption,' as he called it. The phrase is reported by his friend and indulgent critic, Richard Griffith, who having heard Sterne read half of it, noted in his diary: 'It has all the humour and address of the best parts of *Tristram*, and is quite free from the grossness of the worst.'

Its full title, *A Sentimental Journey through France and Italy*, is to this extent misleading: Italy remains unvisited. Whether or not Sterne intended to write any more than the first two volumes we shall never know; in any event he did not live to do so. On 3rd December 1767 he had written to Sir George Macartney: 'I am going to ly-in; being at Christmas at my full reckoning—and unless what I shall bring forth is *press'd* to death by these devils of printers, I shall have the honour of presenting to you *a couple of as clean brats* as ever chaste brain conceiv'd—they are frolicksome too, *mais cela n'empêche pas*.' February 26th, 1768, was publication day of the two volumes. Sterne died on 18th March following. He had been ill all the time he was writing the *Journey*, and had had numerous worries and distractions to contend with.

All the more surprising, then, that it should be by common assent what Saintsbury declared it to be—its

author's 'best work of art, and a singularly successful
and complete work of art in itself.' We may regret that
we were denied Yorick's adventures in Italy; we are also
free to doubt whether at a longer stretch he could have
maintained this new lightness and felicity of touch.
Whatever he may have meant when he called it his
Work of Redemption, it is certainly free from grossness,
though not from impropriety. Remove what it would be
harsh, if just, to call its *double entendre* and suggestiveness,
and half its gaiety would be gone. Not, of course, that
it is ever shocking—at least to readers in this unshock-
able age. More's the pity perhaps, for we have been
shocked into insensitiveness. So accustomed to being
told everything—but everything!—in the crudest terms,
we are losing our faculty for enjoying a *risqué* joke.
There are readers today who have failed to see the point
in the opening of *Tristram Shandy*. They echo, 'Pray
what was your father saying?'

In Sterne's day *A Sentimental Journey* was probably
greater fun than we find it. Where readers then snig-
gered or blushed, we smile faintly and rather at the
subtlety than the sense. As for the sentiment, it moves
us not. We cannot weep over a dead donkey. Our
pleasure is in Sterne's now disciplined waywardness, the
spontaneity of his style, his quick cinematographic
transitions, and his gay tenderness. 'They order, said
I, these things better in France,' he begins: 'these
things' might be made to include the way to tell a
picaresque story and deal with embarrassing situations
—*gauloiserie* at its best. He had had his models, of
course, from Rabelais to Beroalde. Now footloose—or
pretending to be—in France, he can perfect his own
manner without ceasing to be 'in character,' the phil-
andering sentimentalist.

He makes use of actual experience, sometimes of the

experience of others. It was from 'Fish' Craufurd that we got the story which, suitably embellished, he uses as his final curtain, 'The Case of Delicacy.' Nor is he above introducing characters from *Tristram Shandy*—Maria of Moulins (an Ophelia we can well do without) has to be met again for tears to be shed in copious measure. If its earliest readers ever responded to the exhortation to join in the weeping, there could hardly have been a dry leaf in the book. The interest of this encounter is now confined to the fact that it is here we come upon 'God tempers the wind to the shorn lamb,' Sterne's inspired rendering of Maria's French proverb, *A brebis tondue Dieu mesure le vent*. If we also pause, irrelevantly, to consider how popular in English fiction mad and ruined maidens have always been, are we then completely unmoved? Possibly we should have succumbed to the attack upon our sensibilities if Sterne had spared us his reply: 'Shorn indeed! and to the quick, said I; and wast thou in my own land, where I have a cottage, I would take thee to it and shelter thee. . . . When the sun went down I would say my prayers; and when I had done thou shouldst play thy evening song upon thy pipe. . . . Nature melted within me, as I utter'd this; and Maria observing, as I took out my handkerchief, that it was steep'd too much already to be of use, would needs go wash it in the stream. And where will you dry it, Maria? said I. I'll dry it in my bosom, said she; 'twill do me good.' It does *us* no good. Having been forced to harden our hearts and sharpen our wits, we cannot rejoice with Sterne in 'dear sensibility! source inexhausted of all that's precious in our joys, or costly in our sorrows!'

But it is only too easy to yield to the temptation to deride his 'sensibility' as so many before us have done. It was for his bawdiness—so unseemly in a man of his profession—that contemporary critics attacked him.

He had his defenders. There were also those who, like
Horace Walpole, found him boring. Since then not only
has he been more written about than read, there has been
more written about him than he himself wrote about
anything. The little here added to it is more or less for
beginners.

What manner of man he was—or rather would have
liked to be—is seen nowhere better than in *A Sentimental
Journey*. Its design, so he told his friend Mrs James,
was 'to teach us to love the world and our fellow-creatures
better than we do.' To be sure, it inculcates no evil—
unless we scent an example of hypocrisy in such a passage
as: 'I have something within me which cannot bear the
shock of the least indecent insinuation: in the sportability
of chit-chat I have often endeavoured to conquer it, and
with infinite pain have hazarded a thousand things to a
dozen of the sex together—the least of which I could not
venture to a single one to gain heaven.' This because
Monsieur le Count de B—— had said (gaily) 'you are not
come to spy the nakedness of the land—I believe you—
ni encore, I dare say *that* of our women . . .' But *hypocrisy*: is that too strong a word? His letters and the
company he kept bear witness that his 'insinuations'
were not free of improper guile. A verbal libertine, he
wrote with his dress unadjusted, and it would be hypo-
critical to pretend, in words attributed to Queen Victoria,
that 'we are not amused' by his antics. He himself
claimed 'innocence' for them, if we are to credit the
anecdote which Sir Walter Scott had 'from a sure source.'
It appears that 'a Yorkshire lady of fortune and condition' told Sterne she had been informed that *Tristram*
was 'not proper for female perusal.' To this he replied:
'My dear good lady . . . the book is like your young heir
there [pointing to a child of three years old, who was
rolling on the carpet in his white tunics], he shows at

times a good deal of what is usually concealed, but it is all in perfect innocence!'

To dwell too long upon this aspect of Sterne or to suggest that his writings are in perpetual oscillation between mild obscenity and damp sensibility is to do him a stupid injustice while offering little enticement to the prospective reader of *A Sentimental Journey*. It is, all said and done and all allowances made, a delightful book, recapturing and conveying with sunny good humour a holiday mood we all can share. At Calais the brief anatomy (*à la* his beloved Burton) of travellers and travelling leads naturally to a lady, Madame de L——(beautiful and from Brussels) and the possibility of accompanying her in a carriage for two as far as Amiens. Their one-sided conversation is of love. French spontaneous and precipitate gallantry is deprecated. 'Consider then, Madame, continued I, laying my hand upon hers——' What she is asked to consider prompts her to remark, blushing: 'Then I solemnly declare you have been making love to me all this while.' She suffers the Sentimental Traveller to kiss her hand twice, and they part, never to meet again, though, after a comic mischance, they exchange letters in Amiens.

Meanwhile at Montreuil he had engaged a servant, La Fleur, who said he could do nothing but beat a drum and play a march or two upon the fife. 'But you can do something else, La Fleur? said I. *O qu'oui!* he could make Spatterdashes, and play a little upon the fiddle. Bravo! said Wisdom. Why I play a bass myself, said I; we shall do very well.' When they left the inn at Montreuil, '*C'est un garçon de bonne fortune*, said the landlord, pointing through the window to half a dozen wenches who had surrounded La Fleur, and were most kindly taking their leave of him . . .' La Fleur, continued the landlord, 'has but one misfortune in the world

. . . he is always in love.' There could not have been a
warmer testimonial. 'I am heartily glad of it, said I.'

Master and man were to have their amorous adventures
in Paris, the master's inconclusive—or so he would have
us half believe and half doubt. His affairs with the
handsome *grisette* who sold him two pairs of gloves and
with the *fille de chambre* who called upon him at his hotel,
were as virtuous, or otherwise, as we like to make them.
So also with the Piedmontese ('about thirty, with a glow
of health in her cheeks') and her maid, a Lyonoise ('of
twenty, and as brisk and lively a French girl as ever
moved')—what, if anything, happened we are left to
imagine, the episode and the book itself closing with the
words: 'So that when I stretch'd out my hand, I caught
hold of the Fille de Chambre's——'

Fiction, no doubt, most of it, but concocted on a basis
of fact, the interludes of seriousness as distinct from
sentimentality drawn from recollections of his earlier
travels in France, the whole worked over with great care
and nicely calculated to please his large and faithful
public, as indeed it did. That he himself was pleased
with it we may well believe. It continued the projection
of his ideal self. In practice he was probably true to
type as *séducteur jusqu'au bord du lit*. Had all the
women to whom he made epistolary love taken him
seriously he would have fled. As for forthcoming women
who needed no encouragement, he might himself have
written an entertaining Shandean chapter upon them.
But with all his weaknesses as a man and writer, 'we
could not,' as Saintsbury agreeably put it, 'at any price
that could be easily formulated or paid, spare Sterne
from English *literature*.'

The shortcomings of his personal character are em-
phasized by *A Sentimental Journey* because of its connection with *The Journal to Eliza* which follows it in this

edition. On the very first page of the *Journey* Eliza's
name appears in a forced reference to 'the little picture
which I have so long worn, and so often told thee, Eliza,
I would carry with me into my grave. . . .' To the
mystification of readers who were not the author's close
friends and therefore in the know, Eliza is apt to pop up
anywhere. When Madame de L—— has disappointed
him by postponing the telling of her story ('to see her
weep! and though I cannot dry up the fountain of her
tears, what an exquisite sensation is there still left, in
wiping them away from off the cheeks of the first and
fairest of women . . . !') until they meet, if ever, in
Brussels, he reflects: 'It had ever, as I told the reader,
been one of the singular blessings of my life, to be almost
every hour of it miserably in love with some one; and my
last flame happening to be blown out by a whiff of
jealousy on the sudden turn of a corner I had lighted it
up afresh at the pure taper of Eliza. . . .' He continues:
'Eternal fountain of happiness! said I, kneeling down
upon the ground, be thou my witness, and every pure
spirit which tastes it, be my witness also, That I would
not travel to Brussels, unless Eliza went along with me,
did the road lead me towards heaven.' She appears, too,
when he is weeping over Maria of Moulines: '. . . could
the traces be ever worn out of her brain, and those of
Eliza out of mine, she should *not only eat of my bread and
drink of my own cup*, but Maria should lie in my bosom,
and be unto me as a daughter.'

Concurrently he was writing in the *Journal*: 'I have
brought your name *Eliza*! and Picture into my work,
where they will remain when you and I are at rest for
ever. Some Annotator or explainer of my works in this
place will take occasion, to speak of the Friendship which
subsisted so long and faithfully betwixt Yorick and the
Lady he speaks of.' So far the prophecy holds good.

It fails when we come to: 'They were married, and retiring to one of his Livings in Yorkshire, where was a most romantic Situation, they lived and died happily, and are spoken of with honour in the parish to this day.'

Who was Eliza? Much is known of her now—more than Sterne could ever have known. She was his last and greatest love, perhaps. Perhaps only the last object of his affectations. Perhaps his final solace, providing the daydream in which he could escape from his wife. The marriage had not been a successful partnership. Intellectually he had outgrown his wife and outlived his love for her. However innocent his flirtations with other women, she could hardly be expected to approve of them. She was jealous and mercenary—not entirely on her own account: there was her daughter Lydia to consider. At the time when Sterne was writing *A Sentimental Journey* she was more than usually troublesome in her demands. And it was at this point that he met Eliza Draper, she then twenty-three, he older by thirty years. Born in India and sent to school in England, she returned to Bombay and when little over fourteen years of age married a man of thirty-four by whom she had a son and daughter. The family came to England in 1765 for the children's education: her husband, Daniel Draper, an official of the East India Company, returned to Bombay, leaving Eliza behind until April 1767. Sterne met her in Soho at the house of a retired Indian commodore, William James. Their acquaintanceship cannot have extended over more than three months.

She had special attractions for him—youth, for one thing, and vivacity combined with a pretty face and an elegant figure. Her friends, she says, called her the *Belle Indian*. Sterne himself, in a letter, told her: 'You are not handsome, Eliza, nor is yours a face that will please the tenth part of your beholders, but are something more; for I scruple not to tell you, I never saw so intelligent, so animated, so good a countenance. . . . A something in your eyes and voice, you possess in a degree more persuasive than any woman I ever saw, read, or heard of. But it is that bewitching sort of nameless excellence, that men of nice sensibility alone can be touched with.'

As a man of nice sensibility he could write: 'My wife cannot live long . . . and I know not a woman I should like so well for her substitute as yourself. 'Tis true, I am ninety-five in constitution, and you but twenty-five; rather too great a disparity this! but what I want in youth, I will make up in wit and good humour. . . ! This was after Eliza had sailed, called home by her husband. It was a safe proposal to make. Since they had parted he had kept a journal for her. The first instalments are lost; the second (covering the period 13th April to 4th August 1767) he left to be discovered by chance in 1851. It is a strange document, written while Sterne, although ill, was engaged on *A Sentimental Journey*. It is the work of a man not himself yet trying to be: 'I have just been eating my Chicking, sitting over my repast upon it, with Tears—a bitter Sause, Eliza! but I could eat it with no other. When Molly spread the Table Cloath, my heart fainted within me: one solitary plate, one knife, one fork, one Glass! O Eliza! 'twas painfully distressing. I gave a thousand pensive penetrating Looks at the Arm chair thou hast so often graced on these quiet, sentimental Repasts and sighed and laid down my knife and fork, and took out my handkerchief, clap'd it across my face and wept like a child.'

Was Sterne sincere when he wrote this mush? It is almost word for word what he wrote to his wife more than thirty years earlier. Passages from many other letters have also been transferred to the *Journal*. Excuses have been found for him. It has even been suggested that when his daughter prepared his correspondence for publication she foisted on the letters to her mother some passages from the *Journal*. But he had plagiarized from himself before as often as he had 'used' Montaigne or Burton. The best excuse is that of partial derangement. It is odd that although he wrote 'I steal something every day from my sentimental Journey to obey a more sentimental impulse in writing to you,' nothing of the gaiety of the *Journey* is admitted to the *Journal*. The only flash of humour—and that sadly misplaced—comes when he writes: 'I have as whimsical a Story to tell you, and as comically dis-astrous as ever befell one of our family. Shandy's nose, his name, his Sash-Window are fools to it. It will serve at *least* to amuse you . . . I call'd in an able Surgeon and with him an able physician (both my friends) to inspect my disaster. 'Tis a venerial Case, cried my two Scientifick friends. 'Tis impossible at least to be that, replied I, for I have had no commerce whatever with the Sex—not even with my wife, added I, these 15 years.' Amusing to Eliza or not, it is true that the diagnosis was such as he stated. True also that he doctored himself with a French nostrum, *extrait de Saturne*. And only too true that he proved to be incurably ill.

Up to the final entry in the journal he is, with apparent earnestness, making plans for the future of his 'dear Bramine'—a future to be spent with him. After 4th August 1767 there is a gap. His wife, who had been living in France, had returned. In a postscript dated 1st November he tells Eliza: 'I have conquer'd her, as I would every one else, by humanity and Generosity, and she leaves me, more than half in Love with me. She goes into the South of France, her health being in-

supportable in England—and her age, as she now confesses Ten Years more than I thought, being on the edge
of sixty.' This reference to his wife's age has been
regarded as not only caddish but incredible—incredible
because a secret like that could not have been kept so
long in a gossiping community.

Be that as it may, Sterne ends the journal with a some-
what incoherent *cri de cœur:* 'Return, Return! my dear
Eliza! May heaven smooth the Way for thee to send
thee safely to us, and joy for Ever!' As far as we know,
the *cri* did not reach her: she never read the journal
written for her. She may, her biographers suggest, have
forgotten all about him by the time she reached Bombay,
and when she heard of his death was not deeply stirred
by it, may even have felt relieved. But she was per-
turbed when she learned that the widow and daughter
were threatening to publish her letters. The ensuing
disputes need not concern us here. Eliza returned to
England in due course with an aura of romance about
her, not so much because of her friendship with Sterne as
because of the story that she had eloped, per rope-ladder
and waiting boat, with Commodore Sir John Clarke of
H.M.S. *Prudent.* Towards the end of her short life (she
was only thirty-three when she died) she captivated the
Abbé Raynal, who wrote of her as ecstatically as ever
Sterne had done: 'I search for Eliza everywhere: I dis-
cover, I discern some of her features, some of her charms,
scattered among those women whose figure is most
interesting. . . .' Let us leave her there.

> Oh, for it would be a pity
>   To o'erpraise her or to flout her;
> She was wild, and sweet, and witty—
>   Let's not say dull things about her.

Nor about Sterne. If it cannot be said of him what was

said by Johnson of his friend Garrick, that his death eclipsed the gaiety of nations, it can at least be said the gaiety he contributed to life continues to be radiated by his works.

DANIEL GEORGE.

1960.

SELECT BIBLIOGRAPHY

COMPLETE WORKS. *The Works of Laurence Sterne; to which is pre-fixed an account of the Life and Writings of the author,* 7 vols. (Dublin), 1779; 5th edition with additions, 1780; several other editions, notably with illustrations by Darley, 1848; memoir by D. Herbert, 1872; with appendix and several unpublished letters, edited by J. B. Browne, 1873; with life written by himself, 1780, 1803, 1808, 1884, 1891. Works, edited by Professor George Saintsbury, and illustrated by E. J. Wheeler, in 6 vols. (Dent), 1894; another edition, 1903. Translated into French by M. Frénais and A. G. Griffet de la Beaume, 1797; by F. Michel, 1835. The Novels only, with a memoir of the author by Sir Walter Scott, appeared in 1823.

NOVELS. (i) *The Life and Opinions of Tristram Shandy,* 1750; 2nd edition in 9 vols., with autographs of the author, 1760–7; 5th edition, 1779; 10th edition, enlarged and ornamented, 1787; Cooke's edition, with engravings, 1808; with eight etchings from original designs by Harry Furniss, 1883; with introduction by Professor Henry Morley, 1884; by C. Whibley, 1894; edited by Walter Jerrold (Temple Classics), 1899. Translated into French as *La vie et les opinions de Tristram Shandy,* by M. Frénais, 1784; by L. de Wailly, 1842. Translated into German as *Das Leben und die Meynungen des Herrn Tristram Shandy,* 1769; another translation, 1801.

(ii) *A Sentimental Journey through France and Italy, by Mr Yorick,* 1768; many other editions, including those with some account of the life and writings of Laurence Sterne, and an appendix containing several pieces written by Laurence Sterne; also with engravings, 1802; with plates, 1804; stereotype edition, 1808; with memoirs of life and family of Laurence Sterne, 1812; with etchings by E. Hédouin, 1882; with 12 full-page illustrations in photogravure and 220 sketches from designs by Maurice Leloir, 1885; with engravings from designs by Jacque and Fussell, 1888; illustrated by T. H. Robinson, 1897; edited by Walter Jerrold (Temple Classics), 1899; with introduction by H. Paul, 1899; introduction by L. F. Austin, 1903; by Hannaford Bennett, 1905; device of Bruce Rogers, 1905; introduction by Wolmer Whyte, 1907; illustrated by Everard Hopkins, 1910; introduction by Francis Bickley, 1922. Translated into French as *Voyage Sentimental en France,* by M. Frénais, 1770; by M. J. Janin, 1854; by A. Hédouin, 1875; by M. E. Blemont, 1884. Translated into Italian as *Viaggio Sentimentale di Yorick,* by Ugo Foscolo, 1813; by G. Pincherle, 1871. Translated into German as *Herrn Yoricks Reisen durch Franckreich und Italien,* 1769; by A. Lewald, 1842.

SELECT BIBLIOGRAPHY

SERMONS. *The Case of Elijah and the Widow of Zerephath considered:
a charity sermon* (1 Kings xvii. 16), preached on Good Friday, 1747;
The Abuses of Conscience (Hebrews xiii. 18), preached at the summer
assizes at York, 1750; *Of Evil Speaking*, 1762; *Job's account of the
shortness and troubles of life considered* (Job xiv. 1, 2), 1762; *Vindication
of Human Nature* (Romans xiv. 7) and *On setting bounds to our desires*
(2 Kings iv. 13), 1773. *The Sermons of Mr Yorick*, first published in
1761, entered their 5th edition in 1763, and were many times subse-
quently republished.

POLITICAL TRACT. *A Political Romance* (*The History of a good
warm Watch-coat*) *addressed to* ——, *Esq., of York*, 1769; other editions,
1868, 1900. An exact reprint of the first edition, with an introduction
by Wilbur L. Cross, was published in Boston, Mass., in 1914.

LETTERS. *Letters of Laurence Sterne to his most intimate friends;
with a fragment in the manner of Rabelais. To which are prefix'd
memoirs of his life and family by himself, and published by his daughter,
Mrs Medalle*; in 3 vols., 1775. *Sterne's letters to his friends on various
occasions, with his history of a watch-coat, and explanatory notes*, 1775;
Letters from Yorick to Eliza, 1775; translated into German as *Yoricks
Briefe an Elisa*, by J. J. C. Bode, 1775. *Letters from Eliza to Yorick*,
1775. *Original letters never before published*, 1788. *Letters of Yorick
and Elisa: to which is added biographical memoirs of the author and
authoress*, 1807. *Seven Letters written by Sterne and his friends, hitherto
unpublished*, edited by W. D. Cooper, 1844. *Unpublished Letters of
Laurence Sterne*, edited by J. Murray, 1856. *Journal to Eliza*, edited
by Walter Sichel, 1910. *Laurence Sterne's Letter to the Rev. Mr Blake,
with a facsimile*, 1915.

SELECTIONS. Many interesting little selections were made from
Sterne's works, showing the popularity he achieved among his con-
temporaries. Some of these are: *Yorick turned Trimmer; or, The
Gentleman's Jester . . . embellished with 3 copperplate cuts*, 1770 (?);
*Sterne's Witticisms; or, Yorick's Convivial Jester, containing a variety
of* bons mots, 1782; *The Beauties of Sterne* (edited by A. F.), 12th
edition, 1793; 13th edition, 1799; with 8 plates, 1905; *The Beauties of
Sterne*, with caricatures by Rowlandson, from original drawings by
Newton, 1809; with some account of his writings by Sir Walter Scott,
1836. *The Story of My Uncle Toby*, with Life by Percy Fitzgerald,
1871. *Selections from Tristram Shandy*, with unpublished illustrations
in aquatint from the original copperplates engraved in 1820, and an
introductory note by J. Oldcastle, 1888.

BIOGRAPHY, CRITICISM, ETC. *The Clockmakers' Outcry against the
author of Tristram Shandy*, 1760; *Explanatory remarks upon Tristram
Shandy, wherein the morals and politics of the piece are clearly laid open*,
by J. Kunastrokius, 1760; *A Funeral discourse occasioned by the much
lamented death of Mr Yorick: a satire* by C. Flagellan, 1761; *The Life of
Christopher Wagstaffe* [in which insinuations are made about the origin
of Tristram Shandy], 1762; *Illustrations of Sterne*, by John Ferriar,
1798; *The fallacy of French Freedom, and the dangerous tendency of
Sterne's writings*, by Dr D. Whyte, 1799; *Life of Laurence Sterne*, by
P. H. Fitzgerald, 1864; by H. D. Traill, 1882; by Wilbur L. Cross, 1909;
by Walter Sichel, 1910; *L'influence de Laurence Sterne en France au
18me siècle*, by Francis B. Barton, 1911; *Life and Letters*, by Lewis
Melville, 1911; *Sterne and the Novel of his time*, by Charles E. Vaughan
(Cambridge History of English Literature, vol. x), 1913; *Sterne in
Italia*, by G. Rabbizani, 1920; *Sterne's Eliza*, by Arnold Wright and

W. L. Sclater, 1922; *Laurence Sterne and his Novels studied in the light of modern psychology*, by A. de Froe, 1925; *The Politicks of Laurence Sterne*, by L. P. Curtis, 1929; *Perilous Balance*, by W. B. C. Wathew, 1939; *This is Lorence*, by L. C. Hartley, 1943; *Four Portraits*, by P. C. Quennell, 1945; *The Unsentimental Journey of Laurence Sterne*, by E. M. Dilernson, 1948; *Laurence Sterne, a Fellow of Infinite Jest*, by T. Yoseloff, 1948; *Laurence Sterne; The Making of a Humorist*, by Margaret R. B. Shaw, 1957; *Laurence Sterne: from Tristram to Yorick*, by H. Fluchere, 1965; *Laurence Sterne in the Twentieth Century: An Essay and a Bibliography of Sternean Studies, 1900–65*, by L. C. Hartley, 1967.

CONTENTS

A SENTIMENTAL JOURNEY

THROUGH

FRANCE AND ITALY

THEY order, said I, this matter better in France——

You have been in France? said my gentleman, turning quick upon me with the most civil triumph in the world. Strange! quoth I, debating the matter with myself, that one and twenty miles sailing, for 'tis absolutely no further from Dover to Calais, should give a man these rights. I'll look into them: so giving up the argument I went straight to my lodgings, put up half a dozen shirts and a black pair of silk breeches—"the coat I have on," said I, looking at the sleeve, "will do"— took a place in the Dover stage; and the packet sailing at nine the next morning, by three I had got sat down to my dinner upon a fricaseed chicken, so incontestibly in France, that had I died that night of an indigestion, the whole world could not have suspended the effects of the *Droits d'aubaine*;[1] my shirts, and black pair of silk breeches, portmanteau and all must have gone to the King of France, even the little picture which I have so long worn, and so often have told thee, Eliza, I would carry with me into my grave, would have been torn from my neck. Ungenerous! to seize upon the wreck of an unwary passenger, whom your subjects had

[1] All the effects of strangers (Swiss and Scotch excepted) dying in France, are seized by virtue of this law, though the heir be upon the spot—the profit of these contingencies being farmed, there is no redress.

beckon'd to their coast. By heaven! SIRE, it is not well done; and much does it grieve me, 'tis the monarch of a people so civilized and courteous, and so renowned for sentiment and fine feelings, that I have to reason with.

But I have scarce set foot in your dominions——

CALAIS

WHEN I had finished my dinner, and drank the King of France's health, to satisfy my mind that I bore him no spleen, but, on the contrary, high honour for the humanity of his temper, I rose up an inch taller for the accommodation.

No, said I, the Bourbon is by no means a cruel race: they may be misled like other people; but there is a mildness in their blood. As I acknowledged this, I felt a suffusion of a finer kind upon my cheek—more warm and friendly to man, than what Burgundy (at least of two livres a bottle, which was such as I had been drinking) could have produced.

Just God! said I, kicking my portmanteau aside, what is there in this world's goods which should sharpen our spirits, and make so many kind-hearted brethren of us fall out so cruelly as we do by the way?

When man is at peace with man, how much lighter than a feather is the heaviest of metals in his hand! he pulls out his purse, and holding it airily and uncompress'd, looks round him, as if he sought for an object to share it with. In doing this, I felt every vessel in my frame dilate, the arteries beat all chearily together, and every power which sustained life, performed it with so little friction, that 'twould have confounded the most *physical precieuse* in France: with all her materialism, she could scarce have called me a machine.

I'm confident, said I to myself, I should have overset her creed.

The accession of that idea carried Nature, at that time, as high as she could go: I was at peace with the world before, and this finish'd the treaty with myself.

Now, was I a King of France, cried I, what a moment for an orphan to have begg'd his father's portmanteau of me!

THE MONK

CALAIS

I HAD scarce uttered the words, when a poor monk of the order of St. Francis came into the room to beg something for his convent. No man cares to have his virtues the sport of contingencies, or one man may be generous, as another man is puissant—*sed non quo ad hanc*, or, be it as it may,—for there is no regular reasoning upon the ebbs and flows of our humours; they may depend upon the same causes, for aught I know, which influence the tides themselves—'twould oft be no discredit to us, to suppose it was so: I'm sure at least for myself, that in many a case I should be more highly satisfied, to have it said by the world, "I had had an affair with the moon, in which there was neither sin nor shame," than have it pass altogether as my own act and deed, wherein there was so much of both.

But be this as it may. The moment I cast my eyes upon him, I was predetermined not to give him a single sous; and accordingly I put my purse into my pocket, button'd it up, set myself a little more upon my center, and advanced up gravely to him: there was something, I fear, forbidding in my look: I have his figure this moment before my eyes, and think there was that in it which deserved better.

The monk, as I judged from the break in his tonsure, a few scatter'd white hairs upon his temples being all that remained of it, might be about seventy, but from his eyes, and that sort of fire which was in them, which seemed more temper'd by courtesy than years, could be no more than sixty. Truth might lie between. He was certainly sixty-five; and the general air of his countenance, notwithstanding something seem'd to have been planting wrinkles in it before their time, agreed to the account.

It was one of those heads which Guido has often painted—mild, pale, penetrating, free from all commonplace ideas of fat contented ignorance looking downwards upon the earth: it look'd forwards; but look'd, as if it look'd at something beyond this world. How one of his order came by it, heaven above, who let it fall upon a monk's shoulders, best knows; but it would have suited a Bramin, and had I met it upon the plains of Indostan, I had reverenced it.

The rest of his outline may be given in a few strokes; one might put it into the hands of any one to design, for 'twas neither elegant or otherwise, but as character and expression made it so: it was a thin, spare form, something above the common size, if it lost not the distinction by a bend forward in the figure—but it was the attitude of Entreaty; and as it now stands presented to my imagination, it gain'd more than it lost by it.

When he had entered the room three paces, he stood still, and laying his left hand upon his breast (a slender white staff with which he journey'd being in his right), when I had got close up to him, he introduced himself with the little story of the wants of his convent, and the poverty of his order, and did it with so simple a grace, and such an air of depreciation was there in the whole cast of his look and figure, I was bewitch'd not to have been struck with it——

A better reason was, I had predetermined not to give him a single sous.

THE MONK

CALAIS

'Tis very true, said I, replying to a cast upwards with his eyes, with which he had concluded his address; 'tis very true—and heaven be their resource who have no other but the charity of the world, the stock of which, I fear, is no way sufficient for the many *great claims* which are hourly made upon it.

As I pronounced the words *great claims*, he gave a slight glance with his eye downwards upon the sleeve of his tunic. I felt the full force of the appeal. I acknowledge it, said I—a coarse habit, and that but once in three years, with meagre diet, are no great matters; and the true point of pity is, as they can be earn'd in the world with so little industry, that your order should wish to procure them by pressing upon a fund which is the property of the lame, the blind, the aged, and the infirm. The captive who lies down counting over and over again the days of his afflictions, languishes also for his share of it; and had you been of the *order of mercy*, instead of the order of St. Francis, poor as I am, continued I, pointing at my portmanteau, full chearfully should it have been open'd to you, for the ransom of the unfortunate. The monk made me a bow. But of all others, resumed I, the unfortunate of our own country, surely, have the first rights; and I have left thousands in distress upon our own shore. The monk gave a cordial wave with his head as much as to say, No doubt, there is misery enough in every corner of the world, as well as within our convent. But we distinguish, said I, laying my hand upon the sleeve of his tunic, in return for his appeal—we distinguish, my good father! betwixt those who wish only to eat the bread of their own labour and those who eat the bread of other people's, and have no other plan in life, but to get through it in sloth and ignorance, *for the love of God*.

The poor Franciscan made no reply: a hectic of a moment pass'd across his cheek, but could not tarry— Nature seemed to have done with her resentments in him; he shewed none—but letting his staff fall within his arm, he press'd both his hands with resignation upon his breast, and retired.

THE MONK

CALAIS

MY heart smote me the moment he shut the door. Psha! said I, with an air of carelessness, three several times. But it would not do: every ungracious syllable I had utter'd, crowded back into my imagination: I reflected, I had no right over the poor Franciscan, but to deny him; and that the punishment of that was enough to the disappointed, without the addition of unkind language. I considered his grey hairs. His courteous figure seem'd to re-enter and gently ask me what injury he had done me, and why I could use him thus? I would have given twenty livres for an advocate. I have behaved very ill, said I within myself; but I have only just set out upon my travels; and shall learn better manners as I get along.

THE DESOBLIGEANT

CALAIS

WHEN a man is discontented with himself, it has one advantage however, that it puts him into an excellent frame of mind for making a bargain. Now there being no travelling through France and Italy without a chaise, and nature generally prompting us to the thing we are fittest for, I walk'd out into the coach-yard to buy or hire something of that kind to my purpose: an old Desobligeant [1] in the furthest corner of the court hit my fancy at first sight, so I instantly got into it, and finding it in tolerable harmony with my feelings, I ordered the waiter to call Monsieur Dessein, the master of the hotel, but Monsieur Dessein being gone to vespers, and not caring to face the Franciscan, whom I saw on the opposite side of the court, in conference with a lady just arrived at the inn, I drew the taffeta curtain betwixt us, and being determined to write my journey, I took out my pen and ink, and wrote the preface to it in the *Desobligeant.*

PREFACE

IN THE DESOBLIGEANT

IT must have been observed by many a peripatetic philosopher, That Nature has set up by her own un-questionable authority certain boundaries and fences to circumscribe the discontent of man: she has effected her purpose in the quietest and easiest manner, by laying him under almost insuperable obligations to work out

[1] A Chaise, so called in France, from its holding but one person.

his ease, and to sustain his suffering at home. It is there only that she has provided him with the most suitable objects to partake of his happiness, and bear a part of that burthen, which, in all countries and ages, has ever been too heavy for one pair of shoulders. 'Tis true, we are endued with an imperfect power of spreading our happiness sometimes beyond *her* limits, but 'tis so ordered, that, from the want of languages, connections, and dependencies, and from the difference in educations, customs, and habits, we lie under so many impediments in communicating our sensations out of our own sphere, as often amount to a total impossibility.

It will always follow from hence, that the balance of sentimental commerce is always against the expatriated adventurer: he must buy what he has little occasion for, at their own price; his conversation will seldom be taken in exchange for theirs without a large discount —and this, by the bye, eternally driving him into the hands of more equitable brokers, for such conversation as he can find, it requires no great spirit of divination to guess at his party——

This brings me to my point; and naturally leads me (if the see-saw of this *Desobligeant* will but let me get on) into the efficient as well as final causes of travelling——

Your idle people that leave their native country, and go abroad for some reason or reasons which may be derived from one of these general causes——

Infirmity of body,

Imbecility of the mind, or

Inevitable necessity.

The two first include all those who travel by land or by water, labouring with pride, curiosity, vanity, or spleen, subdivided and combined *in infinitum*.

The third class includes the whole army of peregrine

martyrs; more especially those travellers who set out
upon their travels with the benefit of the clergy,
either as delinquents travelling under the direction of
governors recommended by tne magistrate—or young
gentlemen transported by the cruelty of parents
and guardians, and travelling under the direction of
governors recommended by Oxford, Aberdeen, and
Glasgow.

There is a fourth class, but their number is so small,
that they would not deserve a distinction, was it not
necessary in a work of this nature to observe the greatest
precision and nicety, to avoid a confusion of character.
And these men I speak of, are such as cross the seas
and sojourn in a land of strangers, with a view of saving
money for various reasons and upon various pretences:
but as they might also save themselves and others a
great deal of unnecessary trouble by saving their money
at home—and as their reasons for travelling are the
least complex of any other species of emigrants, I shall
distinguish these gentlemen by the name of

Simple Travellers.

Thus the whole circle of travellers may be reduced
to the following *heads*:

Idle Travellers,
Inquisitive Travellers,
Lying Travellers,
Proud Travellers,
Vain Travellers,
Splenetic Travellers,

Then follow

The Travellers of Necessity,
The delinquent and felonious Traveller,
The unfortunate and innocent Traveller,
The simple Traveller,

And last of all (if you please) The Sentimental Traveller (meaning thereby myself), who have travell'd, and of which I am now sitting down to give an account, as much out of *Necessity*, and the *besoin de Voyager*, as any one in the class.

I am well aware, at the same time, as both my travels and observations will be altogether of a different cast from any of my fore-runners; that I might have insisted upon a whole nitch entirely to myself—but I should break in upon the confines of the *Vain* Traveller, in wishing to draw attention towards me, till I have some better grounds for it, than the mere *Novelty of my Vehicle*. It is sufficient for my reader, if he has been a Traveller himself, that with study and reflection hereupon he may be able to determine his own place and rank in the catalogue—it will be one step towards knowing himself, as it is great odds but he retains some tincture and resemblance of what he imbibed or carried out, to the present hour.

The man who first transplanted the grape of Burgundy to the Cape of Good Hope (observe he was a Dutchman) never dreamt of drinking the same wine at the Cape, that the same grape produced upon the French mountains—he was too phlegmatic for that—but undoubtedly he expected to drink some sort of vinous liquor; but whether good, bad, or indifferent, he knew enough of this world to know, that it did not depend upon his choice, but that what is generally called *chance* was to decide his success: however, he hoped for the best: and in these hopes, by an intemperate confidence in the fortitude of his head, and the depth of his discretion, *Mynheer* might possibly overset both in his new vineyard; and by discovering his nakedness, become a laughing-stock to his people.

Even so it fares with the poor Traveller, sailing and

posting through the politer kingdoms of the globe, in pursuit of knowledge and improvements.

Knowledge and improvements are to be got by sailing and posting for that purpose; but whether useful knowledge and real improvements, is all a lottery; and even where the adventurer is successful, the acquired stock must be used with caution and sobriety, to turn to any profit. But as the chances run prodigiously the other way, both as to the acquisition and application, I am of opinion, That a man would act as wisely, if he could prevail upon himself to live contented without foreign knowledge or foreign improvements, especially if he lives in a country that has no absolute want of either—and indeed, much grief of heart has it oft and many a time cost me, when I have observed how many a foul step the inquisitive Traveller has measured to see sights and look into discoveries; all which, as Sancho Pança said to Don Quixote, they might have seen dry-shod at home. It is an age so full of light, that there is scarce a country or corner of Europe, whose beams are not crossed and interchanged with others. Knowledge in most of its branches, and in most affairs, is like music in an Italian street, whereof those may partake, who pay nothing. But there is no nation under heaven—and GOD is my record (before whose tribunal I must one day come and give an account of this work) that I do not speak it vauntingly—but there is no nation under heaven abounding with more variety of learning, where the sciences may be more fitly woo'd, or more surely won, than here; where art is encouraged, and will soon rise high; where Nature (take her altogether) has so little to answer for, and, to close all, where there is more wit and variety of character to feed the mind with. Where then, my dear countrymen, are you going?

We are only looking at this chaise, said they. Your

most obedient servant, said I, skipping out of it, and
pulling off my hat. We were wondering, said one of
them, who, I found, was an *inquisitive Traveller*, what
could occasion its motion. 'Twas the agitation, said
I coolly, of writing a preface. I never heard, said the
other, who was a *simple Traveller*, of a preface wrote in
a *Desobligeant*. It would have been better, said I, in a
Vis à Vis.

As an Englishman does not travel to see Englishmen,
I retired to my room.

CALAIS

I PERCEIVED that something darken'd the passage more
than myself, as I stepp'd along it to my room; it was
effectually Mons. Dessein, the master of the hotel, who
had just returned from vespers, and, with his hat under
his arm, was most complaisantly following me, to put
me in mind of my wants. I had wrote myself pretty
well out of conceit with the *Desobligeant*; and Mons. Dessein speaking of it, with a shrug, as if it would no way
suit me, it immediately struck my fancy that it belong'd
to some *innocent Traveller*, who, on his return home, had
left it to Mons. Dessein's honour to make the most of.
Four months had elapsed since it had finished its career
of Europe in the corner of Mons. Dessein's coach-yard;
and having sallied out from thence but a vampt-up
business at the first, though it had been twice taken to
pieces on Mount Sennis, it had not profited much by
its adventures—but by none so little as the standing
so many months unpitied in the corner of Mons. Dessein's
coach-yard. Much indeed was not to be said for it—but
something might—and when a few words will rescue

misery out of her distress, I hate the man who can be a churl of them.

Now was I the master of this hotel, said I, laying the point of my fore-finger on Mons. Dessein's breast, I would inevitably make a point of getting rid of this unfortunate *Desobligeant*; it stands swinging reproaches at you every time you pass by it.

Mon Dieu ! said Mons. Dessein; I have no interest. Except the interest, said I, which men of a certain turn of mind take, Mons. Dessein, in their own sensations: I'm persuaded, to a man who feels for others as well as for himself, every rainy night, disguise it as you will, must cast a damp upon your spirits. You suffer, Mons. Dessein, as much as the machine.

I have always observed, when there is as much *sour* as *sweet* in a compliment, that an Englishman is eternally at a loss within himself, whether to take it or let it alone: a Frenchman never is: Mons. Dessein made me a bow.

C'est bien vrai, said he. But in this case I should only exchange one disquietude for another, and with loss: figure to yourself, my dear Sir, that in giving you a chaise which would fall to pieces before you had got half way to Paris—figure to yourself how much I should suffer, in giving an ill impression of myself to a man of honour, and lying at the mercy, as I must do, *d'un homme d'esprit*.

The dose was made up exactly after my own prescription; so I could not help taking it, and returning Mons. Dessein his bow, without more casuistry we walk'd together towards his Remise, to take a view of his magazine of chaises.

IN THE STREET

CALAIS

IT must needs be a hostile kind of a world, when the buyer (if it be but of a sorry post-chaise) cannot go forth with the seller thereof into the street, to terminate the difference betwixt them, but he instantly falls into the same frame of mind, and views his conventionist with the same sort of eye, as if he was going along with him to Hyde-park-corner to fight a duel. For my own part, being but a poor swordsman, and no way a match for Monsieur *Dessein*, I felt the rotation of all the movements within me, to which the situation is incident. I looked at Monsieur *Dessein* through and through, eyed him as he walk'd along in profile, then *en face*; thought he look'd like a Jew, then a Turk, disliked his wig, cursed him by my gods, wished him at the devil.

And is all this to be lighted up in the heart for a beggarly account of three or four louis d'ors, which is the most I can be over-reach'd in? Base passion! said I, turning myself about, as a man naturally does upon a sudden reverse of sentiment; base ungentle passion! thy hand is against every man, and every man's hand against thee. Heaven forbid! said she, raising her hand up to her forehead, for I had turned full in front upon the lady whom I had seen in conference with the monk —she had followed us unperceived. Heaven forbid, indeed! said I, offering her my own. She had a black pair of silk gloves, open only at the thumb and two fore-fingers, so accepted it without reserve, and I led her up to the door of the Remise.

Monsieur *Dessein* had *diabled* the key above fifty times, before he found out he had come with a wrong one in his hand: we were as impatient as himself to have

it open'd; and so attentive to the obstacle, that I continued holding her hand almost without knowing it:
so that Monsieur *Dessein* left us together, with her
hand in mine, and with our faces turned towards the
door of the Remise, and said he would be back in
five minutes.

Now a colloquy of five minutes, in such a situation,
is worth one of as many ages, with your faces turned
towards the street: in the latter case, 'tis drawn from
the objects and occurrences without; when your eyes
are fixed upon a dead blank you draw purely from
yourselves. A silence of a single moment upon Mons.
Dessein's leaving us, had been fatal to the situation—
she had infallibly turned about—so I begun the conversation instantly.

But what were the temptations (as I write not to
apologise for the weaknesses of my heart in this tour,
but to give an account of them) shall be described
with the same simplicity, with which I felt them.

THE REMISE DOOR

CALAIS

When I told the reader that I did not care to get out
of the *Desobligeant*, because I saw the monk in close
conference with a lady just arrived at the inn, I told
him the whole truth; for I was full as much restrained
by the appearance and figure of the lady he was talking
to. Suspicion crossed my brain, and said, he was telling
her what had passed; something jarred upon it within
me. I wished him at his convent.

When the heart flies out before the understanding, it
saves the judgment a world of pains. I was certain she

was of a better order of beings; however, I thought no more of her, but went on and wrote my preface.

The impression returned upon my encounter with her in the street; a guarded frankness with which she gave me her hand, shewed, I thought, her good education and her good sense; and as I led her on, I felt a pleasurable ductility about her, which spread a calmness over all my spirits.

Good God! how a man might lead such a creature as this round the world with him!

I had not yet seen her face—'twas not material; for the drawing was instantly set about, and long before we had got to the door of the Remise, *Fancy* had finish'd the whole head, and pleased herself as much with its fitting her goddess, as if she had dived into the TIBER for it. But thou art a seduced, and a seducing slut; and albeit thou cheatest us seven times a day with thy pictures and images, yet with so many charms dost thou do it, and thou deckest out thy pictures in the shapes of so many angels of light, 'tis a shame to break with thee.

When we had got to the door of the Remise, she withdrew her hand from across her forehead, and let me see the original. It was a face of about six and twenty, of a clear transparent brown, simply set off without rouge or powder. It was not critically handsome, but there was that in it, which, in the frame of mind I was in, attached me much more to it—it was interesting. I fancied it wore the characters of a widow'd look, and in that state of its declension, which had passed the two first paroxysms of sorrow, and was quietly beginning to reconcile itself to its loss—but a thousand other distresses might have traced the same lines; I wish'd to know what they had been and was ready to enquire (had the same *bon ton* of conversation permitted, as in

the days of Esdras): *"What aileth thee? and why art
thou disquieted? and why is thy understanding troubled?"*
In a word, I felt benevolence for her; and resolv'd some
way or other to throw in my mite of courtesy, if not
of service.

Such were my temptations—and in this disposition
to give way to them, was I left alone with the lady
with her hand in mine, and with our faces both turned
closer to the door of the Remise than what was
absolutely necessary.

THE REMISE DOOR

CALAIS

THIS certainly, fair lady! said I, raising her hand up a
little lightly as I began, must be one of Fortune's
whimsical doings: to take two utter strangers by their
hands—of different sexes, and perhaps from different
corners of the globe, and in one moment place them
together in such a cordial situation as Friendship
herself could scarce have atchieved for them, had she
projected it for a month.

And your reflection upon it, shows how much, Monsieur, she has embarrassed you by the adventure.

When the situation is what we would wish, nothing
is so ill-timed as to hint at the circumstances which
make it so: you thank Fortune, continued she; you had
reason—the heart knew it, and was satisfied; and who
but an English philosopher would have sent notice of
it to the brain to reverse the judgment?

In saying this she disengaged her hand with a look
which I thought a sufficient commentary upon the text.

It is a miserable picture which I am going to give of
the weakness of my heart, by owning that it suffered a

pain, which worthier occasions could not have inflicted.
I was mortified with the loss of her hand, and the manner
in which I had lost it carried neither oil nor wine to the
wound: I never felt the pain of a sheepish inferiority so
miserably in my life.

The triumphs of a true feminine heart are short upon
these discomfitures. In a very few seconds she laid her
hand upon the cuff of my coat, in order to finish her
reply; so some way or other, God knows how, I regained
my situation.

She had nothing to add.

I forthwith began to model a different conversation
for the lady, thinking from the spirit as well as moral
of this, that I had been mistaken in her character; but
upon turning her face towards me, the spirit which had
animated the reply was fled, the muscles relaxed, and
I beheld the same unprotected look of distress which
first won me to her interest. Melancholy! to see such
sprightliness the prey of sorrow, I pitied her from my
soul; and though it may seem ridiculous enough to a
torpid heart, I could have taken her into my arms, and
cherished her, though it was in the open street, without
blushing.

The pulsations of the arteries along my fingers pressing across hers, told her what was passing within me:
she looked down. A silence of some moments followed.

I fear, in this interval, I must have made some slight
efforts towards a closer compression of her hand, from a
subtle sensation I felt in the palm of my own—not as if
she was going to withdraw hers but as if she thought
about it—and I had infallibly lost it a second time, had
not instinct more than reason directed me to the last
resource in these dangers—to hold it loosely and in a
manner as if I was every moment going to release it, of
myself; so she let it continue till Monsieur *Dessein*

returned with the key; and in the mean time I set
myself to consider how I should undo the ill impressions
which the poor monk's story, in case he had told it her,
must have planted in her breast against me.

THE SNUFF-BOX

CALAIS

THE good old monk was within six paces of us, as the
idea of him crossed my mind; and was advancing
towards us a little out of the line, as if uncertain whether
he should break in upon us or no. He stopp'd, however,
as soon as he came up to us, with a world of frankness:
and having a horn snuff-box in his hand, he presented
it open to me. You shall taste mine, said I, pulling out
my box (which was a small tortoise one) and putting
it into his hand. 'Tis most excellent, said the monk.
Then do me the favour, I replied, to accept of the box
and all, and when you take a pinch out of it, sometimes
recollect it was the peace-offering of a man who once
used you unkindly, but not from his heart.

The poor monk blush'd as red as scarlet. *Mon Dieu !*
said he, pressing his hands together; you never used
me unkindly. I should think, said the lady, he is not
likely. I blush'd in my turn; but from what movements
I leave to the few who feel to analyse. Excuse me,
Madame, replied I, I treated him most unkindly, and
from no provocations. 'Tis impossible, said the lady.
My God! cried the monk, with a warmth of asseveration
which seem'd not to belong to him, the fault was in
me, and in the indiscretion of my zeal. The lady opposed
it, and I joined with her in maintaining it was impossible,
that a spirit so regulated as his, could give offence to any.

I knew not that contention could be rendered so sweet and pleasurable a thing to the nerves as I then felt it. We remained silent without any sensation of that foolish pain which takes place, when in such a circle you look for ten minutes in one another's faces without saying a word. Whilst this lasted, the monk rubb'd his horn box upon the sleeve of his tunick; and as soon as it had acquired a little air of brightness by the friction he made a low bow, and said, 'twas too late to say whether it was the weakness or goodness of our tempers which had involved us in this contest. But be it as it would, he begg'd we might exchange boxes. In saying this, he presented his to me with one hand, as he took mine from me in the other; and having kissed it, with a stream of good-nature in his eyes, he put it into his bosom and took his leave.

I guard this box, as I would the instrumental parts of my religion, to help my mind on to something better: in truth, I seldom go abroad without it: and oft and many a time have I called up by it the courteous spirit of its owner to regulate my own, in the justlings of the world; they had found full employment for his, as I learnt from his story, till about the forty-fifth year of his age, when upon some military services ill requited, and meeting at the same time with a disappointment in the tenderest of passions, he abandoned the sword and the sex together, and took sanctuary, not so much in his convent as in himself.

I feel a damp upon my spirits, as I am going to add, that in my last return through Calais, upon inquiring after Father Lorenzo, I heard he had been dead near three months, and was buried, not in his convent, but, according to his desire, in a little cemetery belonging to it, about two leagues off. I had a strong desire to see where they had laid him—when upon pulling out his little horn box, as I sat by his grave, and plucking up a nettle or two at the head of it, which had no business to grow there, they all struck together so forcibly upon my affections, that I burst into a flood of tears. But I am as weak as a woman; and I beg the world not to smile, but pity me.

THE REMISE DOOR

CALAIS

I HAD never quitted the lady's hand all this time; and had held it so long, that it would have been indecent to have let it go, without first pressing it to my lips: the blood and spirits, which had suffered a revulsion from her, crowded back to her, as I did it.

Now the two travellers, who had spoke to me in the coach-yard, happened at that crisis to be passing by, and observing our communications, naturally took it into their heads that we must be *man and wife*, at least; so stopping as soon as they came up to the door of the Remise, the one of them, who was the inquisitive Traveller, ask'd us if we set out for Paris the next morning? I could only answer for myself, I said; and the lady added, she was for Amiens. We dined there yesterday, said the simple Traveller. You go directly through the town, added the other, in your road to Paris. I was going to return a thousand thanks for the intelligence, *that Amiens was in the road to Paris*; but upon pulling out my poor monk's little horn box to take a pinch of snuff, I made them a quiet bow, and wished them a good passage to Dover. They left us alone.

Now where would be the harm, said I to myself, if I was to beg of this distressed lady to accept of half of my chaise? and what mighty mischief could ensue?

Every dirty passion, and bad propensity in my nature, took the alarm, as I stated the proposition. It will oblige you to have a third horse, said AVARICE, which will put twenty livres out of your pocket. You know not what she is, said CAUTION. Or what scrapes the affair may draw you into, whisper'd COWARDICE.

Depend upon it, Yorick! said DISCRETION, 'twill be said you went off with a mistress, and came by assignation to Calais for that purpose.

You can never after, cried HYPOCRISY aloud, shew your face in the world. Or rise, quoth MEANNESS, in the church. Or be any thing in it, said PRIDE, but a lousy prebendary.

But 'tis a civil thing, said I. And as I generally act from the first impulse, and therefore seldom listen to these cabals, which serve no purpose that I know of, but to encompass the heart with adamant, I turn'd instantly about to the lady.

But she had glided off unperceived, as the cause was pleading, and had made ten or a dozen paces down the street, by the time I had made the determination; so I set off after her with a long stride, to make her the proposal with the best address I was master of; but observing she walk'd with her cheek half resting upon the palm of her hand, with the slow, short-measur'd step of thoughtfulness, and with her eyes, as she went step by step, fixed upon the ground, it struck me, she was trying the same cause herself. God help her! said I, she has some mother-in-law, or tartufish aunt, or nonsensical old woman, to consult upon the occasion, as well as myself: so not caring to interrupt the process, and deeming it more gallant to take her at discretion than surprise, I faced about, and took a short turn or two before the door of the Remise, whilst she walk'd musing on one side.

IN THE STREET

CALAIS

HAVING, on first sight of the lady, settled the affair in my fancy, "that she was of the better order of beings," and then laid it down as a second axiom, as indisputable as the first, that she was a widow, and wore a character of distress, I went no further; I got ground enough for the situation which pleased me, and had she remained close beside my elbow till midnight, I should have held true to my system, and considered her only under that general idea.

She had scarce got twenty paces distant from me, ere something within me called out for a more particular inquiry. It brought on the idea of a further separation. I might possibly never see her more. The heart is for saving what it can; and I wanted the traces through which my wishes might find their way to her, in case I should never rejoin her myself: in a word, I wish'd to know her name, her family's, her condition; and as I knew the place to which she was going, I wanted to know from whence she came: but there was no coming at all this intelligence: a hundred little delicacies stood in the way. I form'd a score different plans—there was no such thing as a man's asking her directly; the thing was impossible.

A little French *debonaire* captain, who came dancing down the street, showed me, it was the easiest thing in the world; for popping in betwixt us, just as the lady was returning back to the door of the Remise, he introduced himself to my acquaintance, and before he had well got announced, begg'd I would do him the honour to present him to the lady. I had not been presented myself, so turning about to her, he did it just as well by asking her, if she had come from Paris? No, she was going that route, she said. *Vous n'êtes pas de Londre ?* She was not, she replied. Then Madame must have come through Flanders—*Apparemment vous êtes Flammande ?* said the French captain. The lady answered, she was. *Peut-être de Lisle ?* added he. She said, she was not of Lisle. Nor Arras? Nor Cambray? Nor Ghent? Nor Brussels? She answered, she was of Brussels.

He had had the honour, he said, to be at the bombardment of it last war—that it was finely situated, *pour cela*—and full of noblesse when the Imperialists were driven out by the French (the lady made a slight curtsy)—so giving her an account of the affair, and of the share he had had in it—he begg'd the honour to know her name—so made his bow.

Et Madame a son Mari ? said he, looking back when he had made two steps, and without staying for an answer danced down the street.

Had I served seven years' apprenticeship to good-breeding, I could not have done as much.

THE REMISE

CALAIS

As the little French captain left us, Mons. Dessein came up with the key of the Remise in his hand, and forthwith let us into his magazine of chaises.

The first object which caught my eye, as Mons. Dessein open'd the door of the Remise, was another old tatter'd *Desobligeant*, and notwithstanding it was the exact picture of that which had hit my fancy so much in the coach-yard but an hour before, the very sight of it stirr'd up a disagreeable sensation within me now; and I thought 'twas a churlish beast into whose heart the idea could first enter, to construct such a machine; nor had I much more charity for the man who could think of using it.

I observed the lady was as little taken with it as myself: so Mons. Dessein led us on to a couple of chaises which stood abreast, telling us, as he recommended them, that they had been purchased by my Lord A. and B. to go the *grand total*, but had gone no further than Paris, so were in all respects as good as new. They were too good—so I pass'd on to a third, which stood behind, and forthwith began to chaffer for the price. But 'twill scarce hold two, said I, opening the door and getting in. Have the goodness, Madame, said Mons. Dessein, offering his arm, to step in. The lady hesitated half a second, and stepp'd in; and the waiter that moment beckoning to speak to Mons. Dessein, he shut the door of the chaise upon us, and left us.

THE REMISE DOOR

CALAIS

C'est bien comique, 'tis very droll, said the lady, smiling, from the reflection that this was the second time we had been left together by a parcel of nonsensical contingencies; *c'est bien comique*, said she.

There wants nothing, said I, to make it so, but the comic use which the gallantry of a Frenchman would put it to—to make love the first moment, and an offer of his person the second.

'Tis their *fort*, replied the lady.

It is supposed so at least, and how it has come to pass, continued I, I know not: but they have certainly got the credit of understanding more of love, and making it better than any other nation upon earth; but for my own part, I think them errant bunglers, and in truth the worst set of marksmen that ever tried Cupid's patience.

To think of making love by *sentiments*!

I should as soon think of making a genteel suit of cloaths out of remnants: and to do it—pop—at first sight by declaration, is submitting the offer and themselves with it, to be sisted with all their *pours* and *contres*, by an unheated mind.

The lady attended as if she expected I should go on.

Consider then, Madame, continued I, laying my hand upon hers——

That grave people hate Love for the name's sake——

That selfish people hate it for their own——

Hypocrites for heaven's——

And that all of us, both old and young, being ten times worse frighten'd than hurt by the very *report*——

What a want of knowledge in this branch of commerce a man betrays, who ever lets the word come out of his lips, till an hour or two at least after the time that his silence upon it becomes tormenting. A course of small, quiet attentions, not so pointed as to alarm, nor so vague as to be misunderstood, with now and then a look of kindness, and little or nothing said upon it, leaves Nature for your mistress, and she fashions it to her mind.

Then I solemnly declare, said the lady, blushing, you have been making love to me all this while.

THE REMISE

CALAIS

MONSIEUR *Dessein* came back to let us out of the chaise,
and acquaint the lady, Count de L——, her brother,
was just arrived at the hotel. Though I had infinite
good-will for the lady, I cannot say, that I rejoiced in
my heart at the event, and could not help telling her
so, for it is fatal to a proposal, Madam, said I, that
I was going to make to you.

You need not tell me what the proposal was, said
she, laying her hand upon both mine, as she interrupted
me. A man, my good Sir, has seldom an offer of kindness
to make to a woman, but she has a presentiment of it
some moments before.

Nature arms her with it, said I, for immediate preservation. But I think, said she, looking in my face,
I had no evil to apprehend, and to deal frankly with
you, had determined to accept it. If I had—(she stopped
a moment)—I believe your good-will would have drawn
a story from me, which would have made pity the only
dangerous thing in the journey.

In saying this, she suffered me to kiss her hand twice,
and with a look of sensibility mixed with a concern, she
got out of the chaise and bid adieu.

IN THE STREET

CALAIS

I NEVER finished a twelve-guinea bargain so expeditiously
in my life: my time seemed heavy upon the loss of the
lady, and knowing every moment of it would be as

two, till I put myself into motion, I ordered post-horses directly, and walked towards the hotel.

Lord! said I, hearing the town-clock strike four, and recollecting that I had been little more than a single hour in Calais.

What a large volume of adventures may be grasped within this little span of life, by him who interests his heart in every thing, and who, having eyes to see what time and chance are perpetually holding out to him as he journeyeth on his way, misses nothing he can *fairly* lay his hands on.

If this won't turn out something, another will. No matter: 'tis an assay upon human nature. I get my labour for my pains—'tis enough—the pleasure of the experiment has kept my senses and the best part of my blood awake, and laid the gross to sleep.

I pity the man who can travel from *Dan* to *Beersheba*, and cry, 'Tis all barren. And so it is; and so is all the world to him, who will not cultivate the fruits it offers. I declare, said I, clapping my hands cheerily together, that was I in a desert, I would find out wherewith in it to call forth my affections. If I could not do better, I would fasten them upon some sweet myrtle, or seek some melancholy cypress to connect myself to. I would court their shade, and greet them kindly for their protection; I would cut my name upon them, and swear they were the loveliest trees throughout the desert: if their leaves wither'd, I would teach myself to mourn, and when they rejoiced, I would rejoice along with them.

The learned SMELFUNGUS travelled from Boulogne to Paris, from Paris to Rome, and so on, but he set out with the spleen and jaundice, and every object he pass'd by was discoloured or distorted. He wrote an account of them, but 'twas nothing but the account of his miserable feelings.

I met Smelfungus in the grand portico of the pantheon —he was just coming out of it. *'Tis nothing but a huge cockpit,*[1] said he. I wish you had said nothing worse of the Venus of Medicis, replied I, for in passing through Florence, I had heard he had fallen foul upon the goddess, and used her worse than a common strumpet, without the least provocation in nature.

I popp'd upon Smelfungus again at Turin, in his return home; and a sad tale of sorrowful adventures he had to tell, "wherein he spoke of moving accidents by flood and field, and of the cannibals which each other eat: the Anthropophagi"—he had been flay'd alive, and bedevil'd, and used worse than St. Bartholomew, at every stage he had come at.

I'll tell it, cried Smelfungus, to the world. You had better tell it, said I, to your physician.

Mundungus, with an immense fortune, made the whole tour; going on from Rome to Naples, from Naples to Venice, from Venice to Vienna, to Dresden, to Berlin, without one generous connection or pleasurable anecdote to tell of; but he had travell'd straight on, looking neither to his right hand or his left, lest Love or Pity should seduce him out of his road.

Peace be to them! if it is to be found; but heaven itself, was it possible to get there with such tempers, would want objects to give it. Every gentle spirit would come flying upon the wings of Love to hail their arrival. Nothing would the souls of Smelfungus and Mundungus hear of, but fresh anthems of joy, fresh raptures of love, and fresh congratulations of their common felicity. I heartily pity them: they have brought up no faculties for this work; and was the happiest mansion in heaven to be allotted to Smelfungus and Mundungus, they

[1] *Vide* S——'s Travels.

would be so far from being happy, that the souls of Smelfungus and Mundungus would do penance there to all eternity.

MONTRIUL

I HAD once lost my portmanteau from behind my chaise, and twice got out in the rain, and one of the times up to the knees in dirt, to help the postillion to tie it on, without being able to find out what was wanting. Nor was it till I got to Montriul, upon the landlord's asking me if I wanted not a servant, that it occurred to me, that that was the very thing.

A servant! That I do most sadly, quoth I. Because, Monsieur, said the landlord, there is a clever young fellow, who would be very proud of the honour to serve an Englishman. But why an English one, more than any other? They are so generous, said the landlord. I'll be shot if this is not a livre out of my pocket, quoth I to myself, this very night. But they have wherewithal to be so, Monsieur, added he. Set down one livre more for that, quoth I. It was but last night, said the landlord, *qu'un my Lord Anglois presentoit un ecu à la fille de chambre. Tant pis, pour Mademoiselle Janatone*, said I.

Now Janatone being the landlord's daughter, and the landlord supposing I was young in French, took the liberty to inform me, I should not have said *tant pis* but, *tant mieux. Tant mieux, toujours, Monsieur*, said he, when there is any thing to be got; *tant pis*, when there is nothing. It comes to the same thing, said I. *Pardonnez moi*, said the landlord.

I cannot take a fitter opportunity to observe, once

for all, that *tant pis* and *tant mieux* being two of the great hinges in French conversation, a stranger would do well to set himself right in the use of them, before he gets to Paris.

A prompt French Marquis at our ambassador's table demanded of Mr. H——, if he was H—— the poet? No, said H—— mildly. *Tant pis*, replied the Marquis.

It is H—— the historian, said another. *Tant mieux*, said the Marquis. And Mr. H——, who is a man of an excellent heart, return'd thanks for both.

When the landlord had set me right in this matter, he called in La Fleur, which was the name of the young man he had spoke of, saying only first, That as for his talents, he would presume to say nothing—Monsieur was the best judge what would suit him; but for the fidelity of La Fleur, he would stand responsible in all he was worth.

The landlord deliver'd this in a manner which instantly set my mind to the business I was upon, and La Fleur, who stood waiting without, in that breathless expectation which every son of nature of us have felt in our turns, came in.

MONTRIUL

I AM apt to be taken with all kinds of people at first sight; but never more so, than when a poor devil comes to offer his service to so poor a devil as myself; and as I know this weakness, I always suffer my judgment to draw back something on that very account—and this more or less, according to the mood I am in, and the case, and I may add the gender too, of the person I am to govern.

When La Fleur entered the room, after every discount I could make for my soul, the genuine look and air of the fellow determined the matter at once in his favour; so I hired him first and then began to inquire what he could do: But I shall find out his talents, quoth I, as I want them; besides, a Frenchman can do every thing.

Now poor La Fleur could do nothing in the world but beat a drum, and play a march or two upon the fife. I was determined to make his talents do: and can't say my weakness was ever so insulted by my wisdom, as in the attempt.

La Fleur had set out early in life, as gallantly as most Frenchmen do, with *serving* for a few years: at the end of which, having satisfied the sentiment, and found moreover, That the honour of beating a drum was likely to be its own reward, as it open'd no further track of glory to him, he retired *à ses terres*, and lived *comme il plaisoit à Dieu*—that is to say, upon nothing.

And so, quoth *Wisdom*, you have hired a drummer to attend you in this tour of yours through France and Italy! Psha! said I, and do not one half of our gentry go with a humdrum *compagnon du voyage* the same round, and have the piper and the devil and all to pay besides? When man can extricate himself with an *equivoque* in such an unequal match he is not ill off. But you can do something else, La Fleur? said I. *O qu'oui !* he could make spatterdashes, and play a little upon the fiddle. Bravo! said Wisdom. Why I play a bass myself, said I; we shall do very well. You can shave, and dress a wig a little, La Fleur? He had all the dispositions in the world. It is enough for heaven! said I, interrupting him, and ought to be enough for me. So supper coming in, and having a frisky English spaniel on one side of my chair, and a French valet, with as much hilarity in his countenance as ever nature painted in one, on the other, I was satisfied to my heart's content with my empire; and if monarchs knew what they would be at, they might be satisfied as I was.

MONTRIUL

As La Fleur went the whole tour of France and Italy with me, and will be often upon the stage, I must interest the reader a little further in his behalf, by saying, that I had never less reason to repent of the impulses which generally do determine me, than in regard to this fellow. He was a faithful, affectionate, simple soul as ever trudged after the heels of a philosopher; and notwithstanding his talents of drum-beating and spatterdash-making, which, though very good in themselves, happened to be of no great service to me, yet was I hourly recompensed by the festivity of his temper. It supplied all defects. I had a constant resource in his looks, in all difficulties and distresses of my own —I was going to have added, of his too; but La Fleur was out of the reach of every thing; for whether it was hunger or thirst, or cold or nakedness, or watchings, or whatever stripes of ill luck La Fleur met with in our journeyings, there was no index in his physiognomy to point them out by—he was eternally the same. So that if I am a piece of a philosopher, which Satan now and then puts into my head I am, it always mortifies the pride of the conceit, by reflecting how much I owe to the complexional philosophy of this poor fellow, for shaming me into one of a better kind. With all this, La Fleur had a small cast of the coxcomb, but he seemed at first sight to be more a coxcomb of nature than of art; and before I had been three days in Paris with him he seemed to be no coxcomb at all.

MONTRIUL

THE next morning, La Fleur entering upon his employment, I delivered to him the key of my portmanteau,
with an inventory of my half a dozen shirts and silk
pair of breeches; and bid him fasten all upon the chaise,
get the horses put to, and desire the landlord to come in
with his bill.

C'est un garçon de bonne fortune, said the landlord,
pointing through the window to half a dozen wenches
who had got round about La Fleur, and were most kindly
taking their leave of him, as the postillion was leading
out the horses. La Fleur kissed all their hands round and
round again, and thrice he wiped his eyes, and thrice he
promised he would bring them all pardons from Rome.

The young fellow, said the landlord, is beloved by
all the town, and there is scarce a corner in Montriul,
where the want of him will not be felt: he has but one
misfortune in the world, continued he, "He is always
in love." I am heartily glad of it, said I; 'twill save me
the trouble every night of putting my breeches under
my head. In saying this, I was making not so much
La Fleur's eloge, as my own, having been in love, with
one princess or other, almost all my life, and I hope
I shall go on so till I die, being firmly persuaded, that
if ever I do a mean action, it must be in some interval
betwixt one passion and another: whilst this interreg-
num lasts, I always perceive my heart locked up, I can
scarce find in it to give Misery a sixpence; and therefore
I always get out of it as fast as I can, and the moment
I am rekindled, I am all generosity and good-will again;
and would do any thing in the world, either for or with
any one, if they will but satisfy me there is no sin in it.

But in saying this, sure I am commending the passion,
not myself.

A FRAGMENT

THE town of Abdera, notwithstanding Democritus lived there, trying all the powers of irony and laughter to reclaim it, was the vilest and most profligate town in all Thrace. What for poisons, conspiracies, and assassinations, libels, pasquinades, and tumults, there was no going there by day; 'twas worse by night.

Now, when things were at the worst, it came to pass, that the Andromeda of Euripides being represented at Abdera, the whole orchestra was delighted with it: but of all the passages which delighted them, nothing operated more upon their imaginations, than the tender strokes of nature, which the poet had wrought up in that pathetic speech of Perseus, *O Cupid, prince of God and men,* etc. Every man almost spoke pure iambics the next day, and talk'd of nothing but Perseus his pathetic address. "O Cupid, prince of God and men." In every street of Abdera, in every house, "O Cupid! Cupid!" in every mouth, like the natural notes of some sweet melody which drops from it whether it will or no, nothing but "Cupid! Cupid! prince of God and men." The fire caught, and the whole city, like the heart of one man, open'd itself to Love.

No pharmacopolist could sell one grain of helebore, not a single armourer had a heart to forge one instrument of death. Friendship and Virtue met together, and kiss'd each other in the street, the golden age returned, and hung over the town of Abdera; every Abderite took his oaten pipe, and every Abderitish woman left her purple web, and chastely sat her down and listened to the song.

'Twas only in the power, says the Fragment, of the God whose empire extendeth from heaven to earth, and even to the depths of the sea, to have done this.

MONTRIUL

WHEN all is ready, and every article is disputed and paid for in the inn, unless you are a little sour'd by the adventure, there is always a matter to compound at the door, before you can get into your chaise, and that is with the sons and daughters of poverty, who surround you. Let no man say, "let them go to the devil." 'Tis a cruel journey to send a few miserables, and they have had sufferings enow without it: I always think it better to take a few sous out in my hand; and I would counsel every gentle traveller to do so likewise; he need not be so exact in setting down his motives for giving them—they will be register'd elsewhere.

For my own part, there is no man gives so little as I do; for few, that I know, have so little to give: but as this was the first public act of my charity in France, I took the more notice of it.

A well-a-way! said I, I have but eight sous in the world, showing them in my hand, and there are eight poor men and eight poor women for 'em.

A poor tatter'd soul, without a shirt on, instantly withdrew his claim, by retiring two steps out of the circle, and making a disqualifying bow on his part. Had the whole parterre cried out, *Place aux dames*, with one voice, it would not have conveyed the sentiment of a deference for the sex with half the effect.

Just Heaven! for what wise reasons hast thou ordered it, that beggary and urbanity, which are at such variance in other countries, should find a way to be at unity in this?

I insisted upon presenting him with a single sous, merely for his *politesse*.

A poor little dwarfish, brisk fellow, who stood over-

against me in the circle, putting something first under
his arm, which had once been a hat, took his snuff-box
out of his pocket, and generously offer'd a pinch on
both sides of him: it was a gift of consequence, and
modestly declined. The poor little fellow press'd it
upon them with a nod of welcomeness. *Prenez en, prenez,*
said he, looking another way; so they each took a pinch.
Pity thy box should ever want one, said I to myself;
so I put a couple of sous into it, taking a small pinch
out of his box to enhance their value, as I did it. He
felt the weight of the second obligation more than of
the first: 'twas doing him an honour, the other was only
doing him a charity, and he made me a bow down to
the ground for it.

Here! said I to an old soldier with one hand, who had
been campaign'd and worn out to death in the service;
here's a couple of sous for thee. *Vive le Roi !* said the
old soldier.

I had then but three sous left: so I gave one, simply
pour l'amour de Dieu, which was the footing on which
it was begg'd. The poor woman had a dislocated hip;
so it could not be well upon any other motive.

Mon cher et tres charitable Monsieur ! There's no
opposing this, said I.

My Lord Anglois ! The very sound was worth the
money—so I gave *my last sous for it.* But in the eagerness
of giving, I had overlooked a *pauvre honteux,* who had
no one to ask a sous for him, and who, I believed, would
have perished ere he could have ask'd one for himself;
he stood by the chaise, a little without the circle, and
wiped a tear from a face which I thought had seen
better days. Good God! said I, and I have not one
single sous left to give him. But you have a thousand!
cried all the powers of nature, stirring within me. So
I gave him—no matter what—I am ashamed to say

how much, now, and was ashamed to think how little, then: so if the reader can form any conjecture of my disposition, as these two fixed points are given him, he may judge within a livre or two what was the precise sum.

I could afford nothing for the rest, but *Dieu vous benisse. Et le bon Dieu vous benisse encore*, said the old soldier, the dwarf, etc. The *pauvre honteux* could say nothing: he pull'd out a little handkerchief, and wiped his face as he turned away—and I thought he thanked me more than them all.

THE BIDET

HAVING settled all these little matters, I got into my post-chaise with more ease than ever I got into a post-chaise in my life; and La Fleur having got one large jack-boot on the far side of a little *bidet*,[1] and another on this (for I count nothing of his legs), he canter'd away before me as happy and as perpendicular as a prince.

But what is happiness! what is grandeur in this painted scene of life! A dead ass, before we had got a league, put a sudden stop to La Fleur's career—his bidet would not pass by it. A contention arose betwixt them, and the poor fellow was kick'd out of his jack-boots the very first kick.

La Fleur bore his fall like a French Christian, saying neither more or less upon it, than, Diable! so presently got up and came to the charge again astride his bidet, beating him up to it as he would have beat his drum.

The bidet flew from one side of the road to the other,

[1] Post-horse.

then back again, then this way, then that way, and in short every way but by the dead ass. La Fleur insisted upon the thing—and the bidet threw him.

What's the matter, La Fleur, said I, with this bidet of thine? *Monsieur*, said he, *c'est un cheval le plus opiniatre du monde*. Nay, if he is a conceited beast, he must go his own way, replied I. So La Fleur got off him, and giving him a good sound lash, the bidet took me at my word, and away he scamper'd back to Montriul. *Peste !* said La Fleur.

It is not *mal-à-propos* to take notice here, that though La Fleur availed himself but of two different terms of exclamation in this encounter, namely, *Diable !* and *Peste !* that there are nevertheless three in the French language; like the positive, comparative, and superlative, one or the other of which serve for every unexpected throw of the dice in life.

Le Diable ! which is the first, and positive degree, is generally used upon ordinary emotions of the mind, where small things only fall out contrary to your expectations, such as, the throwing once doublets, La Fleur's being kick'd off his horse, and so forth; cuckoldom, for the same reason, is always *Le Diable !*

But in cases where the cast has something provoking in it, as in that of the bidet's running away after, and leaving La Fleur aground in jack-boots, 'tis the second degree.

'Tis then *Peste !*

And for the third——

But here my heart is wrung with pity and fellow-feeling, when I reflect what miseries must have been their lot, and how bitterly so refined a people must have smarted, to have forced upon them the use of it.

Grant me, O ye powers which touch the tongue with eloquence in distress!—whatever is my *cast*, grant me but decent words to exclaim in, and I will give my nature way.

But as these were not to be had in France, I resolved to take every evil just as it befel me, without any exclamation at all.

La Fleur, who had made no such covenant with himself, followed the bidet with his eyes till it was got out of sight; and then, you may imagine, if you please, with what word he closed the whole affair.

As there was no hunting down a frightened horse in jack-boots, there remained no alternative but taking La Fleur either behind the chaise, or into it.

I preferred the latter, and in half an hour we got to the post-house at Nampont.

NAMPONT

THE DEAD ASS

AND this, said he, putting the remains of a crust into his wallet, and this should have been thy portion, said he, hadst thou been alive to have shared it with me. I thought by the accent, it had been an apostrophe to his child; but 'twas to his ass, and to the very ass we had seen dead in the road, which had occasioned La Fleur's misadventure. The man seemed to lament it much; and it instantly brought into my mind Sancho's lamentation for his; but he did it with more true touches of nature.

The mourner was sitting upon a stone-bench at the door, with the ass's pannel and its bridle on one side, which he took up from time to time, then laid them down, look'd at them and shook his head. He then took his crust of bread out of his wallet again, as if to eat it;

held it some time in his hand, then laid it upon the bit
of his ass's bridle, looked wistfully at the little arrangement he had made, and then gave a sigh.

The simplicity of his grief drew numbers about him,
and La Fleur amongst the rest, whilst the horses were
getting ready; as I continued sitting in the post-chaise,
I could see and hear over their heads.

He said he had come from Spain, where he had been
from the furthest borders of Franconia; and had got
so far on his return home, when his ass died. Every one
seemed desirous to know what business could have
taken so old and poor a man so far a journey from his
own home.

It had pleased Heaven, he said, to bless him with
three sons, the finest lads in all Germany; but having
in one week lost two of the eldest of them by the small-
pox, and the youngest falling ill of the same distemper,
he was afraid of being bereft of them all; and made a
vow, if Heaven would not take him from him also, he
would go in gratitude to St. Iago in Spain.

When the mourner got thus far on his story, he
stopp'd to pay nature his tribute and wept bitterly.

He said, Heaven had accepted the conditions, and
that he had set out from his cottage with this poor
creature, who had been a patient partner of his journey,
that it had eat the same bread with him all the way, and
was unto him as a friend.

Every body who stood about, heard the poor fellow
with concern. La Fleur offered him money. The mourner
said, he did not want it—it was not the value of the ass,
but the loss of him. The ass, he said, he was assured
loved him; and upon this told them a long story of a
mischance upon their passage over the Pyrenean mountains, which had separated them from each other three
days; during which time the ass had sought him as much

as he had sought the ass, and that they had neither scarce eat or drank till they met.

Thou hast one comfort, friend, said I, at least, in the loss of thy poor beast; I'm sure thou hast been a merciful master to him. Alas! said the mourner, I thought so, when he was alive, but now that he is dead I think otherwise. I fear the weight of myself and my afflictions together have been too much for him—they have shortened the poor creature's days, and I fear I have them to answer for. Shame on the world! said I to myself; did we love each other, as this poor soul but loved his ass, 'twould be something.

NAMPONT

THE POSTILLION

THE concern which the poor fellow's story threw me into required some attention: the postillion paid not the least to it, but set off upon the *pavé* in a full gallop.

The thirstiest soul in the most sandy desert of Arabia could not have wished more for a cup of cold water, than mine did for grave and quiet movements; and I should have had an high opinion of the postillion, had he but stolen off with me in something like a pensive pace. On the contrary, as the mourner finished his lamentation, the fellow gave an unfeeling lash to each of his beasts, and set off clattering like a thousand devils.

I called to him as loud as I could, for heaven's sake to go slower, and the louder I called, the more unmercifully he galloped. The duce take him and his galloping too, said I, he'll go on tearing my nerves to pieces till he has worked me into a foolish passion, and then he'll go slow, that I may enjoy the sweets of it.

The postillion managed the point to a miracle: by the time he had got to the foot of a steep hill about half a league from Nampont, he had put me out of temper with him and then with myself, for being so.

My case then required a different treatment; and a good rattling gallop would have been of real service to me.

Then, prithee, get on; get on, my good lad, said I.

The postillion pointed to the hill. I then tried to return back to the story of the poor German and his ass, but I had broke the clue and could no more get into it again, than the postillion could into a trot.

The duce go, said I, with it all! Here am I sitting as candidly disposed to make the best of the worst, as ever wight was, and all runs counter.

There is one sweet lenitive at least for evils, which Nature holds out to us: so I took it kindly at her hands, and fell asleep; and the first word which roused me was *Amiens*.

Bless me! said I, rubbing my eyes; this is the very town where my poor lady is to come.

AMIENS

THE words were scarce out of my mouth, when the Count de L——'s post-chaise, with his sister in it, drove hastily by: she had just time to make me a bow of recognition—and of that particular kind of it, which told me she had not yet done with me. She was as good as her look; for, before I had quite finished my supper, her brother's servant came into the room with a billet, in which she said she had taken the liberty to charge me with a letter, which I was to present myself to Madame R—— the first morning I had nothing to do at Paris. There was only added, she was sorry, but from what *penchant* she had not considered, that she had been prevented telling me her story, that she still owed it me; and if my route should ever lay through Brussels, and I had not by then forgot the name of Madame de L——, that Madame de L—— would be glad to discharge her obligation.

Then I will meet thee, said I, fair spirit! at Brussels —'tis only returning from Italy through Germany to Holland, by the route of Flanders, home—'twill scarce be ten posts out of my way; but were it ten thousand! with what a moral delight will it crown my journey, in sharing in the sickening incidents of a tale of misery told to me by such a sufferer! to see her weep! and though I cannot dry up the fountain of her tears, what an exquisite sensation is there still left, in wiping them away from off the cheeks of the first and fairest of women, as I'm sitting with my handkerchief in my hand in silence the whole night beside her?

There was nothing wrong in the sentiment; and yet I instantly reproached my heart with it in the bitterest and most reprobate of expressions.

It had ever, as I told the reader, been one of the singular blessings of my life, to be almost every hour of it miserably in love with some one; and my last flame happening to be blown out by a whiff of jealousy on the sudden turn of a corner, I had lighted it up afresh at the pure taper of Eliza but about three months before, swearing as I did it, that it should last me through the whole journey. Why should I dissemble the matter? I had sworn to her eternal fidelity; she had a right to my whole heart; to divide my affections was to lessen them; to expose them, was to risk them: where there is risk, there may be loss:—and what wilt thou have, Yorick! to answer a heart so full of trust and confidence, so good, so gentle, and unreproaching!

I will not go to Brussels, replied I, interrupting myself—but my imagination went on. I recalled her looks at that crisis of our separation, when neither of us had power to say adieu! I look'd at the picture she had tied in a black ribband about my neck and blush'd as I look'd at it. I would have given the world to have kiss'd it, but was ashamed. And shall this tender flower, said I, pressing it between my hands, shall it be smitten to its very root, and smitten, Yorick! by thee, who hast promised to shelter it in thy breast?

Eternal fountain of happiness! said I, kneeling down upon the ground, be thou my witness, and every pure spirit which tastes it, be my witness also, That I would not travel to Brussels, unless Eliza went along with me, did the road lead me towards heaven.

In transports of this kind, the heart, in spite of the understanding, will always say too much.

THE LETTER

AMIENS

FORTUNE had not smiled upon La Fleur; for he had been unsuccessful in his feats of chivalry, and not one thing had offered to signalize his zeal for my service from the time he had entered into it, which was almost four-and-twenty hours. The poor soul burn'd with impatience; and the Count de L——'s servant coming with the letter, being the first practicable occasion which offered, La Fleur had laid hold of it; and in order to do honour to his master, had taken him into a back parlour in the Auberge, and treated him with a cup or two of the best wine in Picardy; and the Count de L——'s servant, in return, and not to be behind-

hand in politeness with La Fleur, had taken him back
with him to the Count's hotel. La Fleur's *prevenancy*
(for there was a passport in his very looks) soon set
every servant in the kitchen at ease with him; and as
a Frenchman, whatever be his talents, has no sort of
prudery in showing them, La Fleur, in less than five
minutes, had pulled out his fife, and leading off the
dance himself with the first note, set the *fille de chambre*,
the *maitre d'hotel*, the cook, the scullion, and all the
household, dogs and cats, besides an old monkey,
a-dancing: I suppose there never was a merrier kitchen
since the flood.

Madame de L——, in passing from her brother's
apartments to her own, hearing so much jollity below
stairs, rung up her *fille de chambre* to ask about it; and
hearing it was the English gentleman's servant who had
set the whole house merry with his pipe, she ordered
him up.

As the poor fellow could not present himself empty,
he had loaden'd himself in going up stairs with a
thousand compliments to Madame de L——, on the
part of his master; added a long apocrypha of inquiries
after Madame de L——'s health; told her, that Monsieur
his master was *au desespoire* for her re-establishment
from the fatigues of her journey; and, to close all, that
Monsieur had received the letter which Madame had
done him the honour—And he has done me the honour,
said Madame de L——, interrupting La Fleur, to send
a billet in return.

Madame de L—— had said this with such a tone of
reliance upon the fact, that La Fleur had not power
to disappoint her expectations. He trembled for my
honour, and possibly might not altogether be uncon-
cerned for his own, as a man capable of being attached
to a master who could be wanting *en egards vis à vis*

d'une femme ! so that when Madame de L—— asked
La Fleur if he had brought a letter—*O qu'oui*, said La
Fleur; so laying down his hat upon the ground, and
taking hold of the flap of his right side pocket with his
left-hand, he began to search for the letter with his
right, then contrary-wise. *Diable !* Then sought every
pocket, pocket by pocket, round, not forgetting his fob.
Peste ! Then La Fleur emptied them upon the floor;
pulled out a dirty cravat, a handkerchief, a comb, a
whip-lash, a night-cap, then gave a peep into his hat.
Quelle etourderie ! He had left the letter upon the table
in the Auberge—he would run for it, and be back with
it in three minutes.

I had just finished my supper when La Fleur came
in to give me an account of his adventure: he told the
whole story simply as it was; and only added, that if
Monsieur had forgot (*par hazard*) to answer Madame's
letter, the arrangement gave him an opportunity to
recover the *faux pas*—and if not, that things were only
as they were.

Now I was not altogether sure of my *etiquette*, whether
I ought to have wrote or no; but if I had, a devil himself
could not have been angry: 'Twas but the officious zeal
of a well-meaning creature for my honour; and however
he might have mistook the road, or embarrassed me in
so doing, his heart was in no fault, I was under no
necessity to write, and what weighed more than all, he
did not look as if he had done amiss.

'Tis all very well, La Fleur, said I. 'Twas sufficient.
La Fleur flew out of the room like lightning, and return'd
with pen, ink, and paper, in his hand; and coming up
to the table, laid them close before me, with such a
delight in his countenance, that I could not help taking
up the pen.

I begun and begun again; and though I had nothing

to say, and that nothing might have been expressed in half a dozen lines, I made half a dozen different beginnings, and could no way please myself.

In short, I was in no mood to write.

La Fleur stepp'd out and brought a little water in a glass to dilute my ink, then fetched sand and seal-wax. It was all one; I wrote, and blotted, and tore off, and burnt, and wrote again. *Le diable l'emporte*, said I half to myself; I cannot write this self-same letter; throwing the pen down despairingly as I said it.

As soon as I had cast down the pen, La Fleur advanced with the most respectful carriage up to the table, and making a thousand apologies for the liberty he was going to take, told me he had a letter in his pocket wrote by a drummer in his regiment to a corporal's wife, which, he durst say, would suit the occasion.

I had a mind to let the poor fellow have his humour. Then prithee, said I, let me see it.

La Fleur instantly pulled out a little dirty pocket book cramm'd full of small letters and billet-doux in a sad condition, and laying it upon the table, and then untying the string which held them all together, run them over one by one, till he came to the letter in question. *La voila*, said he, clapping his hands: so unfolding it first, he laid it before me, and retired three steps from the table whilst I read it.

THE LETTER

MADAME,

  Je suis penetré de la douler la plus vive, et reduit en même temps au desespoir par ce retour imprevû du Corporal qui rend notre entrevue de ce soir la chose du monde la plus impossible.

Mais vive la joie! et toute la mienne sera de penser à vous.

L'amour n'est *rien* sans sentiment.

Et le sentiment est encore *moins* sans amour.

On dit qu'on ne doit jamais se desesperer.

On dit aussi que Monsieur le Corporal monte la garde Mercredi: alors ce sera mon tour.

Chacun à son tour.

En attendant—Vive l'amour! et vive la bagatelle!

Je suis, MADAME,
Avec toutes les sentiments les
plus respectueux et les plus
tendres, tout à vous,

JAQUES ROQUE.

It was but changing the Corporal into the Count and saying nothing about mounting guard on Wednesday, and the letter was neither right or wrong. So to gratify the poor fellow, who stood trembling, for my honour, his own, and the honour of his letter, I took the cream gently off it, and whipping it up my own way, I seal'd it up and sent him with it to Madame de L——, and the next morning we pursued our journey to Paris.

PARIS

WHEN a man can contest the point by dint of equipage, and carry on all floundering before him with half a dozen lackies and a couple of cooks, 'tis very well in such a place as Paris—he may drive in at which end of a street he will.

A poor prince who is weak in cavalry, and whose whole infantry does not exceed a single man, had best quit the field; and signalize himself in the cabinet, if

he can get up into it—I say *up into it*, for there is no
descending perpendicular amongst 'em with a *"Me voici,
mes enfans"* (here I am), whatever many may think.

I own my first sensations, as soon as I was left solitary
and alone in my own chamber in the hotel, were far
from being so flattering as I had prefigured them.
I walked up gravely to the window in my dusty black
coat, and looking through the glass saw all the world in
yellow, blue, and green, running at the ring of pleasure.
The old with broken lances, and in helmets which
had lost their vizards, the young in armour bright
which shone like gold, beplumed with each gay feather
of the east, all—all—tilting at it like fascinated knights
in tournaments of yore for fame and love.

Alas, poor Yorick! cried I, what art thou doing here?
On the very first onset of all this glittering clatter thou
art reduced to an atom. Seek—seek some winding alley,
with a tourniquet at the end of it, where chariot never
rolled or flambeau shot its rays: there thou mayest
solace thy soul in converse sweet with some kind *grisset*
of a barber's wife, and get into such coteries!

May I perish! if I do, said I, pulling out a letter
which I had to present to Madame de R——. I'll wait
upon this lady, the very first thing I do. So I called
La Fleur to go seek me a barber directly, and come back
and brush my coat.

THE WIG

PARIS

WHEN the barber came, he absolutely refused to have
any thing to do with my wig: 'twas either above or
below his art: I had nothing to do, but to take one
ready made of his own recommendation.

But I fear, friend! said I, this buckle won't stand.
You may immerge it, replied he, into the ocean, and
it will stand.

What a great scale is every thing upon in this city!
thought I. The utmost stretch of an English periwig-
maker's ideas could have gone no further than to have
"dipped it into a pail of water." What difference! 'tis
like time to eternity.

I confess I do hate all cold conceptions, as I do the
puny ideas which engender them; and am generally so
struck with the great works of nature, that for my own
part, if I could help it, I never would make a comparison less than a mountain at least. All that can be
said against the French sublime in this instance of it,
is this: that the grandeur is *more* in the *word*; and *less*
in the *thing*. No doubt the ocean fills the mind with
vast ideas; but Paris being so far inland, it was not
likely I should run post a hundred miles out of it, to
try the experiment—the Parisian barber meant nothing.

The pail of water standing beside the great deep,
makes certainly but a sorry figure in speech, but 'twill
be said it has one advantage: 'tis in the next room,
and the truth of the buckle may be tried in it, without
more ado, in a single moment.

In honest truth, and upon a more candid revision of
the matter, *The French expression professes more than
it performs.*

I think I can see the precise and distinguishing marks
of national characters more in these nonsensical *minutiæ*,
than in the most important matters of state; where
great men of all nations talk and stalk so much alike,
that I would not give nine-pence to chuse amongst them.

I was so long in getting from under my barber's
hands, that it was too late to think of going with my
letter to Madame R—— that night: but when a man is

once dressed at all points for going out, his reflections turn to little account; so taking down the name of the Hotel de Modene, where I lodged, I walked forth without any determination where to go. I shall consider of that, said I, as I walk along.

THE PULSE

PARIS

HAIL ye small sweet courtesies of life, for smooth do ye make the road of it! like grace and beauty which beget inclinations to love at first sight: 'tis ye who open this door and let the stranger in.

Pray, Madame, said I, have the goodness to tell me which way I must turn to go to the Opera comique. Most willingly, Monsieur, said she, laying aside her work.

I had given a cast with my eye into half a dozen shops as I came along in search of a face not likely to be disordered by such an interruption; till at last, this hitting my fancy, I had walked in.

She was working a pair of ruffles as she sat in a low chair on the far side of the shop facing the door.

Tres volontiers ; most willingly, said she, laying her work down upon a chair next her, and rising up from the low chair she was sitting in, with so chearful a movement and so chearful a look, that had I been laying out fifty louis d'ors with her, I should have said "This woman is grateful."

You must turn, Monsieur, said she, going with me to the door of the shop, and pointing the way down the street I was to take, you must turn first to your left hand—*mais prenez garde*, there are two turns, and be so good as to take the second—then go down a little way and you'll see a church, and when you are past it, give yourself the trouble to turn directly to the right, and that will lead you to the foot of the *Pont Neuf*, which you must cross; and there any one will do himself the pleasure to shew you.

She repeated her instructions three times over to me, with the same good-natur'd patience the third time as the first; and if *tones and manners* have a meaning, which certainly they have, unless to hearts which shut them out, she seemed really interested, that I should not lose myself.

I will not suppose it was the woman's beauty, notwithstanding she was the handsomest Grisset, I think, I ever saw, which had much to do with the sense I had of her courtesy; only I remember, when I told her how much I was obliged to her, that I looked very full in her eyes and that I repeated my thanks as often as she had done her instructions.

I had not got ten paces from the door, before I found I had forgot every tittle of what she had said; so looking back, and seeing her still standing in the door of the shop as if to look whether I went right or not, I returned back, to ask her whether the first turn was to my right or left, for that I had absolutely forgot. Is it possible? said she, half laughing. 'Tis very possible, replied I, when a man is thinking more of a woman, than of her good advice.

As this was the real truth she took it, as every woman takes a matter of right, with a slight courtesy.

Attendez, said she, laying her hand upon my arm to detain me, whilst she called a lad out of the back-shop to get ready a parcel of gloves. I am just going to send him, said she, with a packet into that quarter, and if you will have the complaisance to step in, it will be ready in a moment, and he shall attend you to the place. So I walk'd in with her to the far side of the shop, and taking up the ruffle in my hand which she laid upon the chair, as if I had a mind to sit, she sat down herself in her low chair, and I instantly sat myself down beside her.

He will be ready, Monsieur, said she, in a moment. And in that moment, replied I, most willingly would I say something very civil to you for all these courtesies. Any one may do a casual act of good-nature, but a continuation of them shows it is a part of the temperature; and certainly, added I, if it is the same blood which comes from the heart, which descends to the extremes (touching her wrist), I am sure you must have one of the best pulses of any woman in the world. Feel it, said she, holding out her arm. So laying down my hat, I took hold of her fingers in one hand, and applied the two fore-fingers of my other to the artery.

Would to heaven! my dear Eugenius, thou hadst passed by, and beheld me sitting in my black coat, and in my lack-a-day-sical manner, counting the throbs of it, one by one, with as much true devotion as if I had been watching the critical ebb or flow of her fever! How wouldst thou have laugh'd and moralized upon my new profession! And thou shouldst have laugh'd and moralized on. Trust me, my dear Eugenius, I should have said, "there are worse occupations in this world *than feeling a woman's pulse.*" But a Grisset's! thou wouldst have said, and in an open shop! Yorick——

So much the better: for when my views are direct, Eugenius, I care not if all the world saw me feel it.

THE HUSBAND

PARIS

I HAD counted twenty pulsations, and was going on fast towards the fortieth, when her husband coming unexpected from a back parlour into the shop, put me a little out of my reckoning. 'Twas nobody but her husband, she said, so I began a fresh score. Monsieur is so good, quoth she, as he pass'd by us, as to give himself the trouble of feeling my pulse. The husband took off his hat, and making me a bow, said, I did him too much honour; and having said that, he put on his hat and walk'd out.

Good God! said I to myself, as he went out, and can this man be the husband of this woman!

Let it not torment the few who know what must have been the grounds of this exclamation, if I explain it to those who do not.

In London a shopkeeper and a shopkeeper's wife seem to be one bone and one flesh: in the several endowments of mind and body, sometimes the one, sometimes the other has it, so as in general to be upon a par, and to tally with each other as nearly as a man and wife need to do.

In Paris, there are scarce two orders of beings more different: for the legislative and executive powers of the shop not resting in the husband, he seldom comes there. In some dark and dismal room behind, he sits commerceless in his thrum night-cap, the same rough son of Nature that Nature left him.

The genius of a people where nothing but the monarchy is *salique*, having ceded this department, with sundry others, totally to the women—by a continual higgling with customers of all ranks and sizes from morning to night, like so many rough pebbles shook long together in a bag, by amicable collisions, they have worn down their asperities and sharp angles, and not only become round and smooth, but will receive, some of them, a polish like a brilliant—Monsieur *le Mari* is little better than the stone under your foot.

Surely, surely, man! it is not good for thee to sit alone—thou wast made for social intercourse and gentle greetings, and this improvement of our natures from it, I appeal to, as my evidence.

And how does it beat, Monsieur? said she. With all the benignity, said I, looking quietly in her eyes, that I expected. She was going to say something civil in return, but the lad came into the shop with the gloves. *A propos*, said I, I want a couple of pair myself.

THE GLOVES

PARIS

THE beautiful Grisset rose up when I said this, and going behind the counter, reach'd down a parcel and untied it: I advanced to the side over-against her: they were all too large. The beautiful Grisset measured them one by one across my hand—it would not alter the dimensions. She begg'd I would try a single pair, which seemed to be the least. She held it open; my hand slipped into it at once. It will not do, said I, shaking my head a little. No, said she, doing the same thing.

There are certain combined looks of simple subtlety, where whim, and sense, and seriousness, and nonsense, are so blended, that all the languages of Babel set loose together could not express them: they are communicated and caught so instantaneously, that you can

scarce say which party is the infector. I leave it to your
men of words to swell pages about it—it is enough in
the present to say again, the gloves would not do; so
folding our hands within our arms, we both loll'd upon
the counter. It was narrow, and there was just room for
the parcel to lay between us.

The beautiful Grisset look'd sometimes at the gloves,
then side-ways to the window, then at the gloves, and
then at me. I was not disposed to break silence—
I follow'd her example: so I look'd at the gloves, then
to the window, then at the gloves, and then at her, and
so on alternately.

I found I lost considerably in every attack. She had
a quick black eye, and shot through two such long and
silken eye-lashes with such penetration, that she look'd
into my very heart and reins. It may seem strange, but
I could actually feel she did.

It is no matter, said I, taking up a couple of the pairs
next me, and putting them into my pocket.

I was sensible the beautiful Grisset had not ask'd
above a single livre above the price—I wish'd she had
ask'd a livre more, and was puzzling my brains how to
bring the matter about. Do you think, my dear Sir,
said she, mistaking my embarrassment, that I could
ask a *sous* too much of a stranger, and of a stranger
whose politeness, more than his want of gloves, has
done me the honour to lay himself at my mercy? *M'en
croyez capable?* Faith! not I, said I; and if you were,
you are welcome. So counting the money into her hand,
and with a lower bow than one generally makes to a shopkeeper's wife, I went out, and her lad with his parcel
followed me.

THE TRANSLATION

PARIS

THERE was nobody in the box I was let into but a kindly old French officer. I love the character, not only because I honour the man whose manners are softened by a profession which makes bad men worse; but that I once knew one—for he is no more—and why should I not rescue one page from violation by writing his name in it, and telling the world it was Captain Tobias Shandy, the dearest of my flock and friends, whose philanthropy I never think of at this long distance from his death but my eyes gush out with tears. For his sake, I have a predilection for the whole corps of veterans; and so I strode over the two back rows of benches, and placed myself beside him.

The old officer was reading attentively a small pamphlet, it might be the book of the opera, with a large pair of spectacles. As soon as I sat down, he took his spectacles off, and putting them into a shagreen case, return'd them and the book into his pocket together. I half rose up, and made him a bow.

Translate this into any civilised language in the world, the sense is this:

"Here's a poor stranger come into the box—he seems as if he knew nobody and is never likely, was he to be seven years in Paris, if every man he comes near keeps his spectacles upon his nose. 'Tis shutting the door of conversation absolutely in his face, and using him worse than a German."

The French officer might as well have said it all aloud: and if he had, I should in course have put the bow I made him into French too, and told him, "I was sensible of his attention, and return'd him a thousand thanks for it."

There is not a secret so aiding to the progress of sociality, as to get master of this *short hand*, and be quick in rendering the several turns of looks and limbs, with all their inflections and delineations, into plain words. For my own part, by long habitude, I do it so mechanically, that when I walk the streets of London, I go translating all the way; and have more than once stood behind in the circle, where not three words have been said, and have brought off twenty different dialogues with me, which I could have fairly wrote down and sworn to.

I was going one evening to Martini's concert at Milan, and was just entering the door of the hall, when the Marquisina di F——— was coming out in a sort of a hurry, she was almost upon me before I saw her; so I gave a spring to one side to let her pass. She had done the same, and on the same side too: so we ran our heads together: she instantly got to the other side to get out: I was just as unfortunate as she had been; for I had sprung to that side, and opposed her passage again. We both flew together to the other side, and then back, and so on. It was ridiculous. We both blush'd intolerably. So I did at last the thing I should have done at first: I stood stock still, and the Marquisina had no more difficulty. I had no power to go into the room, till I had made her so much reparation as to wait and follow her with my eye to the end of the passage. She look'd back twice, and walk'd along it rather sideways, as if she would make room for any one coming up stairs to pass her. No, said I; that's a vile translation: the Marquisina has a right to the best apology I can make her; and that opening is left for me to do it in. So I ran and begg'd pardon for the embarrassment I had given her, saying it was my intention to have made her way. She answered, she was guided by the same intention towards me; so we reciprocally thank'd each other. She was at the top of the stairs; and seeing no *chichesbee* near her, I begg'd to hand her to her coach; so we went down the stairs, stopping at every third step to talk of the concert and the adventure. Upon my word, Madame, said I, when I had handed her in, I made six different efforts to let you go out. And I made six efforts, replied she, to let you enter. I wish to heaven you would make a seventh, said I. With all my heart, said she, making room. Life is too short to be long about the forms of it, so I instantly stepp'd in, and she carried me home with her. And what became of the concert, St. Cecilia, who, I suppose, was at it, knows more than I.

I will only add, that the connection which arose out of the translation, gave me more pleasure than any one I had the honour to make in Italy.

THE DWARF

PARIS

I HAD never heard the remark made by any one in my life, except by one; and who that was will probably come out in this chapter; so that being pretty much unprepossessed, there must have been grounds for what struck me the moment I cast my eyes over the parterre and that was, the unaccountable sport of nature in forming such numbers of dwarfs. No doubt, she sports at certain times in almost every corner of the world; but in Paris, there is no end to her amusements: the goddess seems almost as merry as she is wise.

As I carried my idea out of the Opera comique with

me, I measured every body I saw walking in the streets by it. Melancholy application! especially where the size was extremely little, the face extremely dark, the eyes quick, the nose long, the teeth white, the jaw prominent, to see so many miserables, by force of accidents driven out of their own proper class into the very verge of another, which it gives me pain to write down. Every third man a pigmy!—some by rickety heads and hump backs; others by bandy legs; a third set arrested by the hand of Nature in the sixth and seventh years of their growth; a fourth, in their perfect and natural state like dwarf apple-trees; from the first rudiments and stamina of their existence, never meant to grow higher.

A medical traveller might say, 'tis owing to undue bandages; a splenetic one, to want of air; and an inquisitive traveller, to fortify the system, may measure the height of their houses, the narrowness of their streets, and in how few feet square in the sixth and seventh stories such numbers of the *Bourgoisie* eat and sleep together; but I remember, Mr. Shandy the elder, who accounted for nothing like any body else, in speaking one evening of these matters, averred, that children, like other animals, might be increased almost to any size, provided they came right into the world; but the misery was, the citizens of Paris were so coop'd up, that they had not actually room enough to get them. I did not call it getting any thing, said he; 'tis getting nothing. Nay, continued he, rising in his argument, 'tis getting worse than nothing, when all you have got, after twenty or five-and-twenty years of the tenderest care and most nutritious aliment bestowed upon it, shall not at last be as high as my leg. Now, Mr. Shandy being very short, there could be nothing more said of it.

As this is not a work of reasoning, I leave the solution as I found it, and content myself with the truth only of the remark, which is verified in every lane and by-lane of Paris. I was walking down that which leads from the Carousal to the Palais Royal, and observing a little boy in some distress at the side of the gutter, which ran down the middle of it, I took hold of his hand, and help'd him over. Upon turning up his face to look at him after, I perceived he was about forty. Never mind, said I; some good body will do as much for me, when I am ninety.

I feel some little principles within me, which incline me to be merciful towards this poor blighted part of my species, who have neither size or strength to get on in the world. I cannot bear to see one of them trod upon; and had scarce got seated beside my old French officer, ere the disgust was exercised, by seeing the very thing happen under the box we sat in.

At the end of the orchestra, and betwixt that and the first side-box, there is a small esplanade left, where, when the house is full, numbers of all ranks take sanctuary. Though you stand, as in the parterre, you pay the same price as in the orchestra. A poor defenceless being of this order had got thrust, somehow or other, into this luckless place; the night was hot, and he was surrounded by beings two feet and a half higher than himself. The dwarf suffered inexpressibly on all sides; but the thing which incommoded him most, was a tall corpulent German, near seven feet high, who stood directly betwixt him and all possibility of his seeing either the stage or the actors. The poor dwarf did all he could to get a peep at what was going forwards by seeking for some little opening betwixt the German's arm and his body, trying first one side, then the other; but as the German stood square in the most unaccommodating posture that can be imagined, the dwarf might as well have been placed at the bottom of the deepest draw-well in Paris; so he civilly reach'd up his hand to the German's sleeve, and told him his distress. The German turn'd his head back, look'd down upon him as Goliah did upon David, and unfeelingly resumed his posture.

I was just then taking a pinch of snuff out of my monk's little horn box. And how would thy meek and courteous spirit, my dear monk! so temper'd to *bear and forbear!* how sweetly would it have lent an ear to this poor soul's complaint!

The old French officer, seeing me lift up my eyes with an emotion, as I made the apostrophe, took the liberty to ask me what was the matter. I told him the story in three words, and added, how inhuman it was.

By this time the dwarf was driven to extremes, and in his first transports, which are generally unreasonable, had told the German he would cut off his long queue with his knife. The German look'd back coolly, and told him he was welcome, if he could reach it.

An injury sharpen'd by an insult, be it to whom it will, makes every man of sentiment a party: I could have leap'd out of the box to have redressed it. The old French officer did it with much less confusion; for leaning a little over, and nodding to a centinel, and pointing at the same time with his finger at the distress, the centinel made his way to it. There was no occasion to tell the grievance—the thing told itself; so thrusting back the German instantly with his musket, he took the poor dwarf by the hand, and placed him before him. This is noble! said I, clapping my hands together. And yet you would not permit this, said the old officer, in England.

In England, dear Sir, said I, *we sit all at our ease.*

The old French officer would have set me at unity

with myself, in case I had been at variance, by saying it was a *bon mot*, and as a *bon mot* is always worth something at Paris, he offered me a pinch of snuff.

THE ROSE

PARIS

IT was now my turn to ask the old French officer, "what was the matter?" for a cry of *"Haussez les mains, Monsieur l'Abbé,"* re-echoed from a dozen different parts of the parterre, was as unintelligible to me, as my apostrophe to the monk had been to him.

He told me, it was some poor Abbé in one of the upper loges, who he supposed had got planted perdu behind a couple of grissets, in order to see the opera, and that the parterre espying him, were insisting upon his holding up both his hands during the representation. And can it be supposed, said I, that an ecclesiastic would pick the grissets' pockets? The old French officer smiled, and whispering in my ear, opened a door of knowledge which I had no idea of.

Good God! said I, turning pale with astonishment, is it possible, that a people so smit with sentiment should at the same time be so unclean, and so unlike themselves! *Quelle grossierté !* added I.

The French officer told me it was an illiberal sarcasm at the church, which had begun in the theatre about the time the *Tartuffe* was given in it, by Moliere, but like other remains of Gothic manners, was declining. Every nation, continued he, have their refinements and *grossiertés*, in which they take the lead, and lose it of one another by turns; that he had been in most countries, but never in one where he found not some delicacies, which others seemed to want. *Le* POUR *et le* CONTRE *se trouvant en chaque nation;* there is a balance, said he, of good and bad every where; and nothing but the knowing it is so, can emancipate one-half of the world from the prepossession which it holds against the other; that the advantage of travel, as it regarded the *sçavoir vivre,* was by seeing a great deal both of men and manners; it taught us mutual toleration; and mutual toleration, concluded he, making me a bow, taught us mutual love.

The old French officer delivered this with an air of such candour and good sense, as coincided with my first favourable impressions of his character. I thought I loved the man; but I fear I mistook the object—'twas my own way of thinking—the difference was, I could not have expressed it half so well.

It is alike troublesome to both the rider and his beast if the latter goes pricking up his ears, and starting all the way at every object which he never saw before. I have as little torment of this kind as any creature alive; and yet I honestly confess, that many a thing gave me pain, and that I blush'd at many a word the first month which I found inconsequent and perfectly innocent the second.

Madame de Rambouliet, after an acquaintance of about six weeks with her, had done me the honour to take me in her coach about two leagues out of town. Of all women, Madame de Rambouliet is the most correct; and I never wish to see one of more virtues and purity of heart. In our return back, Madame de Rambouliet desired me to pull the cord. I asked her if she wanted any thing. *Rien que pisser,* said Madame de Rambouliet.

Grieve not, gentle traveller, to let Madame de Rambouliet p—ss on. And, ye fair mystic nymphs! go each

one *pluck your rose*, and scatter them in your path, for
Madame de Rambouliet did no more. I handed Madame
de Rambouliet out of the coach; and had I been the
priest of the chaste CASTALIA, I could not have served
at her fountain with a more respectful decorum.

THE FILLE DE CHAMBRE

PARIS

WHAT the old French officer had delivered upon travelling, bringing Polonius's advice to his son upon the
same subject into my head, and that bringing in Hamlet;
and Hamlet the rest of Shakespeare's works, I stopp'd
at the Quai de Conti in my return home, to purchase
the whole set.

The bookseller said he had not a set in the world.
Comment ! said I; taking one up out of a set which lay
upon the counter betwixt us. He said, they were sent
him only to be got bound, and were to be sent back
to Versailles in the morning to the Count de B——.

And does the Count de B——, said I, read Shakespeare? *C'est un Esprit fort*, replied the bookseller. He
loves English books; and what is more to his honour,
Monsieur, he loves the English too. You speak this so
civilly, said I, that it is enough to oblige an Englishman
to lay out a louis d'or or two at your shop. The bookseller made a bow, and was going to say something,
when a young decent girl about twenty, who by her air
and dress seemed to be *fille de chambre* to some devout
woman of fashion, came into the shop and asked for
Les Egarements du Cœur & de l'Esprit: the bookseller
gave her the book directly; she pulled out a little green
sattin purse, run round with ribband of the same colour,

and putting her finger and thumb into it, she took out the money and paid for it. As I had nothing more to stay me in the shop, we both walk'd out of the door together.

And what have you to do, my dear, said I, with *The Wanderings of the Heart*, who scarce know yet you have one; nor, till love has first told you it, or some faithless shepherd has made it ache, canst thou ever be sure it is so? *Le Dieu m'en garde !* said the girl. With reason, said I, for if it is a good one, 'tis pity it should be stolen; 'tis a little treasure to thee, and gives a better air to your face, than if it was dress'd out with pearls.

The young girl listened with a submissive attention, holding her sattin purse by its ribband in her hand all the time. 'Tis a very small one, said I, taking hold of the bottom of it—she held it towards me—and there is very little in it, my dear, said I; but be but as good as thou art handsome, and heaven will fill it: I had a parcel of crowns in my hand to pay for Shakespeare; and as she had let go the purse entirely, I put a single one in; and tying up the ribband in a bowknot, returned it to her.

The young girl made me more a humble courtesy than a low one—'twas one of those quiet, thankful sinkings, where the spirit bows itself down; the body does no more than tell it. I never gave a girl a crown in my life which gave me half the pleasure.

My advice, my dear, would not have been worth a pin to you, said I, if I had not given this along with it: but now, when you see the crown, you'll remember it, so don't, my dear, lay it out in ribbands.

Upon my word, Sir, said the girl, earnestly, I am incapable. In saying which, as is usual in little bargains of honour, she gave me her hand: *En verité, Monsieur, je mettrai cet argent apart*, said she.

When a virtuous convention is made betwixt man and woman, it sanctifies their most private walks; so notwithstanding it was dusky, yet as both our roads lay the same way, we made no scruple of walking along the Quai de Conti together.

She made me a second courtesy in setting off, and before we got twenty yards from the door, as if she had not done enough before, she made a sort of a little stop to tell me again she thank'd me.

It was a small tribute, I told her, which I could not avoid paying to virtue, and would not be mistaken in the person I had been rendering it to for the world. But I see innocence, my dear, in your face, and foul befal the man who ever lays a snare in its way!

The girl seem'd affected some way or other with what I said. She gave a low sigh. I found I was not empowered to inquire at all after it, so said nothing more till I got to the corner of the Rue de Nevers, where we were to part.

But is this the way, my dear, said I, to the Hotel de Modene? She told me it was, or, that I might go by the Rue de Gueneguault, which was the next turn. Then I'll go, my dear, by the Rue de Gueneguault, said I, for two reasons; first I shall please myself, and next I shall give you the protection of my company as far on your way as I can. The girl was sensible I was civil and said, she wish'd the Hotel de Modene was in the Rue de St. Pierre. You live there? said I. She told me she was *fille de chambre* to Madame R——. Good God! said I, 'tis the very lady for whom I have brought a letter from Amiens. The girl told me that Madame R——, she believed, expected a stranger with a letter, and was impatient to see him. So I desired the girl to present my compliments to Madame R——, and say I would certainly wait upon her in the morning.

We stood still at the corner of the Rue de Nevers whilst this pass'd; we then stopped a moment whilst she disposed of her *Egarements du Cœur*, etc., more commodiously than carrying them in her hand—they were two volumes; so I held the second for her whilst she put the first into her pocket; and then she held her pocket, and I put in the other after it.

'Tis sweet to feel by what fine-spun threads our affections are drawn together.

We set off afresh, and as she took her third step, the girl put her hand within my arm—I was just bidding her—but she did it of herself with that undeliberating simplicity, which show'd it was out of her head that she had never seen me before. For my own part, I felt the conviction of consanguinity so strongly, that I could not help turning half round to look in her face, and see if I could trace out any thing in it of a family likeness. Tut! said I, are we not all relations?

When we arrived at the turning up to the Rue de Gueneguault, I stopp'd to bid her adieu for good and all: the girl would thank me again for my company and kindness. She bid me adieu twice. I repeated it as often; and so cordial was the parting between us, that had it happened any where else, I'm not sure but I should have signed it with a kiss of charity, as warm and holy as an apostle.

But in Paris, as none kiss each other but the men, I did, what amounted to the same thing——

I bid God bless her.

THE PASSPORT

PARIS

WHEN I got home to my hotel, La Fleur told me I had been inquired after by the Lieutenant de Police. The duce take it! said I; I know the reason. It is time the reader should know it, for in the order of things in which it happened, it was omitted; not that it was out of my head; but that, had I told it then, it might have been forgot now, and now is the time I want it.

I had left London with so much precipitation, that it never enter'd my mind that we were at war with France; and had reached Dover, and looked through my glass at the hills beyond Boulogne, before the idea presented itself; and with this in its train, that there was no getting there without a passport. Go but to the end of a street, I have a mortal aversion for returning back no wiser than I set out; and as this was one of the greatest efforts I had ever made for knowledge, I could less bear the thoughts of it; so hearing the Count de —— had hired the packet, I begg'd he would take me in his *suite*. The Count had some little knowledge of me, so made little or no difficulty—only said, his inclination to serve me could reach no farther than Calais, as he was to return by way of Brussels to Paris; however, when I had once pass'd there, I might get to Paris without interruption; but that in Paris I must make friends and shift for myself. Let me get to Paris, Monsieur le Count, said I, and I shall do very well. So I embark'd, and never thought more of the matter.

When La Fleur told me the Lieutenant de Police had been inquiring after me the thing instantly recurred, and by the time La Fleur had well told me, the master of the hotel came into my room to tell me the same thing, with this addition to it, that my passport had been particularly asked after: the master of the hotel concluded with saying, He hoped I had one. Not I, faith! said I.

The master of the hotel retired three steps from me, as from an infected person, as I declared this, and poor La Fleur advanced three steps towards me, and with that sort of movement which a good soul makes to succour a distress'd one. The fellow won my heart by it; and from that single *trait*, I knew his character as perfectly, and could rely upon it as firmly, as if he had served me with fidelity for seven years.

Mon seigneur! cried the master of the hotel—but recollecting himself as he made the exclamation, he instantly changed the tone of it. If Monsieur, said he, has not a passport, (*apparemment*) in all likelihood he has friends in Paris who can procure him one. Not that I know of, quoth I, with an air of indifference. Then, *certes*, replied he, you'll be sent to the Bastile or the Chatelet, *au moins*. Poo! said I, the king of France is a good-natur'd soul—he'll hurt nobody. *Cela n'empeche pas*, said he; you will certainly be sent to the Bastile to-morrow morning. But I've taken your lodgings for a month, answer'd I, and I'll not quit them a day before the time for all the kings of France in the world. La Fleur whispered in my ear, That nobody could oppose the King of France.

Pardi! said my host, *ces Messieurs Anglois sont des gens tres extraordinaires;* and having both said and sworn it, he went out.

THE PASSPORT

THE HOTEL AT PARIS

I COULD not find in my heart to torture La Fleur's with a serious look upon the subject of my embarrassment, which was the reason I had treated it so cavalierly; and to show him how light it lay upon my mind, I dropt the subject entirely; and whilst he waited upon me at supper, talk'd to him with more than usual gaiety about Paris, and of the Opera comique. La Fleur had been there himself, and had followed me through the streets as far as the bookseller's shop; but seeing me come out with the young *fille de chambre*, and that we walk'd down the Quai de Conti together, La Fleur deem'd it unnecessary to follow me a step further, so making his own reflections upon it, he took a shorter cut and got to the hotel in time to be inform'd of the affair of the police against my arrival.

As soon as the honest creature had taken away, and gone down to sup himself, I then began to think a little seriously about my situation.

And here, I know, Eugenius, thou wilt smile at the remembrance of a short dialogue which pass'd betwixt us the moment I was going to set out. I must tell it here.

Eugenius, knowing that I was as little subject to be overburthen'd with money as thought, had drawn me aside to interrogate me how much I had taken care for; upon telling him the exact sum, Eugenius shook his head, and said it would not do; so pull'd out his purse in order to empty it into mine. I've enough in conscience, Eugenius, said I. Indeed, Yorick, you have not, replied Eugenius; I know France and Italy better than you. But you don't consider, Eugenius, said I, refusing his offer, that before I have been three days in Paris, I shall

take care to say or do something or other for which
I shall get clapp'd up into the Bastile, and that I shall
live there a couple of months entirely at the king of
France's expense. I beg pardon, said Eugenius, drily:
really I had forgot that resource.

Now the event I treated gaily came seriously to
my door.

Is it folly, or nonchalance, or philosophy, or pertina-
city—or what is it in me, that, after all, when La Fleur
had gone down stairs, and I was quite alone, I could
not bring down my mind to think of it otherwise than
I had then spoken of it to Eugenius?

And as for the Bastile; the terror is in the word. Make
the most of it you can, said I to myself, the Bastile is
but another word for a tower, and a tower is but another
word for a house you can't get out of. Mercy on the
gouty! for they are in it twice a year—but with nine
livres a day, and pen and ink and paper and patience,
albeit a man can't get out, he may do very well within,
at least for a month or six weeks; at the end of which,
if he is a harmless fellow, his innocence appears, and he
comes out a better and wiser man than he went in.

I had some occasion (I forget what) to step into the
court-yard, as I settled this account; and remember
I walk'd down stairs in no small triumph with the
conceit of my reasoning. Beshrew the *sombre* pencil!
said I vauntingly, for I envy not its power, which paints
the evils of life with so hard and deadly a colouring.
The mind sits terrified at the objects she has magnified
herself, and blackened: reduce them to their proper
size and hue, she overlooks them. 'Tis true, said I, correcting the proposition, the Bastile is not an evil to be
despised; but strip it of its towers, fill up the fossé,
unbarricade the doors—call it simply a confinement,
and suppose 'tis some tyrant of a distemper and not

of a man, which holds you in it—the evil vanishes, and you bear the other half without complaint.

I was interrupted in the hey-day of this soliloquy, with a voice which I took to be of a child, which complained "it could not get out." I look'd up and down the passage, and seeing neither man, woman, or child, I went out without further attention.

In my return back through the passage, I heard the same words repeated twice over; and looking up, I saw it was a starling hung in a little cage. "I can't get out; I can't get out," said the starling.

I stood looking at the bird: and to every person who came through the passage it ran fluttering to the side towards which they approach'd it, with the same lamentation of its captivity. "I can't get out," said the starling. God help thee! said I, but I'll let thee out, cost what it will; so I turned about the cage to get to the door; it was twisted and double twisted so fast with wire, there was no getting it open without pulling the cage to pieces—I took both hands to it.

The bird flew to the place where I was attempting his deliverance, and thrusting his head through the trellis, pressed his breast against it, as if impatient. I fear, poor creature! said I, I cannot set thee at liberty. "No," said the starling, "I can't get out; I can't get out," said the starling.

I vow I never had my affections more tenderly awakened; or do I remember an incident in my life, where the dissipated spirits, to which my reason had been a bubble, were so suddenly call'd home. Mechanical as the notes were, yet so true in tune to nature were they chaunted, that in one moment they overthrew all my systematic reasonings upon the Bastile; and I heavily walk'd up stairs, unsaying every word I had said in going down them.

Disguise thyself as thou wilt, still, Slavery! said I, still thou art a bitter draught! and though thousands in all ages have been made to drink of thee, thou art no less bitter on that account. 'Tis thou, thrice sweet and gracious goddess, addressing myself to LIBERTY, whom all in public or in private worship, whose taste is grateful, and ever will be so, till NATURE herself shall change; no *tint* of words can spot thy snowy mantle, or chymic power turn thy sceptre into iron; with thee to smile upon him as he eats his crust, the swain is happier than his monarch, from whose court thou art exiled. Gracious heaven! cried I, kneeling down upon the last step but one in my ascent, grant me but health, thou great Bestower of it, and give me but this fair goddess as my companion, and shower down thy mitres, if it seems good unto thy divine providence upon those heads which are aching for them

THE CAPTIVE

PARIS

THE bird in his cage pursued me into my room; I sat down close to my table, and leaning my head upon my hand, I began to figure to myself the miseries of confinement. I was in a right frame for it, and so I gave full scope to my imagination.

I was going to begin with the millions of my fellow-creatures, born to no inheritance but slavery: but finding, however affecting the picture was, that I could not bring it near me, and that the multitude of sad groups in it did but distract me——

I took a single captive, and having first shut him up in his dungeon, I then look'd through the twilight of his grated door to take his picture.

I beheld his body half wasted away with long expectation and confinement, and felt what kind of sickness of the heart it was which arises from hope deferr'd. Upon looking nearer I saw him pale and feverish: in thirty years the western breeze had not once fann'd his blood; he had seen no sun, no moon, in all that time; nor had the voice of friend or kinsman breathed through his lattice: his children——

But here my heart began to bleed, and I was forced to go on with another part of the portrait.

He was sitting upon the ground upon a little straw, in the furthest corner of his dungeon, which was alternately his chair and bed: a little calendar of small sticks were laid at the head, notch'd all over with the dismal days and nights he had passed there. He had one of these little sticks in his hand, and with a rusty nail he was etching another day of misery to add to the heap. As I darkened the little light he had, he lifted up a hopeless eye towards the door, then cast it down, shook his head, and went on with his work of affliction. I heard his chains upon his legs, as he turned his body to lay his little stick upon the bundle. He gave a deep sigh; I saw the iron enter into his soul. I burst into tears. I could not sustain the picture of confinement which my fancy had drawn. I started up from my chair, and called La Fleur; I bid him bespeak me a *remise*, and have it ready at the door of the hotel by nine in the morning.

I'll go directly, said I, myself to Monsieur le Duc de Choiseul.

La Fleur would have put me to bed; but not willing he should see any thing upon my cheek which would cost the honest fellow a heart-ach, I told him I would go to bed by myself and bid him go do the same.

THE STARLING

ROAD TO VERSAILLES

I GOT into my *remise* the hour I promised: La Fleur got up behind, and I bid the coachman make the best of his way to Versailles.

As there was nothing in this road, or rather nothing which I look for in travelling, I cannot fill up the blank better than with a short history of this self-same bird, which became the subject of the last chapter.

Whilst the Honourable Mr. —— was waiting for a wind at Dover, it had been caught upon the cliffs before it could well fly, by an English lad who was his groom; who not caring to destroy it, had taken it in his breast into the packet, and by course of feeding it, and taking it once under his protection, in a day or two grew fond of it, and got it safe along with him to Paris.

At Paris the lad had laid out a livre in a little cage for the starling, and as he had little to do better the five months his master staid there, he taught it in his mother's tongue the four simple words (and no more) to which I own'd myself so much its debtor.

Upon his master's going on for Italy the lad had given it to the master of the hotel. But his little song for liberty being in an *unknown* language at Paris, the bird had little or no store set by him, so La Fleur bought both him and his cage for me for a bottle of Burgundy.

In my return from Italy I brought him with me to the country in whose language he had learn'd his notes, and telling the story of him to Lord A——, Lord A begg'd the bird of me. In a week Lord A gave him to Lord B——; Lord B made a present of him to Lord C——; and Lord C's gentleman sold him to Lord D's for a shilling. Lord D gave him to Lord E——, and so on—half round the alphabet. From that rank he pass'd into the lower house, and pass'd the hands of as many commoners. But as all these wanted to *get in*, and my bird wanted to *get out*, he had almost as little store set by him in London as in Paris.

It is impossible but many of my readers must have heard of him; and if any by mere chance have ever seen him, I beg leave to inform them, that that bird was my bird or some vile copy set up to represent him.

I have nothing farther to add upon him, but that from that time to this, I have borne this poor starling as the crest to my arms.

And let the heralds' officers twist his neck about if they dare.

THE ADDRESS

VERSAILLES

I SHOULD not like to have my enemy take a view of my mind when I am going to ask protection of any man; for which reason I generally endeavour to protect myself; but this going to Monsieur le Duc de C—— was an act of compulsion. Had it been an act of choice, I should have done it, I suppose, like other people.

How many mean plans of dirty address, as I went along, did my servile heart form! I deserved the Bastile for every one of them.

Then nothing would serve me, when I got within sight of Versailles, but putting words and sentences together, and conceiving attitudes and tones to wreath myself into Monsieur le Duc de C——'s good graces. This will do, said I. Just as well, retorted I again, as a coat carried up to him by an adventurous taylor, without taking his measure. Fool! continued I; see Monsieur le Duc's face first. Observe what character is written in it; take notice in what posture he stands to hear you; mark the turns and expressions of his body and limbs; and for the tone, the first sound which comes from his lips will give it you; and from all these together you'll compound an address at once upon the spot, which cannot disgust the Duke—the ingredients are his own, and most likely to go down.

Well! said I, I wish it well over. Coward again! as if man to man was not equal throughout the whole surface of the globe; and if in the field, why not face to face in the cabinet too? And trust me, Yorick, whenever it is not so, man is false to himself, and betrays his own succours ten times where nature does it once. Go to the Duc de C—— with the Bastile in thy looks—my life for it, thou wilt be sent back to Paris in half an hour with an escort.

I believe so, said I. Then I'll go to the Duke, by Heaven! with all the gaiety and debonairness in the world.

And there you are wrong again, replied I. A heart at ease, Yorick, flies into no extremes—'tis ever on its center. Well! well! cried I, as the coachman turn'd in at the gates, I find I shall do very well: and by the time he had wheel'd round the court, and brought me up to the door, I found myself so much the better for my own lecture, that I neither ascended the steps like a victim to justice, who was to part with life upon the topmost, nor did I mount them with a skip and a couple of strides, as I do when I fly up, Eliza! to thee, to meet it.

As I entered the door of the saloon, I was met by a person who possibly might be the *maitre d'hotel*, but had more the air of one of the under-secretaries, who

told me the Duc de C—— was busy. I am utterly
ignorant, said I, of the forms of obtaining an audience,
being an absolute stranger, and what is worse in the
present conjuncture of affairs, being an Englishman
too. He replied, that did not increase the difficulty.
I made him a slight bow, and told him, I had something
of importance to say to Monsieur le Duc. The secretary
look'd towards the stairs, as if he was about to leave
me to carry up this account to some one. But I must
not mislead you, said I, for what I have to say is of
no manner of importance to Monsieur le Duc de C——
but of great importance to myself. *C'est une autre affaire*,
replied he. Not at all, said I, to a man of gallantry. But
pray, good Sir, continued I, when can a stranger hope
to have *accesse*? In not less than two hours, said he,
looking at his watch. The number of equipages in the
court-yard seemed to justify the calculation, that
I could have no nearer a prospect, and as walking
backwards and forwards in the saloon, without a soul
to commune with, was for the time as bad as being in
the Bastile itself, I instantly went back to my *remise*,
and bid the coachman to drive me to the *Cordon Bleu*,
which was the nearest hotel.

I think there is a fatality in it: I seldom go to the
place I set out for.

LE PATISSER

VERSAILLES

BEFORE I had got half-way down the street I changed
my mind: as I am at Versailles, thought I, I might as
well take a view of the town; so I pull'd the cord, and
ordered the coachman to drive round some of the

principal streets. I suppose the town is not very large, said I. The coachman begg'd pardon for setting me right, and told me it was very superb, and that numbers of the first dukes and marquisses and counts had hotels. The Count de B——, of whom the bookseller at the Quai de Conti had spoke so handsomely the night before, came instantly into my mind. And why should I not go, thought I, to the Count de B——, who has so high an idea of English books and English men—and tell him my story: so I changed my mind a second time. In truth it was the third; for I had intended that day for Madame de R—— in the Rue St. Pierre, and had devoutly sent her word by her *fille de chambre* that I would assuredly wait upon her. But I am governed by circumstances—I cannot govern them: so seeing a man standing with a basket on the other side of the street, as if he had something to sell, I bid La Fleur go up to him and inquire for the Count's hotel.

La Fleur returned a little pale: and told me it was a Chevalier de St. Louis selling *patés*. It is impossible, La Fleur, said I. La Fleur could no more account for the phænomenon than myself; but persisted in his story: he had seen the croix set in gold, with its red ribband, he said, tied to his button-hole, and had looked into the basket and seen the *patés* which the Chevalier was selling; so could not be mistaken in that.

Such a reverse in man's life awakens a better principle than curiosity: I could not help looking for some time at him as I sat in the *remise*. The more I looked at him, his croix, and his basket, the stronger they wove themselves into my brain. I got out of the *remise*, and went towards him.

He was begirt with a clean linen apron, which fell below his knees, and with a sort of a bib that went half way up his breast; upon the top of this, but a little below the hem, hung his croix. His basket of little *patés* was covered over with a white damask napkin: another of the same kind was spread at the bottom; and there was a look of *propreté* and neatness throughout, that one might have bought his *patés* of him, as much from appetite as sentiment.

He made an offer of them to neither; but stood still with them at the corner of a hotel, for those to buy who chose it, without solicitation.

He was about forty-eight, of a sedate look, something approaching to gravity. I did not wonder. I went up rather to the basket than him, and having lifted up the napkin, and taken one of his *patés* into my hand, I begg'd he would explain the appearance which affected me.

He told me in a few words, that the best part of his life had pass'd in the service, in which, after spending a small patrimony, he had obtain'd a company and the croix with it; but that, at the conclusion of the last peace, his regiment being re-formed, and the whole corps, with those of some other regiments, left without any provision, he found himself in a wide world without friends, without a livre—and indeed, said he, without any thing but this (pointing, as he said it, to his croix). The poor Chevalier won my pity, and he finished the scene with winning my esteem too.

The king, he said, was the most generous of princes, but his generosity could neither relieve or reward every one, and it was only his misfortune to be amongst the number. He had a little wife, he said, whom he loved, who did the *patisserie*; and added, he felt no dishonour in defending her and himself from want in this way, unless Providence had offer'd him a better.

It would be wicked to withhold a pleasure from the good, in passing over what happen'd to this poor Chevalier of St. Louis about nine months after.

It seems he usually took his stand near the iron gates which lead up to the palace, and as his croix had caught the eye of numbers, numbers had made the same inquiry which I had done. He had told the same story, and always with so much modesty and good sense, that it had reach'd at last the king's ears, who hearing the Chevalier had been a gallant officer, and respected by the whole regiment as a man of honour and integrity, he broke up his little trade by a pension of fifteen hundred livres a year.

As I have told this to please the reader, I beg he will allow me to relate another, out of its order, to please myself—the two stories reflect light upon each other and 'tis a pity they should be parted.

THE SWORD

RENNES

WHEN states and empires have their periods of declension, and feel in their turns what distress and poverty is—I stop not to tell the causes which gradually brought the house d'E—— in Brittany into decay. The Marquis d'E—— had fought up against his condition with great firmness; wishing to preserve, and still show to the world some little fragments of what his ancestors had been; their indiscretions had put it out of his power. There was enough left for the little exigencies of *obscurity*, but he had two boys who look'd up to him for *light*: he thought they deserved it. He had tried his sword—it could not open the way; the *mounting* was too expensive, and simple œconomy was not a match for it. There was no resource but commerce.

In any other province in France, save Brittany, this was smiting the root for ever of the little tree his pride and affection wish'd to see re-blossom. But in Brittany, there being a provision for this, he avail'd himself of it; and taking an occasion when the states were assembled at Rennes, the Marquis, attended with his two boys entered the court; and having pleaded the right of an ancient law of the duchy, which, though seldom claim'd, he said, was no less in force, he took his sword from his side. Here, said he, take it; and be trusty guardians of it, till better times put me in condition to reclaim it.

The president accepted the Marquis's sword; he staid a few minutes to see it deposited in the archives of his house, and departed.

The Marquis and his whole family embarked the next day for Martinico, and in about nineteen or twenty years of successful application to business, with some unlook'd-for bequests from distant branches of his house, return'd home to reclaim his nobility and to support it.

It was an incident of good fortune which will never happen to any traveller, but a sentimental one, that I should be at Rennes at the very time of this solemn requisition. I call it solemn—it was so to me.

The Marquis enter'd the court with his whole family. He supported his lady, his eldest son supported his sister, and his youngest was at the other extreme of the line next his mother. He put his handkerchief to his face twice.

There was a dead silence. When the Marquis had approach'd within six paces of the tribunal, he gave the Marchioness to his youngest son, and advancing three steps before his family, he reclaim'd his sword. His sword was given him, and the moment he got it into his hand, he drew it almost out of the scabbard— 'twas the shining face of a friend he had once given up.

He look'd attentively along it, beginning at the hilt, as if to see whether it was the same, when observing a little rust which it had contracted near the point, he brought it near his eye, and bending his head down over it—I think I saw a tear fall upon the place: I could not be deceived by what followed.

"I shall find," said he, "some *other way* to get it off."

When the Marquis had said this, he return'd his sword into its scabbard, made a bow to the guardians of it, and with his wife and daughter, and his two sons following him, walk'd out.

O how I envied him his feelings!

THE PASSPORT

VERSAILLES

I FOUND no difficulty in getting admittance to Monsieur le Count de B——. The set of Shakespeares was laid upon the table, and he was tumbling them over. I walk'd up close to the table, and giving first such a look at the books as to make him conceive I knew what they were, I told him I had come without any one to present me, knowing I should meet with a friend in his apartment, who, I trusted, would do it for me—it is my countryman the great Shakespeare, said I, pointing to his works. *Et ayez la bonté, mon cher ami*, apostrophising his spirit, added I, *de me faire cet honneur-là*.

The Count smiled at the singularity of the introduction; and seeing I look'd a little pale and sickly, insisted upon my taking an arm-chair; so I sat down; and to save him conjectures upon a visit so out of all rule,

I told him simply of the incident in the bookseller's shop, and how that had impelled me rather to go to him with the story of a little embarrassment I was under, than to any other man in France. And what is your embarrassment? let me hear it, said the Count, So I told him the story just as I have told it the reader.

And the master of my hotel, said I, as I concluded it, will needs have it, Monsieur le Count, that I should be sent to the Bastile. But I have no apprehensions, continued I, for in falling into the hands of the most polish'd people in the world, and being conscious I was a true man, and not come to spy the nakedness of the land, I scarce thought I laid at their mercy. It does not suit the gallantry of the French, Monsieur le Count, said I, to show it against invalids.

An animated blush came into the Count de B——'s cheeks as I spoke this. *Ne craignez rien*—Don't fear, said he. Indeed I don't, replied I again. Besides, continued I a little sportingly, I have come laughing all the way from London to Paris, and I do not think Monsieur le Duc de Choiseul is such an enemy to mirth, as to send me back crying for my pains.

My application to you, Monsieur le Count de B—— (making him a low bow), is to desire he will not.

The Count heard me with great good-nature, or I had not said half as much, and once or twice said: *C'est bien dit*. So I rested my cause there, and determined to say no more about it.

The Count led the discourse: we talk'd of indifferent things—of books, and politics, and men, and then of women. God bless them all! said I, after much discourse about them; there is not a man upon earth who loves them so much as I do: after all the foibles I have seen, and all the satires I have read against them, still I love them; being firmly persuaded that a man, who has not

a sort of an affection for the whole sex, is incapable of
ever loving a single one as he ought.

Heh bien ! Monsieur l'Anglois, said the Count, gaily,
you are not come to spy the nakedness of the land—
I believe you—*ni encore*, I dare say *that* of our women;
but permit me to conjecture: if, *par hazard*, they fell
into your way, that the prospect would not affect you.

I have something within me which cannot bear the
shock of the least indecent insinuation: in the sportability of chit-chat I have often endeavoured to conquer
it, and with infinite pain have hazarded a thousand
things to a dozen of the sex together—the least of
which I could not venture to a single one to gain heaven.

Excuse me, Monsieur le Count, said I, as for the
nakedness of your land, if I saw it, I should cast my
eyes over it with tears in them; and for that of your
women (blushing at the idea he had excited in me),
I am so evangelical in this, and have such a fellow-feeling
for whatever is *weak* about them, that I would cover it
with a garment, if I knew how to throw it on. But
I could wish, continued I, to spy the *nakedness* of their
hearts, and through the different disguises of customs,
climates, and religion, find out what is good in them to
fashion my own by—and therefore am I come.

It is for this reason, Monsieur le Count, continued
I, that I have not seen the Palais Royal, nor the Luxem-
bourg, nor the Façade of the Louvre, nor have attempted
to swell the catalogues we have of pictures, statues, and
churches: I conceive every fair being as a temple, and
would rather enter in, and see the original drawings,
and loose sketches hung up in it, than the transfiguration
of Raphael itself.

The thirst of this, continued I, as impatient as that
which inflames the breast of the connoisseur, has led
me from my own home into France, and from France

will lead me through Italy. 'Tis a quiet journey of the heart in pursuit of NATURE, and those affections which arise out of her, which make us love each other, and the world, better than we do.

The Count said a great many civil things to me upon the occasion; and added, very politely, how much he stood obliged to Shakespeare for making me known to him. But, *à-propos*, said he, Shakespeare is full of great things: he forgot a small punctilio of announcing your name—it puts you under a necessity of doing it yourself.

THE PASSPORT

VERSAILLES

THERE is not a more perplexing affair in life to me, than to set about telling any one who I am, for there is scarce any body I cannot give a better account of than myself; and I have often wish'd I could do it in a single word and have an end of it. It was the only time and occasion in my life I could accomplish this to any purpose, for Shakespeare lying upon the table, and recollecting I was in his books, I took up Hamlet, and turning immediately to the grave-diggers' scene in the fifth act, I laid my finger upon YORICK, and advancing the book to the Count, with my finger all the way over the name —*Me voici !* said I.

Now whether the idea of poor Yorick's skull was put out of the Count's mind by the reality of my own, or by what magic he could drop a period of seven or eight hundred years, makes nothing in this account—'tis certain the French conceive better than they combine

—I wonder at nothing in this world, and the less at this; inasmuch as one of the first of our own church, for whose candour and paternal sentiments I have the highest veneration, fell into the same mistake in the very same case. "He could not bear," he said, "to look into the sermons wrote by the king of Denmark's jester." Good my lord! said I; but there are two Yoricks. The Yorick your lordship thinks of has been dead and buried eight hundred years ago: he flourish'd in Horwendillus's court; the other Yorick is myself, who have flourish'd, my lord, in no court. He shook his head. Good God! said I, you might as well confound Alexander the Great with Alexander the Coppersmith, my lord. 'Twas all one, he replied.

If Alexander king of Macedon could have translated your lordship, said I, I'm sure your lordship would not have said so.

The poor Count de B—— fell but into the same *error*.

Et, Monsieur, est il Yorick? cried the Count. *Je le suis*, said I. *Vous? Moi—moi qui ai l'honneur de vous parler, Monsieur le Comte. Mon Dieu!* said he, embracing me: *Vous êtes Yorick!*

The Count instantly put the Shakespeare into his pocket, and left me alone in his room.

THE PASSPORT

VERSAILLES

I COULD not conceive why the Count de B—— had gone so abruptly out of the room, any more than I could conceive why he had put the Shakespeare into his pocket. *Mysteries which must explain themselves are not worth the loss of time which a conjecture about them takes up :* 'twas better to read Shakespeare; so taking up "*Much ado about Nothing,*" I transported myself instantly from the chair I sat in to Messina in Sicily, and got so busy with Don Pedro and Benedict and Beatrice, that I thought not of Versailles, the Count, or the Passport.

Sweet pliability of man's spirit, that can at once surrender itself to illusions, which cheat expectation and sorrow of their weary moments! Long, long since had he number'd out my days, had I not trod so great a part of them upon this enchanted ground; when my way is too rough for my feet, or too steep for my strength, I get off it, to some smooth velvet path which fancy has scattered over with rose-buds of delights; and having taken a few turns in it, come back strengthen'd and refresh'd. When evils press sore upon me, and there is no retreat from them in this world, then I take a new course: I leave it; and as I have a clearer idea of the elysian fields than I have of heaven, I force myself, like Æneas, into them. I see him meet the pensive shade of his forsaken Dido, and wish to recognise it; I see the injured spirit wave her head, and turn off silent from the author of her miseries and dishonours; I lose the feelings for myself in hers, and in those affections which were wont to make me mourn for her when I was at school.

Surely this is not walking in a vain shadow, nor does man disquiet himself in vain *by it*—he oftener does so in trusting the issue of his commotions to reason only. I can safely say for myself, I was never able to conquer any one single bad sensation in my heart so decisively, as by beating up as fast as I could for some kindly and gentle sensation to fight it upon its own ground.

When I had got to the end of the third act, the Count

de B—— entered with my passport in his hand. Mons. le
Duc de C——, said the Count, is as good a prophet, I dare
say, as he is a statesman. *Un homme qui rit*, said the
Duke, *ne sera jamais dangereux*. Had it been for any one
but the king's jester, added the Count, I could not have
got it these two hours. *Pardonnez moi*, Mons. le Count,
said I; I am not the king's jester. But you are Yorick?
Yes. *Et vous plaisantez ?* I answered: Indeed I did jest
—but was not paid for it; 'twas entirely at my own
expense.

We have no jester at court, Mons. le Count, said
I; the last we had was in the licentious reign of
Charles II., since which time our manners have been
so gradually refining, that our court at present is so
full of patriots, who wish for *nothing* but the honours
and wealth of their country; and our ladies are all so
chaste, so spotless, so good, so devout, there is nothing
for a jester to make a jest of.

Voila un persiflage ! cried the Count.

THE PASSPORT

VERSAILLES

As the Passport was directed to all lieutenant-governors,
governors, and commandants of cities, generals of armies,
justiciaries, and all officers of justice, to let Mr. Yorick
the king's jester, and his baggage, travel quietly along,
I own the triumph of obtaining the Passport was not
a little tarnish'd by the figure I cut in it. But there is
nothing unmix'd in this world; and some of the gravest
of our divines have carried it so far as to affirm, that
enjoyment itself was attended even with a sigh, and

that the greatest *they knew of* terminated *in a general way*, in little better than a convulsion.

I remember the grave and learned Bevoriskius, in his Commentary upon the Generations from Adam, very naturally breaks off in the middle of a note to give an account to the world of a couple of sparrows upon the out-edge of his window, which had incommoded him all the time he wrote, and at last had entirely taken him off from his genealogy.

'Tis strange! writes Bevoriskius, but the facts are certain, for I have had the curiosity to mark them down one by one with my pen, but the cock-sparrow, during the little time that I could have finished the other half of this note, has actually interrupted me with the reiteration of his caresses three-and-twenty times and a half.

How merciful, adds Bevoriskius, is heaven to his creatures!

Ill-fated Yorick! that the gravest of thy brethren should be able to write that to the world, which stains thy face with crimson, to copy in even thy study.

But this is nothing to my travels. So I twice—twice beg pardon for it.

CHARACTER

VERSAILLES

AND how do you find the French? said the Count de B——, after he had given me the Passport.

The reader may suppose, that after so obliging a proof of courtesy, I could not be at a loss to say something handsome to the inquiry.

Mais passe, pour cela; Speak frankly, said he: do you
find all the urbanity in the French which the world
give us the honour of? I had found every thing, I said,
which confirmed it. *Vraiment,* said the Count; *les
François sont polis.* To an excess, replied I.

The Count took notice of the word *excesse*; and would
have it I meant more than I said. I defended myself a
long time as well as I could against it; he insisted I had
a reserve, and that I would speak my opinion frankly.

I believe, Mons. le Count, said I, that man has a
certain compass, as well as an instrument; and that
the social and other calls have occasion by turns for
every key in him; so that if you begin a note too high
or too low, there must be a want either in the upper
or under part, to fill up the system of harmony. The
Count de B—— did not understand music, so desired
me to explain it some other way. A polish'd nation, my
dear Count, said I, makes every one its debtor; and
besides, urbanity itself, like the fair sex, has so many
charms, it goes against the heart to say it can do ill;
and yet, I believe, there is but a certain line of perfec-
tion, that man, take him altogether, is impower'd to
arrive at—if he gets beyond, he rather exchanges
qualities than gets them. I must not presume to say,
how far this has affected the French in the subject we
are speaking of, but should it ever be the case of the
English, in the progress of their refinements, to arrive
at the same polish which distinguishes the French, if
we did not lose the *politesse du cœur,* which inclines
men more to humane actions, than courteous ones,
we should at least lose that distinct variety and origin-
ality of character, which distinguishes them, not only
from each other, but from all the world besides.

I had a few of King William's shillings as smooth as
glass in my pocket; and foreseeing they would be of

use in the illustration of my hypothesis, I had got them into my hand, when I had proceeded so far.

See, Mons. le Count, said I, rising up, and laying them before him upon the table; by jingling and rubbing one against another for seventy years together in one body's pocket or another's, they are become so much alike, you can scarce distinguish one shilling from another.

The English, like ancient medals, kept more apart, and passing but few people's hands, preserve the first sharpnesses which the fine hand of Nature has given them: they are not so pleasant to feel, but, in return, the legend is so visible, that at the first look you see whose image and superscription they bear. But the French, Mons. le Count, added I (wishing to soften what I had said), have so many excellencies, they can the better spare this: they are a loyal, a gallant, a generous, an ingenious, and good-temper'd people as is under heaven; if they have a fault, they are too *serious*.

Mon Dieu ! cried the Count, rising out of his chair.

Mais vous plaisantez, said he, correcting his exclamation. I laid my hand upon my breast, and with earnest gravity assured him it was my most settled opinion.

The Count said he was mortified he could not stay to hear my reasons, being engaged to go that moment to dine with the Duc de C——.

But if it is not too far to come to Versailles to eat your soup with me, I beg, before you leave France, I may have the pleasure of knowing you retract your opinion, or, in what manner you support it. But if you do support it, Mons. Anglois, said he, you must do it with all your powers, because you have the whole world against you. I promised the Count I would do myself the honour of dining with him before I set out for Italy; so took my leave.

THE TEMPTATION

PARIS

WHEN I alighted at the hotel, the porter told me a young woman with a bandbox had been that moment enquiring for me. I do not know, said the porter, whether she is gone away or no. I took the key of my chamber of him, and went up stairs; and when I had got within ten steps of the top of the landing before my door, I met her coming easily down.

It was the fair *fille de chambre* I had walked along the Quai de Conti with: Madame de R—— had sent her upon some commission to a *merchante de modes* within a step or two of the Hotel de Modene; and as I had fail'd in waiting upon her, had bid her enquire if I had left Paris; and if so, whether I had not left a letter addressed to her.

As the fair *fille de chambre* was so near my door, she returned back, and went into the room with me for a moment or two while I wrote a card.

It was a fine still evening in the latter end of the month of May. The crimson window-curtains (which were of the same colour as those of the bed) were drawn close; the sun was setting, and reflected through them so warm a tint into the fair *fille de chambre's* face, I thought she blush'd—the idea of it made me blush myself. We were quite alone; and that superinduced a second blush before the first could get off.

There is a sort of a pleasing half-guilty blush, where the blood is more in fault than the man: 'tis sent impetuous from the heart, and virtue flies after it—not to call it back, but to make the sensation of it more delicious to the nerves—'tis associated.

But I'll not describe it. I felt something at first within me which was not in strict unison with the lesson of virtue I had given her the night before. I sought five minutes for a card; I knew I had not one. I took up a pen, I laid it down again, my hand trembled, the devil was in me.

I know as well as any one he is an adversary, whom if we resist he will fly from us. But I seldom resist him at all, from a terror that though I may conquer, I may still get a hurt in the combat—so I give up the triumph for security; and instead of thinking to make him fly, I generally fly myself.

The fair *fille de chambre* came close up to the bureau where I was looking for a card, took up first the pen I cast down, then offer'd to hold me the ink; she offer'd it so sweetly, I was going to accept it—but I durst not. I have nothing, my dear, said I, to write upon. Write it, said she, simply, upon any thing.

I was just going to cry out, Then I will write it, fair girl! upon thy lips.

If I do, said I, I shall perish—so I took her by the hand, and led her to the door, and begg'd she would not forget the lesson I had given her. She said, indeed she would not; and as she uttered it with some earnestness, she turn'd about, and gave me both her hands, closed together, into mine. It was impossible not to compress them in that situation. I wish'd to let them go; and all the time I held them, I kept arguing within myself against it—and still I held them on. In two minutes I found I had all the battle to fight over again, and I felt my legs and every limb about me tremble at the idea.

The foot of the bed was within a yard and a half of the place where we were standing; I had still hold of her hands; and how it happened I can give no account, but I neither ask'd her, nor drew her, nor did I think of the bed, but so it did happen, we both sat down.

I'll just show you, said the fair *fille de chambre*, the little purse I have been making to-day to hold your crown. So she put her hand into her right pocket, which was next me, and felt for it some time, then into the left—"She had lost it." I never bore expectation more quietly. It was in her right pocket at last—she pull'd it out. It was of green taffeta, lined with a little bit of white quilted sattin, and just big enough to hold the crown. She put it into my hand; it was pretty; and I held it ten minutes with the back of my hand resting upon her lap, looking sometimes at the purse, sometimes on one side of it.

A stitch or two had broke out in the gathers of my stock. The fair *fille de chambre*, without saying a word, took out her little housewife, threaded a small needle, and sew'd it up. I foresaw it would hazard the glory of the day; and as she pass'd her hand in silence across and across my neck in the manœuvre, I felt the laurels shake which fancy had wreath'd about my head.

A strap had given way in her walk, and the buckle of her shoe was just falling off. See, said the *fille de chambre*, holding up her foot. I could not from my soul but fasten the buckle in return; and putting in the strap, and lifting up the other foot with it, when I had done, to see both were right—in doing it too suddenly it unavoidably threw the fair *fille de chambre* off her centre, and then——

THE CONQUEST

YES—and then—— Ye whose clay-cold heads and lukewarm hearts can argue down or mask your passions, tell me, what trespass is it that man should have them? or how his spirit stands answerable to the Father of spirits but for his conduct under them.

If Nature has so wove her web of kindness that some threads of love and desire are entangled with the piece, must the whole web be rent in drawing them out? Whip me such stoics, great Governor of nature! said I to myself: Wherever thy providence shall place me for the trials of my virtue, whatever is my danger, whatever is my situation, let me feel the movements which rise out of it, and which belong to me as a man—and if I govern them as a good one, I will trust the issues to thy justice: for thou hast made us, and not we ourselves.

As I finish'd my address, I raised the fair *fille de chambre* up by the hand, and led her out of the room. She stood by me till I lock'd the door and put the key in my pocket—*and then*—the victory being quite decisive, and not till then, I press'd my lips to her cheek, and taking her by the hand again, led her safe to the gate of the hotel.

THE MYSTERY

PARIS

IF a man knows the heart, he will know it was impossible to go back instantly to my chamber: it was touching a cold key with a flat third to it, upon the close of a piece of music, which had call'd forth my affections. Therefore when I let go the hand of the *fille de chambre*, I remain'd at the gate of the hotel for some time, looking at every one who pass'd by, and forming conjectures upon them, till my attention got fix'd upon a single object which confounded all kind of reasoning upon him.

It was a tall figure of a philosophic, serious, adust look, which pass'd and repass'd sedately along the street, making a turn of about sixty paces on each side of the gate of the hotel. The man was about fifty-two, had a small cane under his arm, was dress'd in a dark drab-coloured coat, waistcoat, and breeches, which seem'd to have seen some years service—they were still clean, and there was a little air of frugal *propreté* throughout him. By his pulling off his hat, and his attitude of accosting a good many in his way, I saw he was asking charity; so I got a sous or two out of my pocket ready to give him, as he took me in his turn. He pass'd by me without asking any thing, and yet did not go five steps farther before he ask'd charity of a little woman—I was much more likely to have given of the two. He had scarce done with the woman, when he pull'd his hat off to another who was coming the same way. An ancient gentleman came slowly, and, after him, a young smart one. He let them both pass, and ask'd nothing; I stood observing him half an hour, in which time he had made a dozen turns backwards and forwards, and found that he invariably pursued the same plan.

There were two things very singular in this, which set my brain to work, and to no purpose: the first was, why the man should *only* tell his story to the sex; and secondly, what kind of story it was, and what species of eloquence it could be, which soften'd the hearts of the women, which he knew 'twas to no purpose to practise upon the men.

There were two other circumstances which entangled

this mystery: the one was, he told every woman what he had to say in her ear, and in a way which had much more the air of a secret than a petition; the other was, it was always successful—he never stopp'd a woman, but she pull'd out her purse, and immediately gave him something.

I could form no system to explain the phænomenon.

I had got a riddle to amuse me for the rest of the evening, so I walk'd up stairs to my chamber.

THE CASE OF CONSCIENCE

PARIS

I was immediately followed up by the master of the hotel, who came into my room to tell me I must provide lodgings elsewhere. How so, friend? said I. He answer'd, I had had a young woman lock'd up with me two hours that evening in my bed-chamber, and 'twas against the rules of his house. Very well, said I, we'll all part friends then; for the girl is no worse, and I am no worse, and you will be just as I found you. It was enough, he said, to overthrow the credit of his hotel. *Voyez vous, Monsieur*, said he, pointing to the foot of the bed we had been sitting upon. I own it had something of the appearance of an evidence; but my pride not suffering me to enter into any detail of the case, I exhorted him to let his soul sleep in peace, as I resolved to let mine do that night, and that I would discharge what I owed him at breakfast.

I should not have minded, *Monsieur*, said he, if you had had twenty girls—'Tis a score more, replied I, interrupting him, than I ever reckon'd upon—Provided, added he, it had been but in a morning. And does the difference of the time of the day at Paris make a difference in the sin? It made a difference, he said, in the scandal. I like a good distinction in my heart; and cannot say I was intolerably out of temper with the man. I own it is necessary, re-assumed the master of the hotel, that a stranger at Paris should have the opportunities presented to him of buying lace and silk stockings, and ruffles, *et tout cela*, and 'tis nothing if a woman comes with a bandbox. O' my conscience, said I, she had one; but I never look'd into it. Then *Monsieur*, said he, has bought nothing. Not one earthly thing, replied I. Because, said he, I could recommend one to you who would use you *en conscience*. But I must see her this night, said I. He made me a low bow, and walk'd down.

Now, shall I triumph over this *maitre d'hotel*, cried I—and what then? Then I shall let him see I know he is a dirty fellow. And what then? What then? I was too near myself to say it was for the sake of others. I had no good answer left: there was more of spleen than principle in my project, and I was sick of it before the execution.

In a few minutes the Grisset came in with her box of lace. I'll buy nothing, however, said I, within myself.

The Grisset would show me every thing. I was hard to please: she would not seem to see it; she open'd her little magazine, and laid all her laces one after another before me, unfolded and folded them up again one by one with the most patient sweetness. I might buy or not, she would let me have every thing at my own price; the poor creature seem'd anxious to get a penny; and laid herself out to win me, and not so much in a manner which seem'd artful, as in one I felt simple and caressing.

If there is not a fund of honest cullibility in man, so

much the worse: my heart relented, and I gave up my second resolution as quietly as the first. Why should I chastise one for the trespass of another? If thou art tributary to this tyrant of an host, thought I, looking up in her face, so much harder is thy bread.

If I had not had more than four louis d'ors in my purse, there was no such thing as rising up and showing her the door, till I had first laid three of them out in a pair of ruffles.

The master of the hotel will share the profit with her. No matter! then I have paid only as many a poor soul has *paid* before me, for an act he *could* not do, or think of.

THE RIDDLE

PARIS

WHEN La Fleur came up to wait upon me at supper, he told me how sorry the master of the hotel was for his affront to me in bidding me change my lodgings.

A man who values a good night's rest will not lie down with enmity in his heart, if he can help it, so I bid La Fleur tell the master of the hotel, that I was sorry on my side for the occasion I had given him; and you may tell him, if you will, La Fleur, added I, that if the young woman should call again, I shall not see her.

This was a sacrifice not to him, but myself, having resolved, after so narrow an escape, to run no more risks, but to leave Paris, if it was possible, with all the virtue I enter'd it.

C'est deroger à noblesse, Monsieur, said La Fleur, making me a bow down to the ground as he said it.

Et encore, Monsieur, said he, may change his sentiments; and if (*par hazard*) he should like to amuse himself—
I find no amusement in it, said I, interrupting him.

Mon Dieu! said La Fleur—and took away.

In an hour's time he came to put me to bed, and was more than commonly officious: something hung upon his lips to say to me, or ask me, which he could not get off: I could not conceive what it was, and indeed gave myself little trouble to find it out, as I had another riddle so much more interesting upon my mind, which was that of the man's asking charity before the door of the hotel. I would have given any thing to have got to the bottom of it; and that, not out of curiosity—'tis so low a principle of inquiry, in general, I would not purchase the gratification of it with a two-sous piece—but a secret, I thought, which so soon and so certainly soften'd the heart of every woman you came near, was a secret at least equal to the philosopher's stone: had I had both the Indies, I would have given up one to have been master of it.

I toss'd and turn'd it almost all night long in my brains to no manner of purpose; and when I awoke in the morning, I found my spirit as much troubled with my *dreams*, as ever the king of Babylon had been with his; and I will not hesitate to affirm, it would have puzzled all the wise men of Paris as much as those of Chaldea, to have given its interpretation.

LE DIMANCHE

PARIS

It was Sunday; and when La Fleur came in, in the morning, with my coffee and roll and butter, he had got himself so gallantly array'd, I scarce knew him.

I had covenanted at Montriul to give him a new hat with a silver button and loop, and four louis d'ors *pour s'adoniser*, when we got to Paris; and the poor fellow, to do him justice, had done wonders with it.

He had bought a bright, clean, good scarlet coat, and a pair of breeches of the same—they were not a crown worse, he said, for the wearing. I wish'd him hang'd for telling me—they look'd so fresh, that tho' I knew the thing could not be done, yet I would rather have imposed upon my fancy with thinking I had bought them new for the fellow, than that they had come out of the *Rue de Friperie*.

This is a nicety which makes not the heart sore at Paris.

He had purchased moreover a handsome blue sattin waistcoat, fancifully enough embroidered. This was indeed something the worse for the service it had done, but 'twas clean scour'd, the gold had been touch'd up, and upon the whole was rather showy than otherwise; and as the blue was not violent, it suited with the coat and breeches very well. He had squeez'd out of the money, moreover, a new bag and a solitaire; and had insisted with the *fripier* upon a gold pair of garters to his breeches knees. He had purchased muslin ruffles *bien brodées*, with four livres of his own money and a pair of white silk stockings for five more; and, to top all, nature had given him a handsome figure, without costing him a sous.

He entered the room thus set off, with his hair drest in the first style, and with a handsome *bouquet* in his breast—in a word, there was that look of festivity in every thing about him, which at once put me in mind it was Sunday, and by combining both together, it instantly struck me, that the favour he wish'd to ask of me the night before, was to spend the day as every body in Paris spent it besides. I had scarce made the conjecture, when La Fleur, with infinite humility, but with a look of trust, as if I should not refuse him, begg'd I would grant him the day, *pour faire le galant vis-à-vis de sa maitresse.*

Now it was the very thing I intended to do myself *vis-à-vis* Madame de R——. I had retained the *remise* on purpose for it, and it would not have mortified my vanity to have had a servant so well dress'd as La Fleur was, to have got up behind it: I never could have worse spared him.

But we must *feel*, not argue, in these embarrassments. The sons and daughters of service part with liberty, but not with nature, in their contracts; they are flesh and blood, and have their little vanities and wishes in the midst of the house of bondage, as well as their task-masters. No doubt they have set their self-denials at a price, and their expectations are so unreasonable, that I would often disappoint them, but that their condition puts it so much in my power to do it.

Behold, Behold, I am thy servant ! disarms me at once of the powers of a master.

Thou shalt go, La Fleur! said I.

And what mistress, La Fleur, said I, canst thou have pick'd up in so little a time at Paris? La Fleur laid his hand upon his breast, and said 'twas a *petite demoiselle*, at Monsieur le Count de B——'s. La Fleur had a heart made for society; and, to speak the truth of him, let as few occasions slip him as his master—so that some-how or other, but how Heaven knows—he had con-nected himself with the *demoiselle* upon the landing of the stair-case, during the time I was taken up with my passport; and as there was time enough for me to win the Count to my interest, La Fleur had contrived to make it do to win the maid to his. The family, it seems, was to be at Paris that day, and he had made a party with her, and two or three more of the Count's house-hold, upon the *boulevards*.

Happy people! that once a week at least are sure to lay down all your cares together, and dance and sing, and sport away the weights of grievance, which bow down the spirit of other nations to the earth.

THE FRAGMENT

PARIS

La Fleur had left me something to amuse myself with for the day more than I had bargain'd for, or could have entered either into his head or mine.

He had brought the little print of butter upon a currant-leaf; and as the morning was warm, he had begg'd a sheet of waste paper to put betwixt the currant-leaf and his hand. As that was plate sufficient, I bad him lay it upon the table as it was; and as I resolved to stay within all day, I ordered him to call upon the *trateur*, to bespeak my dinner, and leave me to breakfast by myself.

When I had finished the butter, I threw the currant-leaf out of the window, and was going to do the same by the waste paper, but stopping to read a line first, and that drawing me on to a second and third, I thought it better worth; so I shut the window, and drawing a chair up to it, I sat down to read it.

It was in the old French of Rabelais's time, and for aught I know might have been wrote by him; it was moreover in a Gothic letter, and that so faded and gone off by damps and length of time, it cost me infinite trouble to make any thing of it. I threw it down; and then wrote a letter to Eugenius. Then I took it up again and embroiled my patience with it afresh—and then to cure that, I wrote a letter to Eliza. Still it kept hold of me; and the difficulty of understanding it increased but the desire.

I got my dinner; and after I had enlightened my mind with a bottle of Burgundy, I at it again, and after two or three hours poring upon it, with almost as deep attention as ever Gruter or Jacob Spon did upon a nonsensical inscription, I thought I made sense of it. But to make sure of it, the best way, I imagined, was to turn it into English, and see how it would look then —so I went on leisurely as a trifling man does, sometimes writing a sentence, then taking a turn or two, and then looking how the world went out of the window; so that it was nine o'clock at night before I had done it. I then began and read it as follows.

THE FRAGMENT

PARIS

Now as the Notary's wife disputed the point with the Notary with too much heat—I wish, said the Notary (throwing down the parchment), that there was another Notary here only to set down and attest all this.

And what would you do then, Monsieur? said she, rising hastily up. The Notary's wife was a little fume of a woman, and the Notary thought it well to avoid a hurricane by a mild reply. I would go, answered he, to bed. You may go to the devil, answer'd the Notary's wife.

Now there happening to be but one bed in the house, the other two rooms being unfurnished, as is the custom at Paris, and the Notary not caring to lie in the same bed with a woman who had but that moment sent him pell-mell to the devil, went forth with his hat and cane and short cloak, the night being very windy, and walk'd out ill at ease towards the *Pont Neuf*.

Of all the bridges which ever were built, the whole world who have pass'd over the *Pont Neuf* must own, that it is the noblest, the finest, the grandest, the lightest, the longest, the broadest that ever conjoin'd land and land together upon the face of the terraqueous globe.

By this it seems as if the author of the fragment had not been a Frenchman.

The worst fault which divines and the doctors of the Sorbone can allege against it, is, that if there is but a cap-full of wind in or about Paris, 'tis more blasphemously *sacre Dieu'd* there than in any other aperture of the whole city—and with reason, good and cogent, Messieurs; for it comes against you without crying *garde d'eau*, and with such unpremeditable puffs, that of the few who cross it with their hats on, not one in fifty but hazards two livres and a half, which is its full worth.

The poor Notary, just as he was passing by the sentry, instinctively clapp'd his cane to the side of it, but in raising it up, the point of his cane catching hold of the loop of the centinel's hat, hoisted it over the spikes of the ballustrade clear into the Seine.

'Tis an ill wind, said a boatman, who catch'd it, *which blows nobody any good.*

The sentry, being a Gascon, incontinently twirl'd up his whiskers, and levell'd his harquebuss.

Harquebusses in those days went off with matches; and an old woman's paper lantern at the end of the bridge happening to be blown out, she had borrow'd the sentry's match to light it. It gave a moment's time for the Gascon's blood to run cool, and turn the accident better to his advantage. *'Tis an ill wind,* said he, catching off the Notary's castor, and legitimating the capture with the boatman's adage.

The poor Notary cross'd the bridge, and passing along the rue de Dauphine into the fauxbourg of St. Germain, lamented himself as he walked along in this manner:

Luckless man that I am! said the Notary, to be the sport of hurricanes all my days, to be born to have the storm of ill language levell'd against me and my profession wherever I go, to be forced into marriage by the thunder of the church to a tempest of a woman, to be driven forth out of my house by domestic winds, and despoil'd of my castor by pontific ones, to be here, bare-headed, in a windy night at the mercy of the ebbs and flows of accidents. Where am I to lay my head? Miserable man! what wind in the two-and-thirty points of the whole compass can blow unto thee, as it does to the rest of thy fellow-creatures, good!

As the Notary was passing on by a dark passage, complaining in this sort, a voice call'd out to a girl, to bid her run for the next Notary. Now the Notary being the next, and availing himself of his situation, walk'd up the passage to the door, and passing through an old sort of a saloon, was usher'd into a large chamber, dismantled of every thing but a long military pike, a breast-plate, a rusty old sword, and bandoleer, hung up equidistant in four different places against the wall.

An old personage, who had heretofore been a gentleman, and unless decay of fortune taints the blood along with it, was a gentleman at that time, lay supporting his head upon his hand, in his bed; a little table with a taper burning was set close beside it, and close by the table was placed a chair. The Notary sat him down in it; and pulling out his inkhorn and a sheet or two of paper which he had in his pocket, he placed them before him, and dipping his pen in his ink, and leaning his breast over the table, he disposed every thing to make the gentleman's last will and testament.

Alas! Monsieur le Notaire, said the gentleman, raising himself up a little, I have nothing to bequeath, which will pay the expence of bequeathing, except the history of myself, which I could not die in peace unless I left it as a legacy to the world; the profits arising out of it I bequeath to you for the pains of taking it from me. It is a story so uncommon, it must be read by all mankind; it will make the fortunes of your house. The Notary dipp'd his pen into his inkhorn. Almighty Director of every event in my life! said the old gentleman, looking up earnestly, and raising his hands towards heaven; Thou, whose hand hast led me on through such a labyrinth of strange passages down into this scene of desolation, assist the decaying memory of an old, infirm, and broken-hearted man; direct my tongue by the spirit of thy eternal truth, that this stranger may set down nought but what is written in that Book, from whose records, said he, clasping his hands together, I am to be condemn'd or acquitted! The Notary held up the point of his pen betwixt the taper and his eye.

It is a story, Monsieur le Notaire, said the gentleman,

which will rouse up every affection in nature; it will kill the humane, and touch the heart of cruelty herself with pity——

The Notary was inflamed with a desire to begin, and put his pen a third time into his inkhorn, and the old gentleman turning a little more towards the Notary, began to dictate his story in these words——

And where is the rest of it, La Fleur? said I; he just then entered the room.

THE FRAGMENT AND THE BOUQUET [1]

PARIS

When La Fleur came up close to the table, and was made to comprehend what I wanted, he told me there were only two other sheets of it, which he had wrapt round the stalks of a *bouquet* to keep it together, which he had presented to the *demoiselle* upon the *boulevards*. Then prithee, La Fleur, said I, step back to her to the Count de B——'s hotel, and *see if thou canst get it.* There is no doubt of it, said La Fleur, and away he flew.

In a very little time the poor fellow came back quite out of breath, with deeper marks of disappointment in his looks than could arise from the simple irreparability of the fragment. *Juste ciel!* in less than two minutes that the poor fellow had taken his last tender farewel of her, his faithless mistress had given his *gage d'amour* to one of the Count's footmen, the footman to a young sempstress, and the sempstress to a fidler, with my fragment at the end of it. Our misfortunes

[1] Nosegay.

were involved together: I gave a sigh, and La Fleur echo'd it back again to my ear.

How perfidious! cried La Fleur. How unlucky! said I.

I should not have been mortified, Monsieur, quoth La Fleur, if she had lost it. Nor I, La Fleur, said I, had I found it.

Whether I did or no will be seen hereafter.

THE ACT OF CHARITY

PARIS

THE man who either disdains or fears to walk up a dark entry, may be an excellent good man, and fit for a hundred things; but he will not do to make a good sentimental traveller. I count little of the many things I see pass at broad noon-day, in large and open streets. Nature is shy, and hates to act before spectators; but in such an unobserved corner you sometimes see a single short scene of hers, worth all the sentiments of a dozen French plays compounded together. And yet they are *absolutely* fine; and whenever I have a more brilliant affair upon my hands than common, as they suit a preacher just as well as a hero, I generally make my sermon out of 'em, and for the text: "Cappadocia, Pontus and Asia, Phrygia and Pamphylia" is as good as any one in the Bible.

There is a long dark passage issuing out from the opera comique into a narrow street; 'tis trod by a few who humbly wait for a *fiacre*,[1] or wish to get off quietly o'foot when the opera is done. At the end of it, towards the theatre, 'tis lighted by a small candle, the light of

[1] Hackney-coach.

which is almost lost before you get half-way down, but near the door. 'Tis more for ornament than use: you see it as a fix'd star of the least magnitude; it burns, but does little good to the world, that we know of.

In returning along this passage, I discern'd, as I approach'd within five or six paces of the door, two ladies standing arm in arm with their backs against the wall, waiting, as I imagined, for a *fiacre*. As they were next the door, I thought they had a prior right; so edged myself up within a yard or little more of them, and quietly took my stand. I was in black, and scarce seen.

The lady next me was a tall lean figure of a woman, of about thirty-six; the other of the same size and make, of about forty. There was no mark of wife or widow in any one part of either of them: they seem'd to be two upright vestal sisters, unsapp'd by caresses, unbroke in upon by tender salutations. I could have wish'd to have made them happy—their happiness was destin'd, that night, to come from another quarter.

A low voice, with a good turn of expression, and sweet cadence at the end of it, begg'd for a twelve-sous piece betwixt them, for the love of Heaven. I thought it singular that a beggar should fix the quota of an alms, and that the sum should be twelve times as much as what is usually given in the dark. They both seem'd astonish'd at it as much as myself. Twelve sous! said one. A twelve-sous piece! said the other, and made no reply.

The poor man said, he knew not how to ask less of ladies of their rank; and bow'd down his head to the ground.

Poo! said they; we have no money.

The beggar remained silent for a moment or two, and renew'd his supplication.

Do not, my fair young ladies, said he, stop your good ears against me. Upon my word, honest man! said the younger, we have no change. Then God bless you, said the poor man, and multiply those joys which you can give to others without change! I observed the elder sister put her hand into her pocket. I'll see, said she, if I have a sous. A sous! give twelve, said the supplicant; Nature has been bountiful to you, be bountiful to a poor man.

I would, friend, with all my heart, said the younger, if I had it.

My fair charitable! said he, addressing himself to the elder; what is it but your goodness and humanity which makes your bright eyes so sweet, that they outshine the morning even in this dark passage? and what was it which made the Marquis de Santerre and his brother say so much of you both as they just pass'd by?

The two ladies seemed much affected; and impulsively at the same time they both put their hands into their pocket, and each took out a twelve-sous piece.

The contest betwixt them and the poor supplicant was no more: it was continued betwixt themselves, which of the two should give the twelve-sous piece in charity, and to end the dispute, they both gave it together, and the man went away.

THE RIDDLE EXPLAINED

PARIS

I STEPPED hastily after him: it was the very man whose success in asking charity of the women before the door of the hotel had so puzzled me, and I found at once his secret, or at least the basis of it—'twas flattery.

Delicious essence! how refreshing art thou to nature! how strongly are all its powers and all its weaknesses on thy side! how sweetly dost thou mix with the blood, and help it through the most difficult and tortuous passages to the heart!

The poor man, as he was not straiten'd for time, had given it here in a larger dose: 'tis certain he had a way of bringing it into less form, for the many sudden cases he had to do with in the streets; but how he contrived to correct, sweeten, concentre, and qualify it, I vex not my spirit with the inquiry—it is enough, the beggar gained two twelve-sous pieces, and they can best tell the rest, who have gained much greater matters by it.

PARIS

WE get forwards in the world, not so much by doing services, as receiving them; you take a withering twig, and put it in the ground; and then you water it because you have planted it.

Mons. le Count de B——, merely because he had done me one kindness in the affair of my passport, would go on and do me another, the few days he was at Paris, in making me known to a few people of rank; and they were to present me to others, and so on.

I had got master of my *secret* just in time to turn these honours to some little account; otherwise, as is commonly the case, I should have din'd or supp'd a single time or two round, and then by *translating* French looks and attitudes into plain English, I should presently have seen, that I had gold out of the *couvert* [1]

[1] Plate, napkin, knife, fork, and spoon.

of some more entertaining guest; and in course should
have resigned all my places one after another, merely
upon the principle that I could not keep them. As it
was, things did not go much amiss.

I had the honour of being introduced to the old
Marquis de B——: in days of yore he had signaliz'd
himself by some small feats of chivalry in the *Cour
d'amour*, and had dress'd himself out to the idea of
tilts and tournaments ever since—the Marquis de B——
wish'd to have it thought the affair was somewhere
else than in his brain. "He could like to take a trip to
England," and ask'd much of the English ladies. Stay
where you are, I beseech you, Mons. le Marquis, said
I; Les Messrs. Anglois can scarce get a kind look from
them as it is. The Marquis invited me to supper.

Mons. P—— the farmer-general was just as inquisitive about our taxes. They were very considerable, he
heard. If we knew but how to collect them, said I, making
him a low bow.

I could never have been invited to Mons. P——'s
concerts upon any other terms.

I had been misrepresented to Madame de Q—— as
an *esprit*. Madame de Q—— was an *esprit* herself: she
burnt with impatience to see me, and hear me talk.
I had not taken my seat, before I saw she did not care
a sous whether I had any wit or no—I was let in, to
be convinced she had. I call Heaven to witness I never
once open'd the door of my lips.

Madame de V—— vow'd to every creature she met,
"She had never had a more improving conversation
with a man in her life."

There are three epochas in the empire of a French
woman: She is coquette, then deist, then *devote*. The
empire during these is never lost—she only changes
her subjects. When thirty-five years and more have

unpeopled her dominions of the slaves of love, she re-peoples it with slaves of infidelity, and then with the slaves of the church.

Madame de V—— was vibrating betwixt the first of these epochas: the colour of the rose was fading fast away—she ought to have been a deist five years before the time I had the honour to pay my first visit.

She placed me upon the same sopha with her, for the sake of disputing the point of religion more closely: In short, Madame de V—— told me she believed nothing.

I told Madame de V—— it might be her principle; but I was sure it could not be her interest to level the outworks, without which I could not conceive how such a citadel as hers could be defended—that there was not a more dangerous thing in the world than for a beauty to be a deist; that it was a debt I owed my creed, not to conceal it from her; that I had not been five minutes sat upon the sopha beside her, but I had begun to form designs; and what is it but the senti-ments of religion, and the persuasion they had excited in her breast, which could have check'd them as they rose up?

We are not adamant, said I, taking hold of her hand, and there is need of all restraints, till age in her own time steals in and lays them on us. But, my dear lady, said I, kissing her hand, 'tis too, too soon——

I declare I had the credit all over Paris of unperverting Madame de V——. She affirmed to Mons. D—— and the Abbé M——, that in one half-hour I had said more for revealed religion than all their Encyclopedia had said against it. I was lifted directly into Madame de V——'s *Coterie*, and she put off the epocha of deism for two years.

I remember it was in this *Coterie*, in the middle of a discourse, in which I was showing the necessity of a

first cause, that the young Count de Faineant took me
by the hand to the farthest corner of the room to tell
me my *solitaire* was pinn'd too strait about my neck.
It should be *plus badinant,* said the Count, looking
down upon his own, but a word, Mons. Yorick, *to
the wise——*

And *from the wise,* Mons. le Count, replied I, making
him a bow, *is enough.*

The Count de Faineant embraced me with more
ardour than ever I was embraced by mortal man.

For three weeks together, I was of every man's
opinion I met. *Pardi ! ce Mons. Yorick a autant d'esprit
que nous autres. Il raisonne bien,* said another. *C'est un
bon enfant,* said a third. And at this price I could have
eaten and drank and been merry all the days of my
life at Paris. But 'twas a dishonest *reckoning*—I grew
ashamed of it. It was the gain of a slave—every sentiment of honour revolted against it. The higher I got,
the more was I forced upon my *beggarly system;* the
better the *Coterie,* the more children of Art. I languish'd
for those of Nature: and one night, after a most vile
prostitution of myself to half a dozen different people,
I grew sick, went to bed, order'd La Fleur to get me
horses in the morning to set out for Italy.

MARIA

MOULINES

I NEVER felt what the distress of plenty was in any one
shape till now. To travel it through the Bourbonnois,
the sweetest part of France—in the hey-day of the
vintage, when Nature is pouring her abundance into

every one's lap, and every eye is lifted up—a journey
through each step of which Music beats time to *Labour*,
and all her children are rejoicing as they carry in their
clusters; to pass through this with my affections flying
out, and kindling at every group before me; and every
one of them was pregnant with adventures.

Just Heaven! it would fill up twenty volumes—and
alas! I have but a few small pages left of this to crowd
it into; and half of these must be taken up with the
poor Maria my friend Mr. Shandy met with near
Moulines.

The story he had told of that disorder'd maid affected
me not a little in the reading; but when I got within
the neighbourhood where she lived, it returned so
strong into my mind, that I could not resist an impulse
which prompted me to go half a league out of the
road, to the village where her parents dwelt, to inquire
after her.

'Tis going, I own, like the Knight of the Woeful
Countenance, in quest of melancholy adventures; but
I know not how it is, but I am never so perfectly
conscious of the existence of a soul within me, as when
I am entangled in them.

The old mother came to the door. Her looks told
me the story before she open'd her mouth: she had
lost her husband; he had died, she said, of anguish,
for the loss of Maria's senses, about a month before.
She had feared at first, she added, that it would have
plunder'd her poor girl of what little understanding
was left, but, on the contrary, it had brought her more
to herself. Still she could not rest; her poor daughter, she
said, crying, was wandering somewhere about the
road——

Why does my pulse beat languid as I write this?
and what made La Fleur, whose heart seem'd only to

be tuned to joy, to pass the back of his hand twice across his eyes, as the woman stood and told it? I beckoned to the postillion to turn back into the road.

When we had got within half a league of Moulines, at a little opening in the road leading to a thicket, I discovered poor Maria sitting under a poplar. She was sitting with her elbow in her lap, and her head leaning on one side within her hand; a small brook ran at the foot of the tree.

I bid the postillion go on with the chaise to Moulines and La Fleur to bespeak my supper, and that I would walk after him.

She was dress'd in white, and much as my friend described her, except that her hair hung loose, which before was twisted within a silk net. She had, superadded likewise to her jacket, a pale green ribband, which fell across her shoulder to the waist; at the end of which hung her pipe. Her goat had been as faithless as her lover: and she had got a little dog in lieu of him, which she had kept tied by a string to her girdle: as I look'd at her dog, she drew him towards her with the string. "Thou shalt not leave me, Sylvio," said she. I look'd in Maria's eyes, and saw she was thinking more of her father than of her lover or her little goat; for as she utter'd them, the tears trickled down her cheeks.

I sat down close by her; and Maria let me wipe them away as they fell, with my handkerchief. I then steep'd it in my own, and then in hers, and then in mine, and then I wip'd hers again, and as I did it, I felt such undescribable emotions within me, as I am sure could not be accounted for from any combinations of matter and motion.

I am positive I have a soul; nor can all the books with which materialists have pestered the world ever convince me to the contrary.

MARIA

WHEN Maria had come a little to herself, I ask'd her if she remembered a pale thin person of a man, who had sat down betwixt her and her goat about two years before? She said, she was unsettled much at that time, but remember'd it upon two accounts—that ill as she was, she saw the person pitied her; and next, that her goat had stolen his handkerchief, and she had beat him for the theft. She had wash'd it, she said, in the brook, and kept it ever since in her pocket to restore it to him in case she should ever see him again, which, she added, he had half promised her. As she told me this, she took the handkerchief out of her pocket to let me see it; she had folded it up neatly in a couple of vine-leaves, tied round with a tendril. On opening it, I saw an S. marked in one of the corners.

She had since that, she told me, strayed as far as Rome, and walk'd round St. Peter's once and return'd back; that she found her way alone across the Apennines; had travell'd over all Lombardy without money; and through the flinty roads of Savoy without shoes. How she had borne it, and how she had got supported, she could not tell, but *God tempers the wind*, said Maria, to the shorn lamb.

Shorn indeed! and to the quick, said I; and wast thou in my own land, where I have a cottage, I would take thee to it and shelter thee: thou shouldst eat of my own bread and drink of my own cup; I would be kind to thy Sylvio; in all thy weaknesses and wanderings I would seek after thee and bring thee back. When the sun went down I would say my prayers; and when I had done thou shouldst play thy evening song upon thy pipe, nor would the incense of my sacrifice be worse accepted for entering heaven along with that of a broken heart.

Nature melted within me, as I utter'd this; and Maria observing, as I took out my handkerchief, that it was steep'd too much already to be of use, would needs go wash it in the stream. And where will you dry it, Maria? said I. I'll dry it in my bosom, said she; 'twill do me good.

And is your heart still so warm, Maria? said I.

I touched upon the string on which hung all her sorrows. She look'd with wistful disorder for some time in my face; and then, without saying any thing, took her pipe, and play'd her service to the Virgin. The string I had touch'd ceased to vibrate: in a moment or two Maria returned to herself, let her pipe fall, and rose up.

And where are you going, Maria? said I. She said, to Moulines. Let us go, said I, together. Maria put her arm within mine, and lengthening the string, to let the dog follow—in that order we enter'd Moulines.

MARIA

MOULINES

THO' I hate salutations and greetings in the market place, yet when we got into the middle of this, I stopp'd to take my last look and last farewel of Maria.

Maria, though not tall, was nevertheless of the first order of fine forms. Affliction had touch'd her looks with something that was scarce earthly—still she was feminine, and so much was there about her of all that the heart wishes, or the eye looks for in woman, that could the traces be ever worn out of her brain, and those of Eliza out of mine, she should *not only eat of my bread and drink of my own cup*, but Maria should lie in my bosom, and be unto me as a daughter.

Adieu, poor luckless maiden! Imbibe the oil and wine which the compassion of a stranger, as he journeyeth on his way, now pours into thy wounds—the Being who has twice bruised thee can only bind them up for ever.

THE BOURBONNOIS

THERE was nothing from which I had painted out for myself so joyous a riot of the affections, as in this journey in the vintage, through this part of France; but pressing through this gate of sorrow to it, my sufferings have totally unfitted me: in every scene of festivity I saw Maria in the background of the piece, sitting pensive under her poplar; and I had got almost to Lyons before I was able to cast a shade across her.

Dear sensibility! source inexhausted of all that's precious in our joys, or costly in our sorrows! thou chainest thy martyr down upon his bed of straw, and 'tis thou who lift'st him up to HEAVEN. Eternal fountain of our feelings! 'tis here I trace thee, and this is thy *"divinity which stirs within me"*; not that in some sad and sickening moments, *"my soul shrinks back upon herself, and startles at destruction"*—mere pomp of words! —but that I feel some generous joys and generous cares beyond myself; all comes from thee, great, great SEN-SORIUM of the world! which vibrates, if a hair of our heads but falls upon the ground, in the remotest desert of thy creation. Touch'd with thee, Eugenius draws my curtain when I languish, hears my tale of symptoms, and blames the weather for the disorder of his nerves. Thou giv'st a portion of it sometimes to the roughest peasant who traverses the bleakest mountains. He finds the lacerated lamb of another's flock. This moment I beheld him leaning with his head against his crook, with piteous inclination looking down upon it! Oh! had I come one moment sooner! It bleeds to death—his gentle heart bleeds with it.

Peace to thee, generous swain! I see thou walkest off with anguish. But thy joys shall balance it, for happy is thy cottage, and happy is the sharer of it, and happy are the lambs which sport about you.

THE SUPPER

A SHOE coming loose from the fore-foot of the thill-horse, at the beginning of the ascent of Mount Taurira, the postillion dismounted, twisted the shoe off, and put it in his pocket; as the ascent was of five or six miles, and that horse our main dependence, I made a point of having the shoe fasten'd on again, as well as we could; but the postillion had thrown away the nails, and the hammer in the chaise-box being of no great use without them, I submitted to go on.

He had not mounted half a mile higher, when coming to a flinty piece of road, the poor devil lost a second shoe, and from off his other fore-foot. I then got out of the chaise in good earnest; and seeing a house about a quarter of a mile to the left-hand, with a great deal to do I prevailed upon the postillion to turn up to it. The look of the house, and of every thing about it, as we

drew nearer, soon reconciled me to the disaster. It was
a little farm-house, surrounded with about twenty acres
of vineyard, about as much corn, and close to the house,
on one side, was a *potagerie* of an acre and a half, full
of every thing which could make plenty in a French
peasant's house; and on the other side was a little
wood, which furnished wherewithal to dress it. It was
about eight in the evening when I got to the house, so
I left the postillion to manage his point as he could,
and for mine, I walk'd directly into the house.

The family consisted of an old grey-headed man and
his wife, with five or six sons and sons-in-law, and their
several wives, and a joyous genealogy out of them.

They were all sitting down together to their lentil-
soup; a large wheaten loaf was in the middle of the
table; and a flaggon of wine at each end of it, promised
joy through the stages of the repast—'twas a feast
of love.

The old man rose up to meet me, and with a respectful
cordiality would have me sit down at the table. My heart
was set down the moment I enter'd the room; so I sat
down at once like a son of the family; and to invest
myself in the character as speedily as I could, I instantly
borrowed the old man's knife, and taking up the loaf,
cut myself a hearty luncheon; and as I did it, I saw a
testimony in every eye, not only of an honest welcome,
but of a welcome mix'd with thanks that I had not
seem'd to doubt it.

Was it this; or tell me, Nature, what else it was that
made this morsel so sweet—and to what magic I owe
it, that the draught I took of their flaggon was so
delicious with it, that they remain upon my palate
to this hour?

If the supper was to my taste, the grace which
followed it was much more so.

THE GRACE

WHEN supper was over, the old man gave a knock upon the table with the haft of his knife, to bid them prepare for the dance. The moment the signal was given, the women and girls ran all together into a back apartment to tye up their hair and the young men to the door to wash their faces, and change their sabots; and in three minutes every soul was ready upon a little esplanade before the house to begin. The old man and his wife came out last, and placing me betwixt them, sat down upon a sopha of turf by the door.

The old man had some fifty years ago been no mean performer upon the vielle, and, at the age he was then of, touch'd it well enough for the purpose. His wife sung now-and-then a little to the tune, then intermitted, and join'd her old man again as their children and grand-children danced before them.

It was not till the middle of the second dance, when for some pauses in the movement wherein they all seem'd to look up, I fancied I could distinguish an elevation of spirit different from that which is the cause or the effect of simple jollity. In a word, I thought I beheld *Religion* mixing in the dance—but as I had never seen her so engaged, I should have look'd upon it now as one of the illusions of an imagination which is eternally misleading me, had not the old man, as soon as the dance ended, said that this was their constant way; and that all his life long he had made it a rule, after supper was over, to call out his family to dance and rejoice; believing, he said, that a cheerful and contented mind was the best sort of thanks to Heaven that an illiterate peasant could pay.

Or a learned prelate either, said I.

THE CASE OF DELICACY

WHEN you have gain'd the top of Mount Taurira, you run presently down to Lyons: adieu then to all rapid movements! 'Tis a journey of caution; and it fares better with sentiments, not to be in a hurry with them; so I contracted with a Voiturin to take his time with a couple of mules, and convey me in my own chaise safe to Turin through Savoy.

Poor, patient, quiet, honest people! fear not: your poverty, the treasury of your simple virtues, will not be envied you by the world, nor will your vallies be invaded by it. Nature! in the midst of thy disorders, thou art still friendly to the scantiness thou hast created; with all thy great works about thee, little hast thou left to give, either to the scythe or to the sickle; but to that little thou grantest safety and protection; and sweet are the dwellings which stand so shelter'd.

Let the way-worn traveller vent his complaints upon the sudden turns and dangers of your roads, your rocks, your precipices, the difficulties of getting up, the horrors of getting down, mountains impracticable, and cataracts, which roll down great stones from their summits, and block his road up. The peasants had been all day at work in removing a fragment of this kind between St. Michael and Madane; and by the time my Voiturin got to the place, it wanted full two hours of completing before a passage could any how be gain'd: there was nothing but to wait with patience. 'Twas a wet and tempestuous night: so that by the delay, and that together, the Voiturin found himself obliged to keep up five miles short of his stage at a little decent kind of an inn by the road-side.

I forthwith took possession of my bed-chamber, got

a good fire, order'd supper; and was thanking Heaven it was no worse, when a voiture arrived with a lady in it and her servant-maid.

As there was no other bed-chamber in the house, the hostess, without much nicety, led them into mine, telling them, as she usher'd them in, that there was nobody in it but an English gentleman; that there were two good beds in it, and a closet within the room which held another. The accent in which she spoke of this third bed did not say much for it. However, she said there were three beds, and but three people, and she durst say, the gentleman would do anything to accommodate matters. I left not the lady a moment to make a conjecture about it, so instantly made a declaration that I would do any thing in my power.

As this did not amount to an absolute surrender of my bed-chamber, I still felt myself so much the proprietor, as to have a right to do the honours of it—so I desired the lady to sit down, pressed her into the warmest seat, call'd for more wood, desired the hostess to enlarge the plan of the supper, and to favour us with the very best wine.

The lady had scarce warm'd herself five minutes at the fire, before she began to turn her head back, and give a look at the beds; and the oftener she cast her eyes that way, the more they return'd perplex'd. I felt for her—and for myself; for in a few minutes, what by her looks, and the case itself, I found myself as much embarrassed as it was possible the lady could be herself.

That the beds we were to lie in were in one and the same room, was enough simply by itself to have excited all this, but the position of them, for they stood parallel, and so very close to each other, as only to allow space for a small wicker chair betwixt them, rendered the affair still more oppressive to us. They were fixed up moreover near the fire, and the projection of the chimney on one side, and a large beam which cross'd the room on the other, form'd a kind of recess for them that was no way favourable to the nicety of our sensations. If any thing could have added to it, it was that the two beds were both of them so very small, as to cut us off from every idea of the lady and the maid lying together; which in either of them, could it have been feasible, my lying beside them, though a thing not to be wish'd, yet there was nothing in it so terrible which the imagination might not have pass'd over without torment.

As for the little room within, it offer'd little or no consolation to us; 'twas a damp cold closet, with a half dismantled window-shutter, and with a window which had neither glass or oil paper in it to keep out the tempest of the night. I did not endeavour to stifle my cough when the lady gave a peep into it; so it reduced the case in course to this alternative—that the lady should sacrifice her health to her feelings, and take up with the closet herself, and abandon the bed next mine to her maid, or that the girl should take the closet, &c., &c.

The lady was a Piedmontese of about thirty, with a glow of health in her cheeks. The maid was a Lyonoise of twenty, and as brisk and lively a French girl as ever moved. There were difficulties every way—and the obstacle of the stone in the road, which brought us into the distress, great as it appeared whilst the peasants were removing it, was but a pebble to what lay in our ways now. I have only to add, that it did not lessen the weight which hung upon our spirits, that we were both too delicate to communicate what we felt to each other upon the occasion.

We sat down to supper; and had we not had more generous wine to it than a little inn in Savoy could have furnish'd, our tongues had been tied up, till necessity herself had set them at liberty, but the lady having a few bottles of Burgundy in her voiture, sent down her Fille de Chambre for a couple of them; so that by the time supper was over, and we were left alone, we felt ourselves inspired with a strength of mind sufficient to talk, at least, without reserve upon our situation. We turn'd it every way, and debated and considered it in all kind of lights in the course of a two hours' negotiation; at the end of which the articles were settled finally betwixt us, and stipulated for in form and manner of a treaty of peace—and I believe with as much religion and good faith on both sides, as in any treaty which has yet had the honour of being handed down to posterity.

They were as follow:

First. As the right of the bed-chamber is in Monsieur, and he thinking the bed next to the fire to be the warmest, he insists upon the concession on the lady's side of taking up with it.

Granted, on the part of Madame; with a proviso: that as the curtains of that bed are of a flimsey transparent cotton, and appear likewise too scanty to draw close, that the Fille de Chambre shall fasten up the opening, either by corking pins, or needle and thread, in such manner as shall be deem'd a sufficient barrier on the side of Monsieur.

2dly. It is required on the part of Madame, that Monsieur shall lie the whole night through in his robe de chambre.

Rejected: inasmuch as Monsieur is not worth a robe de chambre; he having nothing in his portmanteau but six shirts and a black silk pair of breeches.

The mentioning the silk pair of breeches made an entire change of the article, for the breeches were accepted as an equivalent for the robe de chambre; and so it was stipulated and agreed upon, that I should lie in my black silk breeches all night.

3dly. It was insisted upon, and stipulated for by the lady, that after Monsieur was got to bed, and the candle and fire extinguished, that Monsieur should not speak one single word the whole night.

Granted; provided Monsieur's saying his prayers might not be deem'd an infraction of the treaty.

There was but one point forgot in this treaty, and that was the manner in which the lady and myself should be obliged to undress and get to bed. There was one way of doing it, and that I leave to the reader to devise; protesting as I do, that if it is not the most delicate in nature, 'tis the fault of his own imagination —against which this is not my first complaint.

Now when we were got to bed, whether it was the novelty of the situation, or what it was, I know not; but so it was, I could not shut my eyes; I tried this side and that, and turn'd and turn'd again, till a full hour after midnight; when Nature and patience both wearing out, O my God! said I.

You have broke the treaty, Monsieur, said the lady, who had no more sleep than myself. I begg'd a thousand pardons, but insisted it was no more than an ejacula- tion. She maintain'd 'twas an entire infraction of the treaty. I maintain'd it was provided for in the clause of the third article.

The lady would by no means give up the point, though she weaken'd her barrier by it; for in the warmth of the dispute, I could hear two or three corking pins fall out of the curtain to the ground.

Upon my word and honour, Madame, said I, stretching my arm out of bed by way of asseveration——

(I was going to have added, that I would not have

trespass'd against the remotest idea of decorum for the world)——

But the Fille de Chambre hearing there were words between us, and fearing that hostilities would ensue in course, had crept silently out of her closet, and it being totally dark, had stolen so close to our beds, that she had got herself into the narrow passage which separated them, and had advanced so far up as to be in a line betwixt her mistress and me——

So that when I stretch'd out my hand, I caught hold of the Fille de Chambre's——

THE JOURNAL TO ELIZA

THE JOURNAL TO ELIZA

THIS Journal wrote under the fictitious names of Yorick and Draper, and sometimes of The Bramin and Bramine, but 'tis a Diary of the miserable feelings of a person separated from a Lady for whose Society he languish'd. The real Names are foreigne, and the account a copy from a French Manuscript, in Mr. S——'s hands, but wrote as it is, to cast a Veil over them. There is a Counterpart, which is the Lady's account [of] what transactions dayly happened, and what Sentiments occupied her mind, during this Separation from her admirer. These are worth reading; the translator cannot say so much in favour of Yorick's, which seem to have little merit beyond their honesty and truth.[1]

CONTINUATION OF THE BRAMINES JOURNAL

([S]he saild 23 [2])

Sunday Ap: 13.[3]

WROTE the last farewel to Eliza by Mr. Wats who sails this day for Bombay, inclosed her likewise the Journal

[1] *The Journal to Eliza,* or *The Continuation of the Bramines Journal*—Sterne's phrase written above the first entry—is printed just as Sterne left it, with its wild chronology and all its vagaries in spelling and punctuation. This descriptive title-page, as well as the *Journal* itself, is in Sterne's own hand.
[2] The mistake in date is obvious.
[3] Sunday fell on 12 April, 1767.

kept from the day we parted, to this; so from hence continue it till the time we meet again. Eliza does the same, so we shall have mutual testimonies to deliver hereafter to each other, That the Sun has not more constantly rose and set upon the earth, than we have thought of and remember'd, what is more chearing than Light itself—eternal Sunshine! Eliza!—dark to me is all this world without thee! and most heavily will every hour pass over my head, till that is come which brings thee, dear Woman back to Albion. Dined with Hall, etc. at the Brawn's Head, the whole Pandamonium assembled; supp'd together at Halls, worn out both in body and mind, and paid a severe reckoning all the night.

Ap: 14. Got up tottering and feeble; then is it Eliza, that I feel the want of thy friendly hand and friendly Council. And yet, with thee beside me, thy Bramin would lose the merit of his virtue: he could not err, but I will take thee upon any terms, Eliza! I shall be happy here, and I will be so just, so kind to thee, I will deserve not to be miserable hereafter—a Day dedicated to Abstinence and reflection, and what object will employ the greatest part of mine full well does my Eliza know.

Munday. Ap: 15.

Worn out with fevers of all kinds, but most, by that fever of the heart with which I'm eternally wasting, and shall waste till I see Eliza again: dreadful Suffering of 15 months! It may be more. Great Controuler of Events! surely thou wilt proportion this, to my Strength, and to that of my Eliza. Pass'd the whole afternoon in reading her Letters, and reducing them to the order in which they were wrote to me; staid the whole evening at home; no pleasure or Interest in either Society or Diversions. What a change, my dear Girl, hast thou made in me! But the Truth is, thou hast only turn'd the tide of my passions a new way—they flow, Eliza, to thee, and ebb from every other Object in this world. And Reason tells me they do right, for my heart has rated thee at a Price, that all the world is not rich enough to purchase thee from me, at. In a high fever all the night.

Ap: 16. And got up so ill, I could not go to Mrs. James as I had promised her. Took James's Powder, however, and lean'd the whole day with my head upon my hand, sitting most dejectedly at the Table with my Eliza's Picture before me, sympathizing and soothing me. O my Bramine! my Friend! my Help-mate!—for that (if I'm a prophet) is the Lot mark'd out for thee; and such I consider thee now, and thence it is, Eliza, I share so righteously with thee in all the evil or good which befalls thee. But all our portion is Evil now, and all our hours grief; I look forwards towards the Elysium we have so often and rapturously talk'd of. Cordelia's spirit will fly to tell thee in some sweet Slumber, the moment the door is open'd for thee and The Bramin of the Vally, shall follow the track wherever it leads him, to get to his Eliza, and invite her to his Cottage.

5 in the afternoon: I have just been eating my Chicking, sitting over my repast upon it, with Tears—a bitter Sause, Eliza! but I could eat it with no other. When Molly spread the Table Cloath, my heart fainted within me: one solitary plate, one knife, one fork, one Glass! O Eliza! 'twas painfully distressing. I gave a thousand

pensive penetrating Looks at the Arm chair thou so often graced on these quiet, sentimental Repasts and sighed and laid down my knife and fork, and took out my handkerchief, clap'd it across my face and wept like a child. I shall read the same affecting account of many a sad Dinner which Eliza has had no power to taste of, from the same feelings and recollections, how She and her Bramin have eat their bread in peace and Love together.

April 17. With my friend Mrs. James in Gerard street, with a present of Colours and apparatus for painting. Long Conversation about thee, my Eliza: sunk my heart with an infamous account of Draper and his detested Character at Bombay. For what a wretch art thou hazarding thy life, my dear friend, and what thanks is his nature capable of returning? Thou wilt be repaid with Injuries and Insults! Still there is a blessing in store for the meek and gentle, and Eliza will not be disinherited of it: her Bramin is kept alive by this hope only, otherwise he is so sunk both in Spirits and looks, Eliza would scarce know him again. Dined alone again to-day; and begin to feel a pleasure in this kind of resigned misery arising from this situation of heart unsupported by aught but its own tenderness. Thou owest me much, Eliza! And I will have patience! for thou wilt pay me all. But the Demand is equal: much I owe thee, and with much shalt thou be requited. Sent for a Chart of the Atlantic Ocean, to make conjectures upon what part of it my Treasure was floating. O! 'tis but a little way off, and I could venture after it in a Boat, methinks. I'm sure I could, was I to know Eliza was in distress. But fate has chalk'd out other roads for us. We must go on with many a weary step, each in his separate heartless track, till Nature——

Ap: 18.

This day set up my Carriage: new Subject of heart-ache. That Eliza is not here to share it with me.

Bought Orm's account of India. Why? Let not my Bramine ask me: her heart will tell her why I do this, and every Thing.

Ap: 19. Poor sick-headed, sick hearted Yorick! Eliza has made a shadow of thee. I am absolutely good for nothing, as every mortal is who can think and talk but upon one thing! How I shall rally my powers alarms me; for Eliza thou has melted them all into one—the power of loving thee and with such ardent affection as triumphs over all other feelings. Was with our faithful friend all the morning; and dined with her and James. What is the Cause, that I can never talk about my Eliza to her, but I am rent in pieces? I burst into tears a dozen different times after dinner, and such affectionate gusts of passion, That she was ready to leave the room, and sympathize in private for us. I weep for you both, said she (in a whisper), for Eliza's anguish is as sharp as yours, her heart as tender, her constancy as great. Heaven join your hands I'm sure together! James was occupied in reading a pamphlet upon the East India affairs, so I answerd her with a kind look, a heavy sigh, and a stream of tears. What was passing in Eliza's breast, at this affecting Crisis? Something kind, and pathetic, I will lay my Life.

8 o'clock. Retired to my room, to tell my dear this: to run back the hours of Joy I have pass'd with her, and meditate upon those which are still in reserve for Us. By this time Mr. James tells me, You will have got as far from me, as the Maderas, and that in two months more, you will have doubled the Cape of good hope.

I shall trace thy track every day in the map, and not allow one hour for contrary Winds, or Currants; every engine of nature shall work together for us. 'Tis the Language of Love, and I can speak no other. And so, good night to thee, and may the gentlest delusions of love impose upon thy dreams, as I forbode they will, this night, on those of thy Bramine.

Ap: 20. Easter Sunday.

Was not disappointed, yet awoke in the most acute pain. Something, Eliza, is wrong with me. You should be ill, out of Sympathy—and yet you are too ill already, my dear friend. All day at home in extream dejection.

Ap: 21. The Loss of Eliza, and attention to that one Idea, brought on a fever—a consequence, I have for some time, forseen, but had not a sufficient Stock of cold philosophy to remedy. To satisfy my friends, call'd in a Physician. Alas! alas! the only Physician, and who carries the Balm of my Life along with her, is Eliza. Why did I suffer thee to go from me? surely thou hast more than once call'd thyself my Eliza, to the same account. 'Twil cost us both dear! but it could not be otherwise. We have submitted; we shall be rewarded. 'Twas a prophetic spirit, which dictated the account of Corporal Trim's uneasy night when the fair Beguin ran in his head, for every night and almost every Slumber of mine, since the day we parted, is a repe[ti]-tion of the same description. Dear Eliza! I am very ill —very ill for thee—but I could still give thee greater proofs of my affection. parted with 12 Ounces of blood, in order to quiet what was left in me. 'Tis a vain experiment. Physicians cannot understand this· 'tis enough for me that Eliza does. I am worn down, my dear Girl, to a shadow, and but that I'm certain thou

wilt not read this, till I'm restored, thy Yorick would
not let the Winds hear his Complaints. 4 o'clock. Sorrowful meal! for 'twas upon our old dish. We shall live to
eat it, my dear Bramine, with comfort.

8 at night. Our dear friend Mrs. James, from the
forbodings of a good heart, thinking I was ill, sent her
maid to enquire after me. I had alarm'd her on Saturday;
and not being with her on Sunday, her friendship supposed the Condition I was in. She suffers most tenderly
for Us, my Eliza! And we owe her more than all the
Sex or indeed both Sexes, if not, all the world put together. Adieu! my sweet Eliza! for this night thy
Yorick is going to waste himself on a restless bed, where
he will turn from side to side a thousand times, and
dream by Intervals of things terrible and impossible:
That Eliza is false to Yorick, or Yorick is false to Eliza.

Ap: 22d. Rose with utmost difficulty. My Physician
order'd me back to bed as soon as I had got a dish of
Tea. Was bled again; my arm broke loose and I half
bled to death in bed before I felt it. O! Eliza! how did
thy Bramine mourn the want of thee to tye up his
wounds, and comfort his dejected heart! Still something bids me hope, and hope, I will, and it shall be the
last pleasurable sensation I part with.

4 o'clock. They are making my bed: how shall I be
able to continue my Journal in it? If there remains a
chasm here, think Eliza, how ill thy Yorick must have
been. This moment received a Card from our dear
friend, beging me to take [care] of a Life so valuable
to my friends, but most so, she adds, to my poor dear
Eliza. Not a word from the Newnhams! but they had

no such exhortations in their hearts, to send thy Bramine. Adieu to em!

Ap: 23. A poor night, and am only able to quit my bed at 4 this afternoon, to say a word to my dear, and fulfill my engagement to her, of letting no day pass over my head without some kind communication with thee—faint resemblance, my dear girl, of how our days are to pass, when one kingdom holds us. Visited in bed by 40 friends, in the Course of the Day. Is not one warm affectionate call, of that friend, for whom I sustain Life, worth 'em all? What thinkest thou, my Eliza?

Ap: 24.
So ill, I could not write a word all this morning— not so much, as Eliza! farewel to thee; I'm going—am a little better.

So shall not depart, as I apprehended, being this morning something better, and my Symptoms become milder, by a tolerable easy night. And now, if I have strength and Spirits to trail my pen down to the bottom of the page, I have as whimsical a Story to tell you, and as comically dis-astrous as ever befell one of our family. Shandy's nose, his name, his Sash-Window, are fools to it. It will serve at *least* to amuse you. The Injury I did myself in catching cold upon James's pouder, fell, you must know, upon the worst part it could, the most painful, and most dangerous of any in the human Body. It was on this Crisis, I call'd in an able Surgeon and with him an able physician (both my friends) to inspect my disaster. Tis a venerial Case, cried my two Scientifick friends. 'Tis impossible at least to be that, replied I, for I have had no commerce whatever with the Sex —not even with my wife, added I, these 15 years. You are . . . however, my good friend, said the Surgeon,

or there is no such Case in the world. What the Devil!
said I, without knowing Woman. We will not reason
about it, said the Physician, but you must undergo a
course of Mercury. I'll lose my life first, said I, and trust
to Nature, to Time, or at the worse to Death. So I put
an end with some Indignation to the Conference; and
determined to bear all the torments I underwent, and
ten times more, rather than submit to be treated as
a *Sinner*, in a point where I had acted like a *Saint*.
Now as the father of mischief would have it, who has
no pleasure like that of dishonouring the righteous, it
so fell out, That from the moment I dismiss'd my Doctors
my pains began to rage with a violence not to be
express'd, or supported. Every hour became more
intollerable. I was got to bed, cried out and raved the
whole night, and was got up so near dead, That my
friends insisted upon my sending again for my Physician and Surgeon. I told them upon the word of a man
of Strict honour, They were both mistaken as to my
case, but tho' they had reason'd wrong, they might act
right; but, that sharp as my sufferings were, I felt
them not so sharp as the Imputation, which a venerial
treatment of my case, laid me under. They answered
that these taints of the blood laid dormant 20 years,
but that they would not reason with me in a matter
wherein I was so delicate, but would do all the office
for which they were call'd in, and namely, to put an
end to my torment, which otherwise would put an end
to me. And so have I been compell'd to surrender
myself, and thus, Eliza, is your Yorick, your Bramine,
your friend with all his sensibilities, suffering the
chastisement of the grossest Sensualist. Is it not a most
ridiculous Embarassment as ever Yorick's Spirit could
be involved in? 'Tis needless to tell Eliza, that nothing
but the purest consciousness of Virtue, could have

tempted Eliza's friend to have told her this Story.
Thou art too good, my Eliza, to love aught but Virtue,
and too discerning not to distinguish the open character
which bears it, from the artful and double one which
affects it. This, by the way, would make no bad anecdote
in T. Shandy's Life. However, I thought at least it
would amuse you, in a country where *less Matters*
serve. This has taken me three Sittings: it ought to be
a good picture—I'm more proud, That it is a true one.
In ten Days I shall be able to get out: my room allways
full of friendly Visitors, and my rapper eternally going
with Cards and enquiries after me. I should be glad of
the Testimonies—without the Tax.

Every thing convinces me, Eliza. We shall live to
meet again, so Take care of your health, to add to the
comfort of it.

Ap: 25. After a tolerable night, I am able, Eliza, to
sit up and hold a discourse with the sweet Picture thou
hast left behind thee of thyself, and tell it how much
I had dreaded the catastrophe, of never seeing its dear
original more in this world. Never did that look of
sweet resignation appear so eloquent as now; it has said
more to my heart, and cheard it up more effectually
above little fears and *may be's* than all the Lectures
of philosophy I have strength to apply to it, in my present
Debility of mind and body. As for the latter, my men of
Science will set it properly agoing again, tho' upon what
principles the Wise Men of Gotham know as much as
they. If they *act right* what is it to me, how *wrong they
think*, for finding my machine a much less tormenting
one to me than before, I become reconciled to my
Situation, and to their Ideas of it. But don't you pity
me, after all, my dearest and my best of friends? I know
to what an amount thou wilt shed over me, this tender

Tax, and 'tis the Consolation springing out of that, of
what a good heart it is which pours this friendly balm
on mine, That has already, and will for ever heal every
evil of my Life. And what is becoming of my Eliza, all
this time! Where is she sailing? What Sickness or
other evils have befallen her? I weep often, my dear
Girl, for thee my Imagination surrounds them with.[1]
What would be the measure of my Sorrow, did I know
thou wast distressed? Adieu, adieu, and trust, my dear
friend, my dear Bramine, that there still wants nothing
to kill me in a few days, but the certainty, That thou
wast suffering, what I am. And yet I know thou art
ill. But when thou returnest back to England, all shall
be set right, so heaven waft thee to us upon the wings
of Mercy—that is, as speedily as the winds and tides
can do thee this friendly office. This is the 7th day
That I have tasted nothing better than Water gruel;
am going, at the solicitation of Hall, to eat of a boil'd
fowl—so he dines with me on it—and a dish of Macaruls.

7 o'clock: I have drank to thy Name, Eliza! ever-
lasting peace and happiness (for my Toast) in the first
glass of Wine I have adventured to drink. My friend
has left me—and I am alone, like thee in thy solitary
Cabbin after thy return from a tasteless meal in the
round house and like thee I fly to my Journal, to tell
thee, I never prized thy friendship so high, or loved thee
more or wish'd so ardently to be a Sharer of all the
weights which Providence has laid upon thy tender
frame Than this moment when upon taking up my
pen, my poor pulse quicken'd, my pale face glowed,
and tears stood ready in my Eyes to fall upon the
paper, as I traced the word Eliza. O Eliza! Eliza! ever

[1] Sterne evidently intended to write "for those my Imagination surrounds thee with."

best and blessed of all thy Sex! blessed in thyself and
in thy Virtues, and blessed and endearing to all who
know thee—to Me, Eliza, most so; because I *know more*
of thee than any other. This is the true philtre by which
Thou hast charm'd me and wilt for ever charm and
hold me thine, whilst Virtue and faith hold this world
together; 'tis the simple Magick, by which I trust, I have
won a place in that heart of thine on which I depend
so satisfied, That Time and distance, or change of every
thing which might allarm the little hearts of little men,
create no unasy suspence in mine. It scorns to doubt,
and scorns to be doubted; 'tis the only exception where
Security is not the parent of Danger.

My Illness will keep me three weeks longer in town.
But a Journey in less time would be hazardous, unless
a short one across the Desert which I should set out
upon to morrow, could I carry a Medicine with me
which I was sure would prolong one month of your
Life—or should it happen——

But why make Suppositions? When Situations happen, 'tis time enough to show thee That thy Bramin
is the truest and most friendly of mortal Spirits, and
capable of doing more for his Eliza, than his pen will
suffer him to promise.

Ap: 26. Slept not till three this morning, was in too
delicious Society to think of it; for I was all the time
with thee besides me, talking over the projess [*sic*] of
our friendship, and turning the world into a thousand
shapes to enjoy it. Got up much better for the Conversation, found myself improved in body and mind
and recruited beyond any thing I lookd for; my Doctors
stroked their beards, and look'd ten per cent. wiser
upon feeling my pulse, and enquiring after my Symptoms.
Am still to run thro' a Course of Van Sweeten's corro-

sive Mercury, or rather Van Sweeten's Course of Mercury is to run thro' me. I shall be sublimated to an etherial Substance by the time my Eliza sees me; she must be sublimated and uncorporated too, to be able to see me. But I was always transparent and a Being easy to be seen thro', or Eliza had never loved me nor had Eliza been of any other *Cast* herself could her Bramine have held *Communion* with her. Hear every day from our worthy sentimental friend, who rejoyces to think that the name of Eliza is still to vibrate upon Yorick's ear. This, my dear Girl, many who loved me dispair'd off. Poor Molly, who is all attention to me, and every day brings in the name of poor Mrs. Draper, told me last night, that She and her Mistress had observed, I had never held up my head, since the Day you last dined with me, That I had seldome laughd or smiled, had gone to no Diversions—but twice or thrice at the most, dined out; That they thought I was broken hearted, for she never enterd the room or passd by the door, but she heard me sigh heavily; That I neither eat or slept or took pleasure in any Thing as before, except writing. The Observation will draw a sigh, Eliza, from thy feeling heart. And yet, so thy heart would wish to have it, 'tis fit in truth We suffer equally nor can it be otherwise, when the causes of anguish in two hearts are so proportion'd, as in ours. Surely, Surely, Thou art mine Eliza! for dear have I bought thee!

Ap: 27. Things go better with me, Eliza! and I shall be reestablished soon, except in bodily weakness; not yet being able to rise from thy arm chair, and walk to the other corner of my room, and back to it again without fatigue. I shall double my Journey to morrow, and if the day is warm the day after be got into my

Carriage and be transported into Hyde park for the advantage of air and exercise. Wast thou but besides me, I could go to Salt hill, I'm sure, and feel the journey short and pleasant. Another Time! . . . the present, alas! is not ours. I pore so much on thy Picture. I have it *off by heart*, dear Girl. Oh 'tis sweet! 'tis kind! 'tis reflecting! 'tis affectionate! 'tis—thine, my Bramine. I say my matins and Vespers to it; I quiet my Murmurs, by the Spirit which speaks in it, "all will end well, my Yorick." I declare, my dear Bramine I am so secured and wrapt up in this Belief, That I would not part with the Imagination, of how happy I am to be with thee, for all the offers of present Interest or Happiness the whole world could tempt me with; in the loneliest cottage that Love and Humility ever dwelt in, with thee along with me, I could possess more refined Content, Than in the most glittering Court; and with thy Love and fidelity, taste truer joys, my Eliza, and make thee also partake of more, than all the senseless parade of this silly world could compensate to either of us. With this, I bound all my desires and worldly views: what are they worth without Eliza? Jesus! grant me but this, I will deserve it. I will make my Bramine as Happy, as Thy goodness wills her; I will be the Instrument of her recompense for the sorrows and disappointments Thou has suffer'd her to undergo; and if ever I am false, unkind or ungentle to her, so let me be dealt with by Thy Justice.

9 o'clock: I am preparing to go to bed, my dear Girl, and first pray for thee, and then to Idolize thee for two wakeful hours upon my pillow. I shall after that, I find, dream all night of thee, for all the day have I done nothing but think of thee. Something tells that thou hast this day, been employed in the same

way. good night, fair Soul, and may the sweet God of
sleep close gently thy eyelids, and govern and direct
thy Slumbers. Adieu, adieu, adieu!

Ap: 28. I was not deceived, Eliza! by my presentiment
that I should find thee out in my dreams; for I have
been with thee almost the whole night, alternately
soothing Thee, or telling thee my sorrows. I have rose
up comforted and strengthened, and found myself so
much better, that I orderd my Carriage, to carry me
to our mutual friend. Tears ran down her cheeks when
she saw how pale and wan I was; never gentle creature
sympathised more tenderly. I beseech you, cried the
good Soul, not to regard either difficulties or expences,
but fly to Eliza directly. I see you will dye without her.
Save yourself for her. How shall I look her in the face?
What can I say to her, when on her return I have to
tell her, That her Yorick is no more! Tell her, my dear
friend, said I, That I will meet her in a better world,
and that I have left this, because I could not live without her; tell Eliza, my dear friend, added I, That I died
broken hearted, and that you were a Witness to it. As
I said this, She burst into the most pathetick flood of
Tears that ever kindly Nature shed. You never beheld
so affecting a Scene: 'twas too much for Nature! Oh!
she is good! I love her as my Sister! and could Eliza
have been a witness, hers would have melted down to
Death and scarse have been brought back, an Extacy
so celestial and savouring of another world. I had like
to have fainted, and to that Degree was my heart and
soul affected, it was with difficulty I could reach the
street door. I have got home, and shall lay all day
upon my Sopha, and to morrow morning, my dear
Girl, write again to thee; for I have not strength to
drag my pen.

Ap: 29.

I am so ill to day, my dear, I can only tell you so. I wish I was put into a Ship for Bombay; I wish I may otherwise hold out till the hour. We might otherwise have met. I have too many evils upon me at once and yet I will not faint under them. Come!—Come to me soon, my Eliza, and save me!

Ap: 30. Better to day, but am too much visited and find my strength wasted by the attention I must give to all concern'd for me. I will go, Eliza, be it but by ten mile Journeys, home to my thatchd Cottage, and there I shall have no respit, for I shall do nothing but think of thee and burn out this weak Taper of Life by the flame thou hast superadded to it. Fare well, my dear. . . . To morrow begins a new month, and I hope to give thee in it, a more sunshiny side of myself. Heaven! how is it with my Eliza?

May 1.

Got out into the park to day. Sheba there on Horseback; pass'd twice by her without knowing her. She stop'd the third time to ask me how I did. I would not have askd you, Solomon! said She, but your Looks affected me, for you're half dead, I fear. I thank'd Sheba very kindly, but without any emotion but what sprung from gratitude. Love, alas! was fled with thee, Eliza! I did not think Sheba could have changed so much in grace and beauty. Thou hadst shrunk, poor Sheba, away into Nothing, but a good natured girl, without powers or charms. I *fear* your wife is dead; quoth Sheba. No, you don't *fear* it, Sheba, said I. Upon my word, Solomon! I would quarrel with You, was you not so ill. If you knew the cause of my Illness, Sheba, replied I, you would quarrel but the more with me. You lie, Solomon! answerd Sheba, for I know the Cause already and am so little out of Charity with You upon it That I give you leave to come and drink Tea with me before you leave Town. You're a good honest Creature, Sheba. No! you Rascal, I am not, but I'm in Love, as much as you can be for your Life. I'm glad of it, Sheba! said I. You Lie, said Sheba, and so canter'd away. O my Eliza, had I ever truely loved another (which I never did) Thou hast long ago, cut the Root of all Affection in me, and planted and water'd and nourish'd it, to bear fruit only for thyself. Continue to give me proofs I have had and shall preserve the same rights over thee, my Eliza! and if I ever murmur at the sufferings of Life after that, Let me be numberd with the ungrateful. I look now forwards with Impatience for the day thou art to get to Madras, and from thence shall I want to hasten thee to Bombay, where heaven will make all things Conspire to lay the Basis of thy health and future happiness. Be true my dear girl, to thy self, and the rights of Self preservation which Nature has given thee. Persevere, be firm, be pliant, be placid, be courteous, but still be true to thy self, and never give up your Life, or suffer the disquieting altercations, or small outrages you may undergo in this momentous point, to weigh a Scruple in the Ballance. Firmness and fortitude and perseverance gain almost impossibilities, and *Skin* for *Skin*, saith Job, *nay all that a Man has, will he give* for his Life." Oh my Eliza! That I could take the Wings of the Morning, and fly to aid thee in *this* virtuous Struggle. Went to Ranelagh at 8 this night, and sat still till ten. Came home ill.

May 2d.

I fear I have relapsed: sent afresh for my Doctor, who has confined me to my sopha, being able neither to walk, stand or sit upright, without aggravating my Symptoms. I'm still to be treated as if I was a Sinner, and in truth have some appearances so strongly implying it, That was I not conscious I had had no Commerce with the Sex these 15 Years, I would decamp to morrow for Montpellier in the South of France, where Maladies of this sort are better treated and all taints more radically driven out of the Blood than in this Country. But if I continue long ill I am still determined to repair there, not to undergo a Cure of a distemper I cannot have, but for the bettering my Constitution by a better Climate. I write this as I lie upon my back, in which posture I must continue, I fear some days. If I am able will take up my pen again before night.

4 o'clock: an hour dedicated to Eliza! for I have dined alone, and ever since the Cloath has been laid, have done nothing but call upon thy dear Name and ask why 'tis not permitted thou shouldst sit down, and share my Macarel and fowl. There would be enough, said Molly as she placed it upon the Table, to have served both You and poor Mrs. Draper. I never bring in the knives and forks, added she, but I think of her. There was no more trouble with you both, than with one of You; I never heard a high or a hasty word from either of You. You were surely made, added Molly, for one another, you are both so kind so quiet and so friendly. Molly furnish'd me with Sause to my Meat, for I wept my plate full, Eliza! and now I have begun, could shed tears till Supper again, and then go to bed weeping for thy absence till morning. Thou hast bewitch'd me with powers, my dear Girl, from which no power shall unloose me, and if fate can put this Journel of my Love into thy hands, before we meet, I know with what warmth it will inflame the kindest of hearts, to receive

me. Peace be with thee, my Eliza, till that happy moment!

9 at night. I shall never get possession of myself, Eliza! at this rate. I want to Call off my Thoughts from thee, that I may now and then apply them to some concerns which require both my attention and genius, but to no purpose. I had a Letter to write to Lord Shelburn, and had got my apparatus in order to begin, when a Map of India coming in my Way I begun to study the length and dangers of my Eliza's Voiage to it, and have been amusing and frightening myself by turns, as I traced the path-way of the Earl of Chatham, the whole afternoon. Good God! what a voiage for any one! But for the poor relax'd frame of my tender Bramine to cross the Line twice, and be subject to the Intolerant heats, and the hazards which must be the consequence of em to such an unsupported Being! O Eliza! 'tis too much! And if thou conquerest these, and all the other difficulties of so tremendous an alienation from thy Country, thy Children and thy friends, 'tis the hand of Providence which watches over thee for most merciful purposes. Let this persuasion, my dear Eliza! stick close to thee in all thy tryals, as it shall in those thy faithful Bramin is put to, till the mark'd hour of deliverance comes. I'm going to sleep upon this religious Elixir. May the Infusion of it distil into the gentlest of hearts, for that Eliza! is thine. Sweet, dear, faithful Girl, most kindly does thy Yorick greet thee with the wishes of a good night and of Millions yet to come.

May 3d Sunday. What can be the matter with me! Something is wrong, Eliza! in every part of me. I do not gain strength; nor have I the feelings of health returning back to me; even my best moments seem merely the efforts of my mind to get well again, because I cannot reconcile myself to the thoughts of never seeing thee, Eliza, more. For something is out of tune in every Chord of me. Still, with thee to nurse and sooth me, I should soon do well. The want of thee is half my distemper, but not the whole of it. I must see Mrs. James to night, tho' I know not how to get there, but I shall not sleep, if I don't talk of you to her, so shall finish this Day's Journal on my return.

May 4th. Directed by Mrs. James how to write Over-Land to thee, my Eliza, would gladly tear out thus much of my Journal to send to thee, but the Chances are too many against its getting to Bombay, or of being deliver'd into your own hands. Shall write a long, long Letter—and trust it to fate and thee. Was not able to say three words at Mrs. James, thro' utter weakness of body and mind; and when I got home could not get up stairs with Molly's aid. Have rose a little better, my dear girl, and will live for thee. Do the same for thy Bramin, I beseech thee. A Line from thee now, in this state of my Dejection, would be worth a kingdome to me!

May 4. Writing by way of Vienna and Bussorah, My Eliza. This and Company took up the day

5th. Writing to Eliza, and trying *l'Extraite de* Saturne upon myself (a French Nostrum).

6th. Dined out for the first time. Came home to enjoy a more harmonious evening with my Eliza, than I could expect at Soho Concert.[1] Every Thing, my dear Girl,

¹ One of the famous concerts at Carlisle House under the management of Mrs. Theresa Cornelys.

has lost its former relish to me, and for thee eternally does it quicken! Writing to thee over Land all day.

7. Continue poorly, my dear, but my blood warms every moment I think of our future Scenes, so must grow strong upon the Idea. What shall I do upon the Reality? O God!

8th. Employ'd in writing to my Dear all day, and in projecting happiness for her, tho in misery myself. O! I have undergone, Eliza!—but the worst is over I hope, so adieu to those Evils, and let me haste the happiness to come.

9th, 10th, and 11th, so unaccountably disorder'd I cannot say more but that I would suffer ten times more and with wishs for my Eliza. Adieu, bless'd Woman!

12th. O Eliza! That my weary head was now laid upon thy Lap ('tis all that's left for it) or that I had thine, reclining upon my bosome, and there resting all its disquietudes. My Bramine, the world or Yorick must perish, before that foundation shall fail thee! I continue poorly, but I turn my Eyes Eastward the oftener, and with more earnestness for it. Great God of Mercy! shorten the Space betwixt us, Shorten the space of our miseries!

13th. Could not get the General post office to take charge of my Letters to You, so gave thirty shillings to a Merchant to further them to Aleppo and from thence to Bassorah, so you will receive 'em (I hope in God) say by Christmas. Surely 'tis not impossible, but I may be made as happy as my Eliza, by some transcript from her, by that time. If not I shall hope, and hope every week, and every hour of it, for Tidings of Comfort.

We taste not of it *now*, my dear Bramine, but we will make full meals upon it hereafter. Cards from 7 or 8 of our Grandies to dine with them before I leave Town; shall go like a Lamb to the Slaughter. *"Man delights not me—nor Woman."*

14. A little better to day, and would look pert, if my heart would but let me. Dined with Lord and Lady Bellasis. So beset with Company, not a moment to write.

15. Undone with too much Society yesterday. You scarse can Conceive, my dear Eliza, what a poor Soul I am; how I shall be got down to Cox only heaven knows, for I am as weak as a Child. You would not like me the worse for it, Eliza, if you was here; My friends like me, the more, and Swear I shew more true fortitude and eveness of temper in my Suffering than Seneca, or Socrates. I am, my Bramin,[1] resigned.

16. Taken up all day with worldly matters, just as my Eliza was the week before her departure. Breakfasted with Lady Spencer; caught her with the character of your Portrait; caught her passions still more with that of yourself, and my Attachment to the most amiable of Beings. Drove at night to Ranelagh; staid an hour; return'd to my Lodgings, dissatisfied.

17. At Court. Every thing in this world seems in Masquerade, but thee, dear Woman, and therefore I am sick of all the world but thee. One Evening *so spent, as the Saturday's which preeceeded our Separation would sicken all the Conversation of the world; I relish no Converse since.* When will the like return? Tis hidden

---

[1] Just as Sterne sometimes refers to himself as the Bramine, so he here carelessly addresses Eliza as the Bramin.

from us both, for the wisest ends, and the hour will
come my Eliza! when We shall be convinced, that every
event has been order'd for the best for Us. Our fruit
is not ripen'd, the accidents of time and Seasons will
ripen every Thing *together* for Us. A little better to day,
or could not have wrote this. Dear Bramine, rest thy
Sweet Soul in peace!

18. Laid sleepless all night, with thinking of the
many dangers and sufferings, my dear Girl! that thou
art exposed to, from the Voiage and thy sad state of
health, but I find I must think no more upon them.
I have rose wan and trembling with the Havock they
have made upon my nerves. 'Tis death to me to apprehend for you; I must flatter my Imagination, That
every Thing goes well with You. Surely no evil can
have befallen you, for if it had I had felt some monitory
sympathetic Shock within me, which would have spoke
like Revelation. So farewell to all tormenting *May be's*
in regard to my Eliza. She is well; she thinks of her
Yorick with as much Affection and true esteem as ever,
and values him as much above the World, as he values
his Bramine.

19.
Packing up, or rather Molly for me, the whole day.
Tormenting, had not Molly all the time talk'd of poor
Mrs. Draper, and recounted every Visit She had made
me, and every repast she had shared with me; how
good a Lady! How sweet a temper! how beautiful!
how genteel! how gentle a Carriage—and how soft and
engaging a look! The poor girl is bewitch'd with us
both, infinitely interested in our Story, tho' She knows
nothing of it but from her penetration and Conjectures.
She says, however, 'tis Impossible not to be in Love

with her: In heart felt truth, Eliza! I'm of Molly's opinion.

20. Taking Leave of all the Town, before my departure to morrow.

21. Detaind by Lord and Lady Spencer who had made a party to dine and sup on my account. Impatient to set out for my Solitude: there the Mind, Eliza! gains strength, and learns to lean upon herself, and seeks refuge in its own Constancy and Virtue. In the world it seeks or accepts of a few treacherous supports —the feign'd Compassion of one, the flattery of a second, the Civilities of a third, the friendship of a fourth. They all deceive and bring the Mind back to where mine is retreating—that is Eliza! to itself, to thee who art my second self, to retirement, reflection and Books. When The Stream of Things, dear Bramine, Brings Us both together to this Haven, will not your heart take up its rest for ever? and will not your head Leave the world to those who can make a better thing of it—if there are any who know how. Heaven take thee, Eliza! under it's Wing. Adieu! adieu!

22d.
Left Bond Street and London with it, this Morning. What a Creature I am! my heart has ached this week to get away, and still was ready to bleed in quitting a Place where my Connection with my dear dear Eliza began. Adieu to it! till I am summon'd up to the Downs by a Message, to fly to her, for I think I shall not be able to support Town without you, and would chuse rather to sit solitary here till the end of the next Summer, to be made happy altogether, than seek for happiness, or even suppose I can have it, but in Eliza's Society.

23d.[1] Bear my Journey badly: ill and dispirited all the Way. Staid two days on the road at the Archbishop of Yorks. Show'd his Grace and his Lady and Sister your portrait, with a short but interesting Story of my friendship for the Original. Kindly nursed and honour'd both. Arrived at my Thatchd Cottage the 28th of May.

29th and 30th. Confined to my bed, so emaciated, and unlike what I was, I could scarse be angry with thee, Eliza, if thou Coulds not remember me, did heaven send me across thy way. Alas! poor Yorick! *"Remember thee ! Pale Ghost, remember thee, whilst Memory holds a seat in this* distracted World, Remember thee. Yes, from the Table of her Memory, shall just Eliza wipe away all trivial men, and leave a throne for Yorick. Adieu, dear constant Girl, adieu, adieu, and Remember my Truth and eternal fidelity; Remember how I Love; remember what I suffer. Thou art mine, Eliza, by Purchace had I not earn'd thee with a bitter price.

31.
Going this day upon a long course of Corrosive Mercury, which in itself, is deadly poyson, but given in a certain preparation, not very dangerous, I was forced to give it up in Town, from the terrible Cholicks both in Stomach and Bowels—but the Faculty thrust it down my Throat again. These Gentry have got it into their Nodelles, That mine is *an Ecclesiastick* Rheum as the French call it, God help em! I submit as my Uncle Toby did, in drinking Water, upon the wound he received in his Groin. *Merely for quietness sake.*

June 1.
The Faculty, my dear Eliza! have mistaken my Case;

[1] Only the first clause can belong to the twenty-third.

why not yours? I wish I could fly to you and attend you
but one month as a physician: You'll Languish and dye
where you are, if not by the climate—most certainly
by their *Ignorance of your Case*, and the unskilful
Treatment you must be a martyr to in such a place as
Bombay. I'm Languishing here myself with every Aid
and help, and tho' I shall conquer it yet, have had a
cruel struggle. Would, my dear friend, I could ease
yours, either by my Advice, my attention, my Labour,
my purse—They are all at your Service, such as they are,
and that you know, Eliza, or my friendship for you is
not worth a rush.

June 2d.

This morning surpriz'd with a Letter from my Lydia:
that She and her Mama are coming to pay me a Visit,
but on Condition I promise not to detain them in England beyond next April, when they purpose, by my
Consent, to retire into France, and establish themselves
for Life. To all which I have freely given my parole of
Honour, and so shall have them with me for the Summer.
From October to April they take Lodgings in York,
when they Leave me for good and all, I suppose.

☞ Every thing for the best! Eliza. This unexpected
visit, is neither a visit of friendship or form, but 'tis a
visit, such as I know you will never make me, of pure
Interest, to pillage what they can from me. In the first
place to sell a small estate I have of sixty pounds a
year and lay out the purchase money in joint annuitys
for them in the French Funds. By this they will obtain
200 pounds a year, to be continued to the longer Liver,
and as it rids me of all future care, and moreover transfers
their Income to the Kingdom where they purpose to
live, I'm truly acquiescent, tho' I lose the Contingency
of surviving them. But 'tis no matter: I shall have

enough, and a hundred or two hundred Pounds for Eliza
when ever She will honour me with putting her hand
into my Purse. In the main time, I am not sorry for
this visit, as every Thing will be finally settled between
us by it; only, as their Annuity will be too strait, I shall
engage to remit them a 100 Guineas a year more, during
my Wife's Life, and then I will think, Eliza, of living
for myself and the Being I love as much. But I shall
be pillaged in a hundred small Items by them which
I have a Spirit above saying, *no* to: as Provisions of
all sorts of Linnens—for house use, Body use, printed
Linnens for Gowns; Mazareens of Teas; Plate (all I have
but 6 Silver Spoons). In short, I shall be pluck'd bare,
all but of your Portrait and Snuff Box and your other
dear Presents, and the neat furniture of my thatch'd
Palace, and upon these I set up Stock again, Eliza.
What say you, Eliza! shall we join our *little capitals
together?* Will Mr. Draper give us leave? He may
safely, if your *Virtue* and Honour are only concern'd:
'twould be safe in Yorick's hands, as in a Brother's.
I would not wish Mr. Draper to allow you above half
I allow Mrs. Sterne—Our Capital would be too great,
and tempt us from the Society of poor Cordelia, who
begins to wish for you.

By this time, I trust you have doubled the Cape of
Good Hope, and sat down to your writing Drawer; and
look'd in Yorick's face, as you took out your Journal;
to tell him so. I hope he seems to smile as kindly upon
you Eliza, as ever. Your Attachment and Love for me,
will make him do so to eternity. If ever he should
change his Air, Eliza! I charge you catechize your own
Heart—oh! twil never happen!

June 3d. Cannot write my Travels, or give one half
hour's close attention to them, upon Thy account my

dearest friend. Yet write I must, and what to do with
You whilst I write I declare I know not. I want to have
you ever before my Imagination, and cannot keep you
out of my heart or head. In short thou enter'st my
Library Eliza! (as thou one day shalt) without tapping
or sending for by thy own Right of ever being close to
thy Bramine. Now I must shut you out sometimes, or
meet you Eliza! with an empty purse upon the Beach.
Pity my entanglements from other passions, my Wife
with me every moment of the Summer; think without
restraint upon a Fancy that should Sport and be in
all points at its ease. O had I, my dear Bramine, this
Summer, to soften and modulate my feelings, to enrich
my fancy, and fill my heart brim full with bounty, my
Book would be worth the reading.

It will be by stealth if I am able to go on with my
Journal at all: It will have many Interruptions and
Heyho's! most sentimentally utter'd. Thou must take
it as it pleases God, as thou must take the Writer
Eternal Blessings be about You, Eliza! I am a little
better, and now find I shall be set right in all points.
My only anxiety is about You: I want to prescribe for
you, My Eliza, for I think I understand your *Case*
better than all the Faculty. Adieu, adieu.

June 4.

Hussy! I have employ'd a full hour upon your sweet
sentimental Picture and a couple of hours upon yourself,
and with as much kind friendship, as the hour You
left me. I deny it: Time lessens no Affections which
honour and merit have planted. I would give more, and
hazard more now for your happiness than in any one
period, since I first learn'd to esteem you. Is it so with
thee, my friend? has absence weaken'd my Interest,
has time worn out any Impression, or is Yorick's name

less Musical in Eliza's ears? My heart smites me, for asking the question. 'Tis Treason against thee, Eliza, and Truth—Ye are dear Sisters, and your Brother Bramin Can never live to see a Separation amongst Us. What a similitude in our Trials whilst asunder! Providence has order'd every Step better, than we could have order'd them, for the particular good we wish each other. This you will comment upon and find the *Sense of* without my explanation.

I wish this Summer and Winter with all I am to go through with in them, in business and Labour and Sorrow, well over. I have much to compose and much to discompose me; have my Wife's projects and my own Views arising out of them, to harmonize and turn to account; I have Millions of heart aches to suffer and reason with—and in all this Storm of Passions, I have but one small Anchor, Eliza! to keep this weak Vessel of mine from perishing. I trust all I have to it, as I trust Heaven, which cannot leave me, without a fault, to perish. May the same just Heaven, my Eliza, be that eternal Canopy which shall shelter thy head from evil *till we* meet. Adieu, adieu, adieu.

June 5.

I sit down to write this day in good earnest, so read, Eliza! quietly besides me. I'll not give you a Look except one of kindness. Dear Girl! if thou lookest so bewitching once more I'll turn thee out of my Study. You may bid me defiance, Eliza. You cannot conceive how much and how universally I'm pitied, upon the Score of this unexpected Visit from France: my friends think it will kill me. If I find myself in danger I'll fly to you to Bombay. Will Mr. Draper receive me? He ought, but he will never know what reasons make it his *Interest* and *Duty*. We must leave all, all to that

Being who is infinitely removed above all Straitness of heart . . . and is a friend to the friendly, as well as to the friendless.

June 6. Am quite alone in the depth of that sweet Recesse, I have so often described to You. 'Tis sweet in itself, but You never come across me but the perspective brightens up, and every Tree and Hill and Vale and Ruin about me smiles as if you was amidst 'em. Delusive moments! how pensive a price do I pay for you. Fancy sustains the Vision whilst She has strength, but Eliza! Eliza is not with me! I sit down upon the first Hillock Solitary as a sequester'd Bramin; I wake from my delusion to a thousand Disquietudes, which many talk of, my Eliza! but few feel; then weary my Spirit with thinking, plotting, and projecting, and when I've brought my System to my mind am only Doubly miserable, That I cannot execute it.

Thus, Thus, my dear Bramine, are we lost at present in this tempest. Some Haven of rest will open to us assuredly. God made us not for Misery! and Ruin: He has orderd all our Steps and influenced our Attachments for what is worthy of them. It must end well, Eliza!

June 7.
I have this week finish'd a sweet little apartment which all the time it was doing, I flatter'd the most delicious of Ideas, in thinking I was making it for You. 'Tis a neat little simple elegant room, overlook'd only by the Sun—just big enough to hold a Sopha for us, a Table, four Chairs, a Bureau, and a Book case. They are to be all yours, Room and all, and there, Eliza! shall I enter ten times a day to give thee Testimonies of my Devotion. Was't thou this moment sat down, it would

be the sweetest of earthly Tabernacles. I shall enrich it, from time to time, for thee, till Fate lets me lead thee, by the hand Into it, and then it can want no Ornament. 'Tis a little oblong room with a large Sash at the end, a little elegant fireplace, with as much room to dine around it, as in Bond street. But in sweetness and Simplicity and silence beyond any thing. Oh, my Eliza! I shall see thee surely Goddesse of this Temple, and the most sovereign one, of all I have and of all the powers heaven has trusted me with. They were lent me, Eliza! only for thee, and for thee, my dear Girl, shall be kept and employ'd. You know *what rights* You have over me. Wish to heaven I could Convey the Grant more amply than I have *done*, but 'tis the same: 'tis register'd where it will longest last, and that is in the feeling and most sincere of human hearts. You know I mean this reciprocally, and whenever I mention the Word Fidelity and Truth, in Speaking of your Reliance on mine, I always Imply the same Reliance upon the same Virtues in my Eliza. I love thee, Eliza! and will love thee for ever. Adieu.

June 8.

Begin to recover, and sensibly to gain strength every day, and have such an appetite as I have not had for some Years. I prophecy I shall be the better, for the very Accident which has occasiond my Illness and that the Medicines and Regimen I have submitted to will make a thorough Regeneration of me, and that I shall have more health and strength, than I have enjoy'd these ten years. Send me such an account of thyself, Eliza, by the first sweet Gale. But 'tis impossible You should from Bombay—'twil be as fatal to You, as it has been to thousands of your Sex. England and Retirement in it, can only save you. Come! Come away!

June 9th. I keep a post chaise and a couple of fine horses, and take the Air every day in it. I go out and return to my Cottage, Eliza! alone. 'Tis melancholly, what should be matter of enjoyment; and the more so for that reason. I have a thousand things to remark and say as I roll along, but I want you to say them to. I could some times be wise and often Witty, but I feel it a reproach to be the latter whilst Eliza is so far from hearing me, and what is Wisdome to a foolish weak heart like mine! 'Tis like the Song of Melody to a broken Spirit. You must teach me fortitude, my dear Bramine, for with all the tender qualities which make you the most precious of Women and most wanting of all other Women of a kind of protector, yet you have a passive kind of sweet Courage which bears you up—more than any one Virtue I can summon up in my own Case. We were made with Tempers for each other, Eliza! and you are bless'd with such a certain turn of Mind and reflection that if Self love does not blind me I resemble no Being in the world so nearly as I do you. Do you wonder, then, I have such friendship for you? For my own part, I should not be astonished, Eliza, if you was to declare "You was up to the ears in Love with Me."

June 10th.

You are stretching over now in the Trade Winds from the Cape to Madras (I hope), but I know it not. Some friendly Ship you possibly have met with, and I never read an account of an India Man arrived, but I expect that it is the Messenger of the news my heart is upon the rack for. I calculate, That you will arrive at Bombay by the beginning of October. By February, I shall surely hear from you thence, but from Madrass sooner. I expect you, Eliza, in person, by September and shall scarse go to London till March—for what have I to do

there, when (except printing my Books) I have no Interest
or Passion to gratify? I shall return in June to Coxwould
and there wait for the glad Tidings of your arrival in
the Downs. Won't You write to me, Eliza? by the first
Boat? Would you not wish to be greeted by your
Yorick upon the Beech?—or be met by him to hand you
out of your postchaise, to pay him for the Anguish he
underwent, in handing you into it? I know your answers:
my Spirit is with You. Farewel, dear friend.

June 11.

I am every day negociating to sell my little Estate
besides me to send the money into France to purchace
peace to myself and a certainty of never having it
interrupted by Mrs. Sterne; who, when She is sensible
I have given her all I can part with, will be at rest
herself. Indeed, her plan to purchace annuities in
France, is a pledge of Security to me, That She will
live her days out there; otherwise She could have no
end in transporting this two thousand pounds out of
England, nor would I consent but upon that plan. But
I may be at rest, if my imagination will but let me!
Hall says 'tis no matter where she lives: If we are but
separate, 'tis as good as if the Ocean rolled between us.
And so I should argue to another Man. But, 'tis an
Idea which won't do so well for me, and tho' nonsensical
enough, Yet I shall be most at rest when there is that
Bar between Us, was I never so sure I should never be
interrupted by her in England. But I may be at rest,
I say, on that head, for they have left all their Cloaths
and plate and Linnen behind them in France, and have
join'd in the most earnest Entreaty, That they may
return and fix in France—to which I have give my
word and honour. You will be bound with me Eliza!
I hope, for performance of my promise. I never yet

broke it, in cases where Interest or pleasure could have tempted me. And shall hardly do it now, when tempted only by misery. In Truth, Eliza! thou art the Object to which every act of mine is directed. You interfere in every Project. I rise, I go to sleep with this on my Brain: how will my dear Bramine approve of this? which way will it conduce to make her happy? and how will it be a proof of my affection to her? Are all the Enquiries I make—your Honour, your Conduct, your Truth and regard for my esteem I know will equally direct every Step and Movement of your Desires; and with that Assurance, is it, my dear Girl, That I sustain Life. But when will those Sweet eyes of thine, run over these Declarations? How, and with whom are they to be entrusted; to be conveyed to You? Unless Mrs. James's friendship to us finds some expedient, I must wait till the first evening I'm with You when I shall present You with them as a better Picture of me, than Cosway could do for You. . . . Have been dismally ill all day, owing to my course of Medicines which are too strong and forcing for this gawsy Constitution of mine. I mend with them, however. Good God! how is it with You?

June 12. I have return'd from a delicious walk of Romance, my Bramine, which I am to tread a thousand times over with You swinging upon my arm—'tis to my Convent—and I have pluckd up a score [of] Bryars by the roots which grew near the edge of the foot way, that they might not scratch or incommode you. Had I been sure of your taking that walk with me the very next day, I could not have been more serious in my employment. Dear Enthusiasm? thou bringst things forward in a moment, which Time keeps for Ages back. I have you ten times a day besides me; I talk to you,

Eliza, for hours together; I take your Council; I hear your reasons; I admire you for them! To this magic of a warm Mind, I owe all that's worth living for, during this State of our Trial. Every Trincket you gave or exchanged with me has its force: your Picture is Yourself, all Sentiment, Softness and Truth. It speaks, it listens, 'tis conc'rned, it resignes. Dearest Original! how like unto thee does it seem—and will seem till thou makest it vanish, by thy presence. I'm but so, so, but advancing in health to meet you, to nurse you, to nourish you against you come—for I fear, You will not arrive, but in a State that calls out to Yorick for support. Thou art Mistress, Eliza, of all the powers he has to sooth and protect thee; for thou art Mistress of his heart, his affections, and his reason—and beyond that, except a paltry purse, he has nothing worth giving thee.

June 13.

This has been a year of presents to me, my Bramine. How many presents have I received from You in the first place? Lord Spencer has loaded me with a grand Ecritoire of 40 Guineas. I am to receive this week a fourty Guinea-present of a gold Snuff Box, as fine as Paris can fabricate one with an Inscription on it, more valuable, than the Box itself. I have a present of a portrait (which by the by I have immortalized in my Sentimental Journey), worth them both. I say nothing of a gold Stock buccle and Buttons, tho' I rate them above rubies, because they were Consecrated by the hand of Friendship, as She fitted them to me. I have a present of the Sculptures upon poor Ovid's Tomb, who died in Exile, tho' he wrote so well upon the Art of Love: These are in six beautiful Pictures executed on Marble at Rome, and these, Eliza, I keep sacred as Ornaments for your Cabinet, on Condition I hang them up. And last of all, I have had a present, Eliza! this Year, of a Heart so finely set, with such rich materials and Workmanship, That Nature must have had the chief hand in it. If I am able to keep it; I shall be a rich man; If I lose it I shall be poor indeed—so poor! I shall stand begging at your gates. But what can all these presents portend? That it will turn out a fortunate earnest, of what is to be given me hereafter.

June 14.

I want you to comfort me, my dear Bramine and reconcile my mind to 3 months' misery. Some days I think lightly of it; on others my heart sinks down to the earth. But this is the last Trial of conjugal Misery, and I wish it was to begin this moment, That it might run its period the faster; for, sitting as I do, expecting sorrow is suffering it. I am going to Hall to be philosophizd with for a week or ten Days on this point, but one hour with you would calm me more and furnish me with stronger Supports under this weight upon my Spirits, than all the world put together. Heaven! to what distressful Encountres hast thou thought fit to expose me! and was it not, that thou hast bless'd me with a chearfulness of disposition and thrown an object in my way: That is: to render that Sun Shine perpetual, Thy dealings with me would be a mystery.

June 15. From morning to night every moment of this day held in Bondage at my friend Lord ffauconberg's, so have but a moment left to close the day, as I do every one, with wishing thee a sweet night's rest. Would I was at the feet of your Bed fanning breezes to You, in your Slumbers! Mark! you will dream of me this night, and if it is not recorded in your Journal, I'll say, you could not recollect it the day following. Adieu.

June 16.

My Chaise is so large, so high, so long, so wide, so Crawford's-like, That I am building a coach house on purpose for it. Do you dislike it for this gigantick size? Now I remember, I heard you once say You hated a small post Chaise, which you must know determined my Choice to this, because I hope to make you a present of it; and if you are squeamish I shall be as squeamish as You, and return you all your presents, but one which I cannot part with, and what that is I defy you to guess. I have bought a milch Asse this afternoon and purpose to live by Suction, to save the expences of houskeeping and have a Score or two guineas in my purse, next.

June 17.

I have brought your name *Eliza !* and Picture into my work,[1] where they will remain when you and I are at rest for ever. Some Annotator or explainer of my works in this place will take occasion, to speak of the Friendship which subsisted so long and faithfully betwixt Yorick and the Lady he speaks of. Her Name, he will tell the world, was Draper: a Native of India, married there to a gentleman in the India Service of that Name, who brought her over to England for the recovery of her health in the Year 65, where She continued to April the Year 1767. It was about three months before her Return to India, That our Author's acquaintance and hers began. Mrs. Draper had a great thirst for knowledge, was handsome, genteel, engaging, and of such gentle dispositions and so enlighten'd an understanding, That Yorick (whether he made much opposition is not known) from an acquaintance soon became her Admirer. They caught fire at each other at the same time, and they would often say, without reserve to the world, and

[1] *A Sentimental Journey.*

without any Idea of saying wrong in it, That their Affections for each other were *unbounded*. Mr. Draper dying in the Year . . . This Lady return'd to England and Yorick the Year after becoming a Widower, They were married, and retiring to one of his Livings in Yorkshire, where was a most romantic Situation, they lived and died happily, and are spoke of with honour in the parish to this day.

June 18.

How do you like the History of this couple, Eliza? Is it to your mind? or shall it be written better some sentimental Evening after your return? 'Tis a rough sketch, but I could make it a pretty picture, as the outlines are just. We'll put our heads together and try what we can do. This last Sheet had put it out of my power, ever to send you this Journal to India. I had been more guarded but that You have often told me, 'twas in vain to think of writing by Ships which sail in March, as you hoped to be upon your return again by their arrival at Bombay. If I can write a Letter I will, but this Journal must be put into Eliza's hands by Yorick only. God grant you to read it soon!

June 19.

I never was so well and alert, as I find myself this day, tho' with a face as pale and clear as a Lady after her Lying-in. Yet you never saw me so Young by 5 Years, and If you do not leave Bombay soon You'l find me as young as Yourself at this rate of going on. Summon'd from home. Adieu.

June 20.

I think, my dear Bramine, That nature is turn'd upside down, for Wives go to visit Husbands at greater

perils and take longer journies to pay them this Civility
now a days out of ill Will than good. Mine is flying post
a Journey of a thousand Miles—with as many miles to
go back—merely to see how I do, and whether I am fat
or lean. And how far are you going to see your Help-
mate, and at such hazards to Your life, as few Wives'
best affections would be able to surmount! But Duty
and Submission, Eliza, govern thee; by what impulses
my Rib is bent towards me I have told you, and yet
I would to God, Draper but received and treated you
with half the courtesy and good nature. I wish you was
with him, for the same reason I wish my Wife at Coxwould: That She might the sooner depart in peace.
She is ill of a Diarhea which she has from a weakness
on her bowels ever since her paralytic Stroke. Travelling
post in hot weather, is not the best remedy for her, but
my girl says she is determined to venture. She wrote
me word in Winter, She would not leave France, till
her end approach'd. Surely this journey is not prophetick!
but 'twould invert the order of Things on the other side
of this Leaf—and what is to be on the next *Leaf* The
Fates, Eliza, only can tell us. Rest satisfied.

June 21.

Have left off all medicines, not caring to tear my
frame to pieces with 'em, as I feel perfectly well. Set
out for Crasy Castle to morrow morning, where I stay
ten days; take my Sentimental Voyage and this Journal
with me, as certain as the two first Wheels of my
Chariot—I cannot go on without them. I long to see
yours. I shall read it a thousand times over If I get it
before your arrival. What would I now give for it, tho'
I know there are *circumstances* in it, That will make my
heart bleed and waste within me. *But if all blows over—*
'tis enough; we will not recount our Sorrows, but to

shed tears of Joy over them. O Eliza! Eliza! Heaven
nor any Being it created, never so possessd a Man's
heart as thou possessest mine. Use it kindly, Hussy:
that is, eternally be true to it.

June 22. I've been as far as York to day with no
Soul with me in my Chase, but your Picture, for it has
a *Soul*, I think, or something like one which has talk'd
to me and been the best Company I ever took a Journey
with—always excepting a Journey I once took with
a friend of yours to Salt hill, and Enfield Wash. The
pleasure I had in those Journies, have left *Impressions*
upon my Mind, which will last my Life. You may tell
her as much when You see her; she will not take it ill.
I set out early to morrow morning to see Mr. Hall, but
take my Journal along with me.

June 24th.

As pleasant a Journey as I am capable of taking,
Eliza! without thee. Thou shalt take it with me when
time and tide serve hereafter, and every other Journey
which ever gave me pleasure, shall be rolled over again
with thee besides me. Amo's Vale shall look gay again
upon Eliza's Visit, and the Companion of her Journey
will grow young again as he sits upon her Banks with
Eliza seated besides him. I have this and a thousand
little parties of pleasure and systems of living out of
the comon high road of Life, hourly working in my
fancy for you. There wants only the *Dramatis Personæ*
for the performance: the play is wrote, the Scenes are
painted, and the Curtain ready to be drawn up. The
whole Piece waits for thee, my Eliza.

June 25. In a course of continual visits and Invita-
tions here *Bombay-Lascelles* dined here to day (his

Wife yesterday brought to bed). He is a poor sorry soul! but has taken a house two miles from Crasy Castle. What a Stupid, selfish, unsentimental set of Beings are the Bulk of our Sex! by Heaven! not one man out of 50, informd with feelings or endow'd either with heads or hearts able to possess and fill the mind of such a Being as thee, with one Vibration like its own. I never see or converse with one of my Sex but I give this point a reflection: how would such a creature please my Bramine? I assure thee, Eliza, I have not been able to find one, whom I thought could please You. The turn of Sentiment with which I left your Character possess'd must improve, hourly upon You: Truth, fidelity, honour and Love mix'd up with Delicacy, garrantee one another, and a taste so improved as yours, by so delicious fare, can never degenerate. 1 shall find you, my Bramine, if possible, more valuable and lovely than when you first caught my esteem and kindness for You; and tho' I see not this change, I give you so much Credit for it that at this moment, my heart glowes more warmly as I think of you, and I find myself more your Husband than contracts can make us. I stay here till the 29th—had intended a longer Stay, but much company and Dissipation rob me of the only comfort my mind takes, which is in retirement, where I can think of You, Eliza! and enjoy you quietly and without Interruption. 'Tis the way We must expect all that is to be had of *real* enjoyment in this vile world, which being miserable itself, seems so confederated against the happiness of the Happy, that they are forced to secure it in private. Vanity must still be had; and that, Eliza! every thing with it, which Yorick's sense, or generosity has to furnish to one he loves so much as thee—need I tell thee—Thou wilt be as much a Mistress of as thou art eternally of thy Yorick. Adieu, adieu!

June 26: eleven at night. Out all the day; dined with a large Party; shew'd your Picture from the fullness of my heart; highly admired. Alas! said I, did you but see the Original! Good night.

June 27.

Ten in the morning, with my Snuff open at the Top of this sheet, and your gentle sweet face opposite to mine, and saying "what I write will be cordially read." Possibly you may be precisely engaged at this very hour, the same way, and telling me some interesting Story about your health, your sufferings, your heart aches, and other Sensations which friendship, absence, and uncertainty create within you. For my own part, my dear Eliza, I am a prey to every thing in its turn, and was it not for that sweet clew of hope which is perpetual opening me a way which is to lead me to thee thro' all this Labyrinth—was it not for this, my Eliza! how could I find rest for this bewildered heart of mine? I should wait for you till September came, and if you did not arrive with it, should sicken and die. But I will live for thee, so count me Immortal. 3 India Men arrived within ten days: will none of 'em bring me tidings of You? But I am foolish—but ever thine, my dear, dear Bramine.

June 28.

O what a tormenting night have my dreams led me about You, Eliza! Mrs. Draper a Widow, with a hand at Liberty to give,—and gave it to another! She told me I must acquiese; it could not be otherwise. Acquiese! cried I, waking in agonies. God be prais'd, cried I; 'tis a dream! Fell asleep after; dream'd You was married to the Captain of the Ship; I waked in a fever. But 'twas the Fever in my blood which brought on this painful chain of Ideas, for I am ill to day and for want of more cheary Ideas, I torment my Eliza with these, whose Sensibility will suffer, if Yorick could dream but of her Infidelity! And I suffer, Eliza, in my turn, and think my self at present little better than an old woman or a Dreamer of Dreams in the Scripture Language. I am going to ride myself into better health and better fancies with Hall, whose Castle lying near the Sea We have a Beach as even as a mirrour of 5 miles in Length before it, where we dayly run races in our Chaises; with one wheel in the Sea, and the other in the Sand. O Eliza, with what fresh ardour and impatience when I'm viewing the element, do I sigh for thy return! But I need no *mementos* of my Destitution and misery for want of thee. I carry them about me, and shall not lay them down—for I worship and I do Idolize these tender sorrows till I meet thee upon the Beech and present the handkerchiefs staind with blood which broke out from my heart upon your departure. This token of what I felt at that Crisis, Eliza, shall never, never be wash'd out. Adieu, my dear Wife; you are still mine, notwithstanding all the Dreams and Dreamers in the world. Mr. Lascells dined with us. Mem. I have to tell you a Conversation; I will not write it.

June 29. Am got home from Halls to Coxwould. O 'tis a delicious retreat! both from its beauty, and air of Solitude; and so sweetly does every thing about it invite your mind to rest from its Labours and be at peace with itself and the world That 'tis the only place, Eliza, I could live in at this juncture. I hope one day, You will like it as much as your Bramine. It shall be decorated and made more worthy of You by the time fate encourages me to look for you. I have made you a sweet Sitting Room (as I told You) already, and am projecting a good Bed-Chamber adjoining it, with a pretty dressing room for You, which connects them together, and when they are finish'd, will be as sweet a set of romantic apartments, as You ever beheld. The Sleeping room will be very large; The dressing room, thro' which You pass into your Temple, will be little, but Big enough to hold a dressing Table, a couple of chairs, with room for your Nymph to stand at her ease both behind and on either side of you, with spare Room to hang a dozen petticoats, gowns, etc, and Shelves for as many Bandboxes. Your little Temple I have described, and what it will hold—but if it ever holds You and I, my Eliza, the Room will not be too little for us, but We shall be *too big* for the Room.

June 30. 'Tis now a quarter of a year (wanting 3 days) since You sail'd from the Downs. In one month more You will be (I trust) at Madras, and there you will stay I suppose 2 long long months, before you set out for Bombay. 'Tis there I shall want to hear from you, most impatiently because the most interesting Letters must come from Eliza when she is there. At present, I can hear of your health, and tho' that of all accounts affects me most, yet still I have hopes taking their Rise from that, and those are: What Impression you can make upon Mr. Draper, towards setting you at Liberty and leaving you to pursue the best measures for your preservation—and these are points, I would go to Aleppo, to know certainty.[1] I have been possess'd all day and night with an opinion, That Draper will change his behaviour totally towards you, That he will grow friendly and caressing, and as he knows your nature is easily to be won with gentleness, he will practice it

[1] This is probably a slip for "certainly," though Sterne may have intended "for a certainty."

to turn you from your purpose of quitting him. In short, when it comes to the point of your going from him to England, it will have so much the face, if not the reality, of an alienation on your side from India for ever, as a place you cannot live at, that he will part with You by no means, he can prevent. You will be cajolled, my dear Eliza, thus out of your Life. But what serves it to write this, unless means can be found for You to read it? If you come not I will take the Safest Cautions I can to have it got to You, and risk every thing, rather than You should not know how much I think of You and how much stronger hold you have got of me, than ever. Dillon has obtain'd his fair Indian and has this post wrote a kind Letter of enquiry after Yorick and his Bramine. He is a good Soul and interests himself much in our fate. I have wrote him a whole Sheet [1] of paper about us—it ought to have been copied into this Journal, but the uncertainty of your ever reading it, makes me omit that, with a thousand other things, which when we meet, shall beguile us of many a long winters night. *Those precious Nights !*—my Eliza! You rate them as high as I do and look back upon the manner the hours glided over our heads in them, with the same Interest and Delight as the Man you *spent them with*. They are all that remains to us, except the *Expectation* of their return. The Space between us is a dismal Void, full of doubts and suspence. Heaven and its kindest Spirits, my dear, rest over your thoughts by day and free them from all disturbance at night. Adieu, adieu, Eliza! I have got over this Month—so fare wel to it, and the Sorrows it has brought with it. The next month, I prophecy will be worse.

July 1. But who can foretell what a month may

[1] This letter is probably lost.

produce, Eliza? I have no less than seven different chances, not one of which is improbable, and any one of ['em] would set me much at Liberty—and some of 'em render me compleatly happy, as they would facilitate and open the road to thee. What these chances are I leave thee to conjecture, my Eliza. Some of them You cannot divine, tho' I once hinted them to You, but those are pecuniary chances arising out of my Prebend and so not likely to stick in thy brain nor could they occupy mine a moment, but on thy account. . . . I hope before I meet thee, Eliza, on the Beach, to have every thing plann'd; that depends on me properly— and for what depends upon Him who orders every Event for us, to Him I leave and trust it. We shall be happy at last, I know: 'tis the Corner Stone of all my Castles and 'tis all I bargain for. I am perfectly recover'd, or more than recover'd, for never did I feel such Indications of health or Strength and promptness of mind, notwithstanding the Cloud hanging over me of a Visit and all its tormenting consequences. Hall has wrote an affecting little poem upon it—the next time I see him, I will get it, and transcribe it in this Journal, for You. . . . He has persuaded me to trust her with no more than fifteen hundred pounds into Franc[e]—'twil purchase 150 pounds a year—and to let the rest come annually from myself. The advice is wise enough. If I can get her off with it, I'll summon up the Husband a little (if I can) and keep the 500 pounds remaining for emergencies. Who knows, Eliza, what sort of Emergencies may cry out for it? I conceive some, and you, Eliza, are not backward in Conception, so may conceive others. *I wish I was in Arno's Vale!*

July 2d. But I am in the Vale of Coxwould and wish You saw in how princely a manner I live in it—'tis a

Land of Plenty. I sit down alone to Venison, fish or wild foul, or a couple of fouls, with curds, and strawberrys and cream, and all the simple clean plenty which a rich Vally can produce; with a Bottle of wine on my right hand (as in Bond street) to drink your health. I have a hundred hens and chickens about my yard, and not a parishoner catches a hare a rabbit or a Trout but he brings it as an offering. In short, 'tis a golden Vally and will be the golden Age when You govern the rural feast, my Bramine, and are the Mistress of my table and spread it with elegancy and that natural grace and bounty with which heaven has distinguish'd You. . . .

Time goes on slowly; every thing stands still; hours seem days and days seem Years whilst you lengthen the Distance between us. From Madras to Bombay I shall think it shortening—and then desire and expectation will be upon the rack again. Come; come!

July 3d.

Hail! Hail! my dear Eliza! I steal something every day from my sentimental Journey to obey a more sentimental impulse in writing to you and giving you the present Picture of myself, my wishes, my Love, my sincerity, my hopes, my fears. Tell me, have I varied in any one Lineament, from the first sitting to this last; have I been less warm, less tender and affectionate than you expected or could have wish'd me in any one of 'em, or, however varied in the expressions of what I was and what I felt, have I not still presented the same air and face towards thee? Take it as a Sample of what I ever shall be, My dear Bramine, and that is, such as my honour, my Engagements and promisses and desires have fix'd me. I want You to be on the other side of my little table, to hear how sweetly your Voice will be in Unison to all this. I want to hear what You have to say to your Yorick upon this Text: what heavenly Consolation would drop from your Lips, and how pathetically you would enforce your Truth and Love upon my heart to free it from every Aching doubt. Doubt! did I say? But I have none—and as soon would I doubt the Scripture I have preach'd on as question thy promisses or suppose one Thought in thy heart during thy absence from me, unworthy of my Eliza. For if thou art false, my Bramine, the whole world and Nature itself are lyars, and I will trust to nothing on this side of heaven—but turn aside from all Commerce with expectation, and go quietly on my way alone towards a State where no disappointments can follow me. You are grieved when I talk thus; it implies what does not exist in either of us, so cross it out if thou wilt, or leave it as a part of the picture of a heart that again Languishes for Possession and is disturbed at every Idea of its uncertainty. So heaven bless thee and ballance thy passions better than I have power to regulate mine. Farewel, my dear Girl, I sit in dread of tomorrow's post which is to bring me an account when *Madame* is to arrive.

July 4th. Hear nothing of her—so am tortured from post to post, for I want to know certainly *the day and hour of this Judgment.* She is moreover ill, as my Lydia writes me word, and I'm impatient to know whether 'tis that or what other Cause detains her, and keeps me in this vile state of Ignorance. I'm pitied by every Soul in proportion as her Character is detested and her Errand known. She is coming, every one says, to flea poor Yorick or stay him, and I am spirited up by every friend I have to sell my life dear and fight valiantly in defence both of my property and Life. Now my Maxim, Eliza, is quietly [*sic*] in three:[1] "Spare my Life, and take all I have["]. If she is not content to decamp with that One Kingdome shall not hold us; for If she will not betake herself to France, I will. But these, I verlily [*sic*] believe my fears and nothing more, for she will be as impatient to quit England as I could wish her; but of this you will know more, before I have gone thro' this month's Journal. I get 2000 pounds for my Estate —that is, I had the offer this morning of it and think 'tis enough. When that is gone I will begin saving for thee, but in Saving myself for thee, That and every other kind Act is implied. Get on slowly with my Work, but my head is too full of other Matters; yet will I finish it before I see London, for I am of too scrupulous honour to break faith with the world. Great Authors make no scruple of it, but if they are great Authors I'm sure they are little Men. And I'm sure also of another Point which concerns yourself—and that is, Eliza, that You shall never find me one hair breadth a less Man than you . . .[2] Farewell: I love thee eternally.

July 5. Two letters from the South of France by this post, by which by some fatality, I find not one of my Letters have got to them this month. This gives me concern because it has the aspect of an unseasonable unkindness in me: to take no notice of what had the appearance at least of a Civility in desiring to pay me a Visit. My daughter, besides, has not deserved ill of me—and tho' her mother has, I would not ungenerously take that Opportunity, which would most overwhelm her, to give any mark of my resentment. I have besides long since forgiven her, and am the more inclined now

[1] Sterne apparently intended "is quickly wrote in three words."

[2] Erasure.

as she proposes a plan, by which I shall never more be disquieted. In these 2 last, she renews her request to have leave to live where she has transfer'd her fortune, and purposes, with my leave she says, to end her days in the South of France. To all which I have just been writing her a Letter of Consolation and good will, and to crown my professions, intreat her to take post with my girl to be here time enough to enjoy York races; and so having done my duty to them, I continue writing, to do it to thee Eliza who art the *Woman of my heart*, and for whom I am ordering and planning this, and every thing else. Be assured, my Bramine, that ere every thing is ripe for our Drama, I shall work hard to fit out and decorate a little Theatre for us to act on. But not before a crouded house—no, Eliza! it shall be as secluded as the elysian fields. Retirement is the nurse of Love and kindness, and I will Woo and caress thee in it in such sort, that every thicket and grotto we pass by *shall* solicit the remembrance of the mutual pledges We have exchanged of Affection with one another. Oh! these expectations make me sigh as I recite them, and many a heart-felt Interjection! do they cost me, as I saunter alone in the tracks we are to tread together hereafter. Still I think thy heart is with me, and whilst I think so, I prefer it to all the Society this world can offer. And 'tis in truth, my dear, oweing to this that tho I've received half a dozen Letters to press me to join my friends at Scarborough, that I've found pretences not to quit You *here* and sacrifice the many sweet occasions I have of giving my thoughts up to You,—for Company I cannot rellish *since I have tasted* my dear Girl, the *sweets of thine.*

July 6.

Three long Months and three long days are passed

and gone, since my Eliza sighed on taking her Leave of
Albion's Cliffs, and of all in Albion, which was dear to
her! How oft have I smarted at the Idea, of that last
longing Look by which thou badest adieu to all thy
heart sufferd at that dismal Crisis. 'Twas the Separation
of Soul and Body and equal to nothing but what passes
on that tremendous Moment. And like it in one Consequence, that thou art in another world; where I
would give a world to follow thee, or hear even an
account of thee. For this I shall write in a few days to
our dear friend Mrs. James: she possibly may have
heard a single Syllable or two about You. But it cannot
be; the same must have been directed towards Yorick's
ear, to whom you would have wrote the Name of
Eliza, had there been no time for more. I would almost
now compound with Fate, and was I sure Eliza only
breathd I would thank heaven and acquiesce. I kiss
your Picture, your Shawl, and every trinket I exchanged
with You every day I live. Alas! I shall soon be debarrd
of that. In a fortnight I must lock them up and clap
my seal and yours upon them in the most secret Cabinet
of my Bureau. You may divine the reason, Eliza!
Adieu! adieu!

July 7.
But not Yet: for I will find means to write to you
every night whilst my people are here—if I sit up till
midnight, till they are asleep. I should not dare to face
you, if I was worse than my word in the smallest Item,
and this Journal I promised You, Eliza, should be kept
without a chasm of a day in it; and had I my time to
myself and nothing to do but gratify my propensity,
I should write from sun rise to sun set to thee. But a
Book to write, a Wife to receive and make Treaties
with, an estate to sell, a Parish to superintend, and a

disquieted heart perpetually to reason with, are eternal calls upon me. And yet I have you more in my mind than ever, and in proportion as I am thus torn from your embraces, *I cling the closer to the Idea of you.* Your Figure is ever before my eyes; the sound of your voice vibrates with its sweetest tones the live long day in my ear—I can see and hear nothing but my Eliza. Remember this, when you think my Journal too short and compare it not with thine, which tho' it will exceed it in length, can do no more than equal it in Love and truth of esteem. For esteem thee I do beyond all the powers of eloquence to tell thee how much, and I love thee, my dear Girl, and prefer thy Love, to me more than the whole world.

Night: have not eat or drunk all day thro' vexation of heart at a couple of ungrateful unfeeling Letters from that Quarter, from whence, had it pleas'd God, I should have lookd for all my Comforts. But He has will'd they should come from the East, and he knows how I am satisfyed with all his Dispensations; but with none, my dear Bramine, so much as this, with which Cordial upon my Spirits I go to bed, in hopes of seeing thee in my Dreams.

July 8th.

Eating my fowl, and my trouts and my cream and my strawberries, as melancholly as a Cat; for want of you. By the by, I have got one which sits quietly besides me, purring all day to my sorrows and looking up gravely from time to time in my face, as if she knew my Situation. How soothable my heart is, Eliza, when such little things sooth it! for in some pathetic sinkings I feel even some support from this poor Cat. I attend to her purrings and think they harmonize me: they are *pianissimo* at least, and do not disturb me. Poor Yorick! to be driven, with all his sensibilities, to these resources! All powerful Eliza, that has had this Magical authority over him; to bend him thus to the dust! But I'll have my revenge, Hussy!

July 9. I have been all day making a sweet Pavillion in a retired Corner of my garden,—but my Partner and Companion and friend for whom I make it, is fled from me, and when she return to me again, Heaven who first brought us together, best knows. When that hour is foreknown what a Paradise will I plant for thee! Till then I walk as Adam did whilst there was no help-meet found for it, and could almost wish a day's Sleep would come upon me till that Moment When I can say as he did: *"Behold the Woman Thou has given me for Wife."* She shall be call'd La Bramine. Indeed, Indeed, Eliza! my Life will be little better than a dream, till we approach nearer to each other. I live scarse conscious of my existence, or as if I wanted a vital part and could not live above a few hours. And yet I live, and live, and live on, for thy Sake, and the sake of thy truth to me which I measure by my own;—and I fight against every evil and every danger, that I may be able to support and shelter thee from danger and evil also. Upon my word, dear Girl, thou owest me much—but 'tis cruel to dun thee when thou art not in a condition to pay. I think Eliza has not run off in her Yorick's debt.

July 10.
I cannot suffer you to be longer upon the Water: in 10 days' time, You shall be at Madrass. The element roles in my head as much as yours, and I am sick at the sight and smell of it—for all this, my Eliza, I feel in Imagination and so strongly I can bear it no longer.

On the 20th therefore Inst. I begin to write to you as a terrestrial Being. I must deceive myself and think so I will notwithstanding all that Lascelles has told me, but there is no truth in him. I have just kiss'd your picture—even that sooths many an anxiety. I have found out the Body is too little for the head: it shall not be rectified, till I sit by the Original, and direct the Painter's Pencil and that done, will take a Scamper to *Enfield* and see your dear children—if You tire by the Way, there are *one or two* places to rest at. I never stand out. God bless thee—I am thine as *ever*.

July 11.

Sooth me, calm me, pour thy healing Balm, Eliza, into the sorest of hearts. I'm pierced with the Ingratitude and unquiet Spirit of a restless unreasonable Wife whom neither gentleness or generosity can conquer. She has now enter'd upon a new plan of waging War with me, a thousand miles. Thrice a week this last month, has the quietest man under heaven been outraged by her Letters: I have offer'd to give her every Shilling I was worth except my preferment, to be let alone and left in peace by her. Bad Woman! nothing must now purchace this, unless I borrow 400 pounds to give her and carry into France. More! I would perish first, my Eliza! ere I would give her a shilling of another man's, which I must do if I give her a shilling more than I am worth. How I now feel the want of thee! my dear Bramine, my generous unworldly honest creature. I shall die for want of thee for a thousand reasons. Every emergency and every Sorrow each day brings along with it tells me what a Treasure I am bereft off. Whilst I want thy friendship and Love to keep my head up sinking, God's will be done. But I think she will send me to my grave. She will now keep me in torture till the end of September, and writes me word to day She will delay her Journey two Months beyond her first Intention. It keeps me in eternal suspence all the while, for she will come unawars at last upon me, and then adieu to the dear sweets of my retirement.

How cruelly are our Lots drawn, my dear—both made for happiness, and neither of us made to taste it! In feeling so acutely for my own disappointment I drop blood for thine, I call thee in to my Aid—and thou wantest mine as much! Were we together we should recover, but never, never till then *nor by any other Recipe.*

July 12.

Am ill all day with the Impressions of Yesterday's account; can neither eat or drink or sit still and write or read. I walk like a disturbed Spirit about my Garden, calling upon heaven and thee, to come to my Succour. Couldst Thou but write one word to me, it would be worth half the world to me. My friends write me millions —and every one invites me to flee from my Solitude and come to them. I obey the commands of my friend Hall who has sent over on purpose to fetch me, or he will come himself for me—so I set off to morrow morning to take Sanctuary in Crasy Castle. The news papers have sent me there already by putting in the following paragraph.

"We hear from Yorkshire, That Skelton Castle is the present Rendevouz, of the most brilliant Wits of the Age—the admired Author of Tristram, Mr. Garrick, etc. beening [*sic*] there; and Mr. Coleman and many other men of Wit and Learning being every day expected." When I get there, which will be to-morrow night, my Eliza will hear from her Yorick—her Yorick who loves her more than ever.

July 13. Skelton Castle. Your picture has gone round the Table after supper—and your health after it, my invaluable friend! Even the Ladies, who hate grace in another, seemed struck with it in You. But Alas! you are as a dead Person, and Justice (as in all such Cases) is paid you in course: when thou returnest it will be render'd more sparingly, but I'll make up all deficiences by honouring You more than ever Woman was honourd by man. Every good Quality That ever good heart possess'd thou possessest, my dear Girl; and so sovereignly does thy temper and sweet sociability, which harmonize all thy other properties make me thine, that whilst thou art true to thyself and thy Bramin he thinks thee worth a world—and would give a World was he master of it, for the undisturbed possession of thee. Time and Chance are busy throwing this Die for me: a fortunate Cast, or two, at the most, makes our fortune—it gives us each other, and then for the World, I will not give a pinch of Snuff. Do take care of thyself. Keep this prospect before thy eyes; have a view to it in all your Transactions, Eliza; In a word, Remember You are mine and stand answerable for all you say and do to me. I govern myself by the same Rule, and such a History of myself can I lay before you as shall create no blushes, but those of pleasure. 'Tis midnight—and so sweet Sleep to thee the remaining hours of it. I am more thine, my dear Eliza! than ever—but that cannot be.

July 14.

Dining and feasting all day at Mr. Turner's; his Lady a fine Woman herself, in love with your picture. O my dear Lady, cried I, did you but know the Original! But what is she to you, Tristram? Nothing; but that I am in Love with her. Et cætera . . ., said She. No,

I have given over dashes, replied I. I verily think my
Eliza I shall get this Picture set, so as to wear it, as
I first purposed, about my neck. I do not like the place
'tis in; it shall be nearer my heart—Thou art ever in
its centre. Good night.

July 15—From home (Skelton Castle) from 8 in the
morning till late at Supper. I seldom have put thee
off, my dear Girl—and yet to morrow will be as bad.

July 16.
For Mr. Hall has this Day left his Crasy Castle to
come and sojourn with me at Shandy Hall for a few
days—for so they have long christen'd our retired
Cottage. We are just arrived at it, and whilst he is
admiring the premises I have stole away to converse
a few minutes with thee, and in thy own dressing room
—for I make every thing thine and call it so, before
hand, that thou art to be mistress of hereafter. This
Hereafter, Eliza, is but a melancholly term—but the
Certainty of its coming to us, brightens it up. Pray do
not forget my prophecy in the Dedication of the Alma-
nack: I have the utmost faith in it myself. But by what
impulse my mind was struck with 3 Years, heaven,
whom I believe it's author, best knows. But I shall
see your face before—but that I leave to You and to
the Influence such a Being must have over all inferior
ones. We are going to dine with the Arch Bishop [1] to-
morrow, and from thence to Harrogate for three days,
whilst thou dear Soul art pent up in sultry Nastiness
without Variety or change of face or Conversation.
Thou shalt have enough of both when I cater for thy
happiness Eliza—and if an Affectionate husband and
400 pounds a year in a sweeter Vally than that of

[1] Robert Hay Drummond.

Jehosophat will do—less thou shalt never have, but
I hope more, and were it millions 'tis the same; 'twould
be laid at thy feet. Hall is come in in raptures with
every thing. And so I shut up my Journal for to-day and
to-morrow for I shall not be able to open it where I go.
Adieu, my dear Girl.

18. Was yesterday all the day with our Archbishop.
This good Prelate, who is one of our most refined Wits
and the most of a gentleman of our order, oppresses me
with his kindness. He shews in his treatment of me,
what he told me upon taking my Leave: that he loves
me, and has a high Value for me. His Chaplains tell me,
he is perpetually talking of me and has such an opinion
of my head and heart that he begs to stand Godfather
for my next Literary production, so has done me the
honour of putting his name in a List which I am most
proud of because my Eliza's name is in it. I have just
a moment to scrawl this to thee, being at York—where
I want to be employd in taking you a little house,
where the prophet may be accommodated with a
"Chamber in the Wall apart with a stool & a Candlestick";
where his Soul can be at rest from the distractions of
the world, and lean only upon his kind hostesse, and
repose all his Cares, and melt them *along with hers* on
her sympathetic bosom.

July 19. Harrogate Spaws. Drinking the waters here
till the 26th—to no effect, but a cold dislike of every
one of your sex. I did nothing, but make comparisons
betwixt thee, my Eliza, and every woman I saw and
talk'd to. Thou hast made me so unfit for every one
else than [1] I am thine as much from necessity, as Love;
I am thine by a thousand sweet ties, the least of which

    [1] Evidently a slip for *that*.

shall never be relax'd. Be assured, my dear Bramine,
of this, and repay me in so doing the Confidence
I repose in thee—your absence, your distresses, your
sufferings, your conflicts, all make me rely but the
more upon that fund in you, which is able to sustain
so much weight. Providence I know will relieve you
from one part of it, and it shall be the pleasure of my
days to ease my dear friend of the other. I Love thee,
Eliza, more than the heart of Man ever loved Woman's;
I even love thee more than I did, the day thou badest
me farewel! Farewell! Farewell! to thee again. I'm
going from hence to York Races.

July 27. Arrived at York, where I had not been
2 hours before My heart was overset with a pleasure,
which beggard every other, that fate could give me
save thyself: It was thy dear Packets from Iago. I
cannot give vent to all the emotions I felt even before
I opend them, for I knew thy hand and my seal—which
was only in thy possession. O, 'tis from my Eliza, said
I. I instantly shut the door of my Bed-chamber, and
orderd myself to be denied, and spent the whole evening,
and till dinner the next day, in reading over and over
again the most interesting account and the most endearing one that ever tried the tenderness of man. I read
and wept, and wept and read till I was blind; then grew
sick, and went to bed—and in an hour call'd again for
the Candle to read it once more. As for my dear Girl's
pains and her dangers I cannot write about them,
because I cannot write my feelings or express them
any how to my mind, O Eliza! but I will talk them over
with thee with a sympathy that shall woo thee, so
much better than I have ever done That we will both
be gainers in the end. *I'll love thee for the dangers thou
hast past,* and thy Affection shall go hand in hand with

me, because I'll pity thee as no man ever pitied Woman. But Love like mine is never satisfied—else your second Letter from Iago is a Letter so warm, so simple, so tender, I defy the world to produce such another. By all that's kind and gracious! I will entreat thee, Eliza, so kindly that thou shalt say, I merit much of it—nay, all—for my merit to thee is my truth.

I now want to have this week of nonsensical Festivity over that I may get back, with my picture which I ever carry about me to my retreat and to Cordelia. When the days of our Afflictions are over, I oft amuse my fancy, with an Idea, that thou wilt come down to me by Stealth, and hearing where I have walk'd out to, surprize me some sweet Shiney night at Cordelia's grave, and catch me in thy Arms over it. O my Bramin! my Bramin!

July 31. Am tired to death with the hurrying pleasures of these Races: I want still and *silent* ones—so return home to morrow, in search of them. I shall find them as I sit contemplating over thy passive picture; sweet Shadow! of what is to come! for 'tis all I can now grasp. First and best of woman kind! remember me, as I remember thee. 'Tis asking a great deal, my Bramine! but I cannot be satisfied with less. Farwell; fare happy till fate will let me cherish thee myself. O my Eliza! thou writest to me with an Angel's pen, and thou wouldst win me by thy Letters, had I never seen thy face or known thy heart.

August 1. What a sad Story thou hast told me of thy Sufferings and Despondences from St. Iago, till thy meeting with the Dutch Ship. 'Twas a sympathy above Tears—I trembled every Nerve as I went from line to line, and every moment the account comes across me, I suffer all I felt, over and over again. Will providence suffer all this anguish without end and without pity? "*It no can be.*" I am tried, my dear Bramine, in the furnace of Affliction as much as thou. By the time we meet, We shall be fit only for each other, and should cast away upon any other Harbour.

August 2. My wife uses me most unmercifully. Every Soul advises me to fly from her, but where can I fly If I fly not to thee? The Bishop of Cork and Ross [1] has made me great offers in Ireland, but I will take no step without thee and till heaven opens us some track. He is the best of feeling tender hearted men, knows our Story, sends You his Blessing, and says if the Ship you return in touches at Cork (which many India men do), he will take you to his palace, till he can send for me to join You. He only hopes, he says, to join us together for ever. But more of this good man, and his attachment to me hereafter and of and [*sic*] couple of Ladies in the family, etc., etc.

Augt. 3. I have had an offer of exchanging two pieces of preferment I hold here (but sweet Cordelia's Parish is not one of 'em) for a living of 350 pounds a year in Surry about 30 miles from London, and retaining Coxwould and my Prebendaryship, which are half as much more. The Country also is sweet. But I will not, I cannot take any step, unless I had thee, my Eliza, for whose sake I live, to consult with, and till the road is open for me as my heart wishes to advance. With thy sweet light Burden in my Arms, I could get up fast the hill of preferment, if I chose it, but without thee I feel Lifeless, and if a Mitre was offer'd me, I would not have it, till I could have thee too, to make it sit easy upon

[1] Dr. Jemmet Brown, whom Sterne met at Scarborough.

my brow. I want kindly to smooth thine, and not only wipe away thy tears but dry up the Sourse of them for ever.

Augst. 4. Hurried backwards and forwards about the arrival of Madame, this whole week, and then farewel I fear to this journal till I get up to London and can pursue it as I wish. At present all I can write would be but the History of my miserable feelings. She will be ever present and if I take up my pen for thee, something will jarr within me as I do it that I must lay it down again. I will give you one general account of all my sufferings together, but not in Journals. I shall set my wounds a-bleeding every day afresh by it and the Story cannot be too short, so worthiest, best, kindest and most affectionate of Souls, farewell. Every Moment will I have thee present and sooth my sufferings with the looks my fancy shall cloath thee in. Thou shalt lye down and rise up with me—about my bed and about my paths, and shalt see out all my Ways. Adieu, adieu, and remember one eternal truth, My dear Bramine, which is not the worse, because I have told it thee a thousand times before: That I am thine, and thine only, and for ever.

L. STERNE.

[Postscript.]

Nov: 1st. All, my dearest Eliza, has turnd out more favourable than my hopes. Mrs. S. and my dear Girl have been 2 Months with me and they have this day left me to go to spend the Winter at York, after having settled every thing to their heart's content. Mrs. Sterne retires into France, whence she purposes not to stir, till her death, and never, has she vow'd, will give me another sorrowful or discontented hour. I have conquerd her, as I would every one else, by humanity and Generosity, and she leaves me, more than half in Love with me. She goes into the South of France, her health being insupportable in England—and her age, as she now confesses ten Years more than I thought, being on the edge of sixty. So God bless and make the remainder of her Life happy, in order to which I am to remit her three hundred guineas a year, and give my dear Girl two thousand pounds with which all Joy, I agree to,—but 'tis to be sunk into an annuity in the French Loans.

And now, Eliza! Let me talk to thee. But What can I say, What can I write, But the Yearnings of heart wasted with looking and wishing for thy Return? Return, Return! my dear Eliza! May heaven smooth the Way for thee to send thee safely to us, and joy for Ever.

LETTERS TO ELIZA

LETTERS TO ELIZA

LETTER I

ELIZA will receive my books with this. The sermons came all hot from the heart: I wish that I could give them any title to be offered to yours. The others came from the head. I am more indifferent about their reception.

I know not how it comes about, but I am half in love with you. I ought to be wholly so; for I never valued (or saw more good qualities to value) or thought more of one of your sex than of you; so adieu.

Yours faithfully,

If not affectionately,

L. STERNE.

LETTER II

I CANNOT rest, Eliza, though I shall call on you at half-past twelve, till I know how you do. May thy dear face smile, as thou risest, like the sun of this morning. I was much grieved to hear of your alarming indisposition yesterday; and disappointed too, at not being let in. Remember, my dear, that a friend has the same right as a physician. The etiquettes of this town (you'll say) say otherwise. No matter! Delicacy and propriety do not always consist in observing their frigid doctrines.

I am going out to breakfast, but shall be at my

lodgings by eleven; when I hope to read a single line under thy own hand, that thou art better, and wilt be glad to see thy Bramin.

9 o'clock.

LETTER III

I GOT thy letter last night, Eliza, on my return from Lord Bathurst's, where I dined, and where I was heard (as I talked of thee an hour without intermission) with so much pleasure and attention, that the good old Lord toasted your health three different times; and now he is in his eighty-fifth year, says he hopes to live long enough to be introduced as a friend to my fair Indian disciple, and to see her eclipse all other nabobesses as much in wealth, as she does already in exterior and (what is far better) in interior merit. I hope so too. This nobleman is an old friend of mine. You know he was always the protector of men of wit and genius; and has had those of the last century, Addison, Steele, Pope, Swift, Prior, &c., &c., always at his table. The manner in which his notice began of me, was as singular as it was polite. He came up to me, one day, as I was at the Princess of Wales's court. "I want to know you, Mr. Sterne; but it is fit you should know, also, who it is that wishes this pleasure You have heard, continued he, of an old Lord Bathurst, of whom your Popes and Swifts have sung and spoken so much: I have lived my life with geniuses of that cast; but have survived them; and, despairing ever to find their equals, it is some years since I have closed my accounts, and shut up my books, with thoughts of never opening them again; but you have kindled a desire in me of opening them once more before I die; which I now do; so go home and dine with me." This nobleman, I say, is a prodigy; for at eighty-five he has all the wit and promptness of a man of thirty. A disposition to be pleased, and a power to please others, beyond whatever I knew: added to which, a man of learning, courtesy, and feeling.

He heard me talk of thee, Eliza, with uncommon satisfaction; for there was only a third person, and of sensibility, with us. And a most sentimental afternoon, till nine o'clock, have we passed! But thou, Eliza, wert the star that conducted and enliven'd the discourse. And when I talked not of thee, still didst thou fill my mind, and warmed every thought I uttered, for I am not ashamed to acknowledge I greatly miss thee. Best of all good girls! the sufferings I have sustained the whole night on account of thine, Eliza, are beyond my power of words. Assuredly does Heaven give strength proportioned to the weight he lays upon us! Thou hast been bowed down, my child, with every burden that sorrow of heart, and pain of body, could inflict upon a poor being; and still thou tellest me, thou art beginning to get ease; thy fever gone, thy sickness, the pain in thy side vanishing also. May every evil so vanish that thwarts Eliza's happiness, or but awakens thy fears for a moment! Fear nothing, my dear! Hope every thing; and the balm of this passion will shed its influence on thy health, and make thee enjoy a spring of youth and cheerfulness, more than thou hast hardly yet tasted.

And so thou hast fixed thy Bramin's portrait over thy writing-desk; and wilt consult it in all doubts and difficulties. Grateful and good girl! Yorick smiles contentedly over all thou dost; his picture does not do justice to his own complacency.

Thy sweet little plan and distribution of thy time, how worthy of thee! Indeed, Eliza, thou leavest me nothing to direct thee in; thou leavest me nothing to require, nothing to ask but a continuation of that conduct which won my esteem, and has made me thy friend for ever.

May the roses come quick back to thy cheeks, and the rubies to thy lips! But trust my declaration, Eliza, that thy husband (if he is the good, feeling man I wish him) will press thee to him with more honest warmth and affection, and kiss thy pale, poor dejected face with more transport, than he would be able to do, in the best bloom of all thy beauty; and so he ought, or I pity him. He must have strange feelings, if he knows not the value of such a creature as thou art!

I am glad Miss Light [1] goes with you. She may relieve you from many anxious moments. I am glad your ship-mates are friendly beings. You could least dispense with what is contrary to your own nature, which is soft and gentle, Eliza. It would civilize savages. Though pity were it thou shouldst be tainted with the office! How canst thou make apologies for thy last letter? 'tis most delicious to me, for the very reason you excuse it. Write to me, my child, only such. Let them speak the easy carelessness of a heart that opens itself, any how, and every how, to a man you ought to esteem and trust. Such, Eliza, I write to thee, and so I should ever live with thee, most artlessly, most affectionately, if Providence permitted thy residence in the same section of the globe: for I am, all that honour and affection can make me,   THY BRAMIN.

---

[1] Miss Light afterwards married George Stratton, Esq., late in the service of the East-India Company at Madras.

LETTER IV

I WRITE this, Eliza, at Mr. James's, whilst he is dressing, and the dear girl, his wife, is writing, beside me, to thee. I got your melancholy billet before we sat down to dinner. 'Tis melancholy indeed, my dear, to hear so piteous an account of thy sickness! Thou art encountered with evils enow, without that additional weight! I fear it will sink thy poor soul, and body with it, past recovery. Heaven supply thee with fortitude! We have talked of nothing but thee, Eliza, and of thy sweet virtues, and endearing conduct, all the afternoon. Mrs. James, and thy Bramin, have mixed their tears a hundred times, in speaking of thy hardships, thy goodness, thy graces. The ——'s, by heavens, are worthless! I have heard enough to tremble at the articulation of the name. How could you, Eliza, leave them (or suffer them to leave you rather) with impressions the least favourable? I have told thee enough to plant disgust against their treachery to thee, to the last hour of thy life! Yet still thou toldest Mrs. James at last, that thou believest they affectionately love thee. Her delicacy to my Eliza, and true regard to her ease of mind, have saved thee from hearing more glaring proofs of their baseness. For GOD's sake, write not to them; nor foul thy fair character with such polluted hearts. *They* love thee! What proof? Is it their actions that say so? or their zeal for those attachments, which do thee honour, and make thee happy? or their tenderness for thy fame? No. But they *weep* and say *tender things*. Adieu to all such for ever. Mrs. James's honest heart revolts against the idea of ever returning them one visit. I honour her, and I honour thee, for almost every act of thy life, but this blind partiality for an unworthy being.

Forgive my zeal, dear girl, and allow me a right which arises only out of that fund of affection I have, and shall preserve for thee to the hour of my death! Reflect, Eliza, what are my motives for perpetually advising thee? think whether I can have any, but what proceed from the cause I have mentioned! I think you are a very deserving woman; and that you want nothing but firmness and a better opinion of yourself to be the best female character I know. I wish I could inspire you with a share of that vanity your enemies lay to your charge (though to me it has never been visible); because I think, in a well-turned mind, it will produce good effects.

I probably shall never see you more; yet I flatter myself you'll sometimes think of me with pleasure; because you must be convinced I love you, and so interest myself in your rectitude, that I had rather hear of any evil befalling you, than your want of reverence for yourself. I had not power to keep this remonstrance in my breast. It's now out; so adieu. Heaven watch over my Eliza!

Thine,

YORICK.

LETTER V

To whom should Eliza apply in her distress, but to her friend who loves her? why then, my dear, do you apologize for employing me? Yorick would be offended, and with reason, if you ever sent commissions to another, which he could execute. I have been with Zumps; and your piano forté must be tuned from the brass middle

string of your guittar, which is C. I have got you a
hammer too, and a pair of plyers to twist your wire
with; and may every one of them, my dear, vibrate
sweet comfort to my hopes! I have bought you ten
handsome brass screws, to hang your necessaries upon:
I purchased twelve; but stole a couple from you to put
up in my own cabin, at Coxwould. I shall never hang,
or take my hat off one of them, but I shall think of you.
I have bought thee, moreover, a couple of iron screws,
which are more to be depended on than brass, for
the globes.

I have written, also, to Mr. Abraham Walker, pilot
at Deal, that I had dispatched these in a packet, directed
to his care; which I desired he would seek after, the
moment the Deal machine arrived. I have, moreover,
given him directions, what sort of an arm-chair you
would want, and have directed him to purchase the
best that Deal could afford, and take it, with the parcel,
in the first boat that went off. Would I could, Eliza,
so supply all thy wants, and all thy wishes! It would
be a state of happiness to me. The journal is as it
should be, all but its contents. Poor, dear, patient
being! I do more than pity you; for I think I lose both
firmness and philosophy, as I figure to myself your
distresses. Do not think I spoke last night with too
much asperity of ——; there was cause; and besides,
a good heart ought not to love a bad one; and, indeed,
cannot. But, adieu to the ungrateful subject.

I have been this morning to see Mrs. James. She loves
thee tenderly, and unfeignedly. She is alarmed for thee.
She says thou looked'st most ill and melancholy on
going away. She pities thee. I shall visit her every Sunday, while I am in town. As this may be my last letter,
I earnestly bid thee farewell. May the God of Kindness
be kind to thee, and approve himself thy protector,

now thou art defenceless! And, for thy daily comfort, bear in thy mind this truth, that whatever measure of sorrow and distress is thy portion, it will be repaid to thee in a full measure of happiness, by the Being thou hast wisely chosen for thy eternal friend.

Farewell, farewell, Eliza! whilst I live, count upon me as the most warm and disinterested of earthly friends.

YORICK.

LETTER VI

MY DEAREST ELIZA!

I began a new journal this morning; you shall see it; for if I live not till your return to England, I will leave it you as a legacy. 'Tis a sorrowful page; but I will write cheerful ones; and could I write letters to thee, they should be cheerful ones too: but few, I fear, will reach thee! However, depend upon receiving something of the kind by every post; till then, thou wavest thy hand, and bid'st me write no more.

Tell me how you are; and what sort of fortitude Heaven inspires you with. How are you accommodated, my dear? Is all right? Scribble away, any thing, and every thing, to me. Depend upon seeing me at Deal, with the James's, should you be detained there by contrary winds. Indeed, Eliza, I should with pleasure fly to you, could I be the means of rendering you any service, or doing you kindness. Gracious and merciful GOD! consider the anguish of a poor girl. Strengthen and preserve her in all the shocks her frame must be exposed to. She is now without a protector, but thee! Save her from all accidents of a dangerous element, and give her comfort at the last.

My prayer, Eliza, I hope, is heard; for the sky seems to smile upon me, as I look up to it. I am just returned from our dear Mrs. James's, where I have been talking of thee for three hours. She has got your picture, and likes it: but Marriot, and some other judges, agree that mine is the better, and expressive of a sweeter character. But what is that to the original? yet I acknowledge that hers is a picture for the world, and mine is calculated only to please a very sincere friend, or sentimental philosopher. In the one, you are dressed in smiles, and with all the advantages of silks, pearls, and ermine; in the other, simple as a vestal, appearing the good girl nature made you; which, to me, conveys an idea of more unaffected sweetness, than Mrs. Draper, habited for conquest, in a birth-day suit, with her countenance animated, and her dimples visible. If I remember right, Eliza, you endeavoured to collect every charm of your person into your face, with more than *common* care, the day you sat for Mrs. James. Your colour, too, brightened; and your eyes shone with more than usual brilliancy. I then requested you to come simple and unadorned when you sat for me, knowing (as I see with *unprejudiced* eyes) that you could receive no addition from the silk-worm's aid, or jeweller's polish. Let me now tell you a truth, which, I believe, I have uttered before. When I first saw you, I beheld you as an object of compassion, and as a very plain woman. The mode of your dress (tho' fashionable) disfigured you. But nothing now could render you such, but the being solicitous to make yourself admired as a handsome one. You are not handsome, Eliza, nor is yours a face that will please the tenth part of your beholders, but are something more; for I scruple not to tell you, I never saw so intelligent, so animated, so good a countenance; nor was there (nor ever will be) that man of sense, tenderness, and feeling, in your company three hours, that was not (or will not be) your admirer, or friend, in consequence of it; that is, if you assume, or assumed, no character foreign to your own, but appeared the artless being nature designed you for. A something in your eyes, and voice, you possess in a degree more persuasive than any woman I ever saw, read, or heard of. But it is that bewitching sort of nameless excellence, that men of nice sensibility alone can be touched with.

Were your husband in England, I would freely give him five hundred pounds (if money could purchase the acquisition) to let you only sit by me two hours in a day, while I wrote my Sentimental Journey. I am sure the work would sell so much the better for it, that I should be reimbursed the sum more than seven times told. I would not give nine pence for the picture of you the Newnhams have got executed. It is the resemblance of a conceited, made-up coquette. Your eyes, and the shape of your face (the latter the most perfect oval I ever saw), which are perfections that must strike the most indifferent judge, because they are equal to any of GOD's works in a similar way, and finer than any I beheld in all my travels, are manifestly injured by the affected leer of the one, and strange appearance of the other; owing to the attitude of the head, which is a proof of the artist's, or your friend's false taste. The ——'s, who verify the character I once gave of teazing, or sticking like pitch, or birdlime, sent a card that they would wait on Mrs. —— on Friday. She sent back, she was engaged. Then to meet at Ranelagh, to-night. She answered, she did not go. She says, if she allows the least footing, she never shall get rid of the acquaintance; which she is resolved to drop at once. She knows them. She knows they are not her friends, nor yours; and the first use they would make of being with her, would be to sacrifice you to her (if they could) a second time. Let her not then; let her not, my dear, be a greater friend to thee, than thou art to thyself. She begs I will reiterate my request to you, that you will not write to them. It will give her, and thy Bramin, inexpressible pain. Be assured, all this is not without reason on her side, I have my reasons too; the first of which is, that I should grieve to excess, if Eliza wanted that fortitude her Yorick has built so high upon. I said I never more would mention the name to thee; and had I not received it, as a kind of charge, from a dear woman that loves you, I should not have broke my word. I will write again to-morrow to thee, thou best and most endearing of girls! A peaceful night to thee. My spirit will be with thee through every watch of it.

Adieu.

LETTER VII

I THINK you could act no otherwise than you did with the young soldier. There was no shutting the door against him, either in politeness or humanity. Thou tellest me he seems susceptible of tender impressions: and that before Miss Light has sailed a fortnight, he will be in love with her. Now I think it a thousand times more likely that he attaches himself to thee, Eliza; because thou art a thousand times more amiable. Five months with Eliza; and in the same room; and an amorous son ot Mars besides! *"It can no be, masser."* The sun, if he could avoid it, would not shine upon a dunghill; but his rays are so pure, Eliza, and celestial, I never heard that they were polluted by it. Just such will thine be, dearest child, in this, and every such situation you will be exposed to, till thou art fixed for life. But thy discretion, thy wisdom, thy honour, the spirit of thy Yorick, and thy own spirit, which is equal to it, will be thy ablest counsellors.

Surely, by this time, something is doing for thy accommodation. But why may not clean washing and rubbing do instead of painting your cabin, as it is to be hung? Paint is so pernicious, both to your nerves and lungs, and will keep you so much longer, too, out of your apartment; where, I hope, you will pass some of your happiest hours.

I fear the best of your shipmates are only genteel by comparison with the contrasted crew, with which thou must behold them. So was—you know who!—from the same fallacy that was put upon the judgment, when— but I will not mortify you. If they are decent, and distant, it is enough; and as much as it is to be expected. If any of them are more, I rejoice; thou wilt want every aid; and 'tis thy due to have them. Be cautious only, my dear, of intimacies. Good hearts are open and fall naturally into them. Heaven inspire thine with forti- tude, in this, and every deadly trial. Best of GOD's works, farewell! Love me, I beseech thee; and remember me for ever!

I am, my Eliza, and will ever be, in the most compre- hensive sense,

Thy friend,
YORICK.

P.S. Probably you will have an opportunity of writing to me by some Dutch or French ship, or from the Cape de Verd Islands. It will reach me somehow.

LETTER VIII

MY DEAR ELIZA!

Oh! I grieve for your cabin. And the fresh paint-ing will be enough to destroy every nerve about thee. Nothing so pernicious as white lead. Take care of yourself, dear girl; and sleep not in it too soon. It will be enough to give you a stroke of an epilepsy. I hope you will have left the ship; and that my Letters may meet, and greet you, as you get out of your post-chaise, at Deal. When you have got them all, put them, my dear, into some order. The first eight or nine are num-bered: but I wrote the rest without that direction to thee; but thou wilt find them out, by the day or hour, which, I hope, I have generally prefixed to them. When they are got together, in chronological order, sew them together under a cover. I trust they will be a perpetual refuge to thee, from time to time; and that thou wilt (when weary of fools, and uninteresting discourse) retire, and converse an hour with them, and me.

I have not had power, or the heart, to aim at enliven-ing any one of them with a single stroke of wit or humour; but they contain something better; and what you will feel more suited to your situation—a longdetail of much advice, truth, and knowledge. I hope, too, you will perceive loose touches of an honest heart in every one of them; which speaks more than the most studied periods; and will give thee more ground of trust and reliance upon Yorick, than all that laboured eloquence could supply. Lean then thy whole weight, Eliza, upon them and upon me. "May poverty, distress, anguish, and shame, be my portion, if ever I give thee reason to repent the knowledge of me!" With this assevera-tion, made in the presence of a just God, I pray to him, that so it may speed with me, as I deal candidly and honourably with thee! I would not mislead thee, Eliza; I would not injure thee, in the opinion of a single individual, for the richest crown the proudest monarch wears.

Remember, that while I have life and power, whatever is mine, you may style, and think, yours. Though sorry should I be, if ever my friendship was put to the test thus, for your own delicacy's sake. Money and counters are of equal use, in my opinion; they both serve to set up with.

I hope you will answer me this letter; but if thou art debarred by the elements, which hurry thee away, I will write one for thee; and knowing it is such a one as thou would'st have written, I will regard it as my Eliza's.

Honour, and happiness, and health, and comforts of every kind, sail along with thee, thou most worthy of girls! I will live for thee, and my Lydia, be rich for the dear children of my heart, gain wisdom, gain fame, and happiness, to share with them, with thee, and her, in my old age. Once for all, adieu. Preserve thy life; steadily pursue the ends we proposed; and let nothing rob thee of those powers Heaven has given thee for thy well-being.

What can I add more, in the agitation of mind I am in, and within five minutes of the last postman's bell, but recommend thee to Heaven, and recommend myself to Heaven with thee, in the same fervent ejaculation, "that we may be happy, and meet again; if not in this world, in the next." Adieu, I am thine, Eliza, affectionately, and everlastingly,

YORICK.

LETTER IX

I wish to God, Eliza, it was possible to postpone the voyage to India for another year. For I am firmly persuaded within my own heart, that thy husband could never limit thee with regard to time.

I fear that Mr. B—— has exaggerated matters. I like not his countenance. It is absolutely killing. Should evil befal thee, what will he not have to answer for? I know not the being that will be deserving of so much pity, or that I shall hate more. He will be an outcast, alien. In which case I will be a father to thy children, my good girl! Therefore take no thought about them.

But, Eliza, if thou art so very ill, still put off all thoughts of returning to India this year. Write to your husband, tell him the truth of your case. If he is the generous, humane man you describe him to be, he cannot but applaud your conduct. I am credibly informed, that his repugnance to your living in England arises only from the dread, which has entered his brain, that thou mayest run him in debt beyond thy appointments, and that he must discharge them. That such a creature should be sacrificed for the paltry consideration of a few hundreds, is too, too hard! Oh! my child! that I could, with propriety, indemnify him for every charge, even to the last mite, that thou hast been of to him! With joy would I give him my whole subsistence—nay, sequester my livings, and trust the treasures Heaven has furnished my head with, for a future subsistence.

You owe much, I allow, to your husband, you owe something to appearances, and the opinion of the world; but, trust me, my dear, you owe much likewise to yourself. Return, therefore, from Deal, if you continue ill. I will prescribe for you, gratis. You are not the first woman, by many, I have done so for, with success. I will send for my wife and daughter, and they shall carry you in pursuit of health, to Montpelier, the wells of Bançois, the Spa, or whither thou wilt. Thou shalt direct them, and make parties of pleasure in what corner of the world fancy points out to thee. We shall fish upon the banks of Arno, and lose ourselves in the sweet labyrinths of its vallies. And then thou should'st warble to us, as I have once or twice heard thee, "I'm lost, I'm lost" —but we should find thee again, my Eliza. Of a similar nature to this, was your physician's prescription: "Use gentle exercise, the pure southern air of France, or milder Naples, with the society of friendly, gentle beings." Sensible man! He certainly entered into your feelings. He knew the fallacy of medicine to a creature whose ILLNESS HAS ARISEN FROM THE AFFLICTION OF HER MIND. Time only, my dear, I fear you must trust to, and have your reliance on; may it give you the health so enthusiastic a votary to the charming goddess deserves!

I honour you, Eliza, for keeping secret some things, which, if explained, had been a panegyric on yourself. There is a dignity in venerable affliction which will not allow it to appeal to the world for pity or redress. Well have you supported that character, my amiable, philosophic friend! And, indeed, I begin to think you have as many virtues as my Uncle Toby's widow. I don't mean to insinuate, hussey, that *my* opinion is no better founded than his was of Mrs. Wadman; nor do I conceive it possible for any *Trim* to convince me it is equally fallacious. I am sure, while I have my reason, it is not. Talking of widows, pray, Eliza, if ever you are such, do not think of giving yourself to some wealthy nabob, because I design to marry you myself. My wife cannot live long—she has sold all the provinces in France already—and I know not the woman I should like so well for her substitute as yourself. 'Tis true, I am ninety-five in constitution, and you but twenty-five; rather too great a disparity this! but what I want in youth, I will make up in wit and good humour. Not Swift so loved his Stella, Scarron his Maintenon, or Waller his Sacharissa, as I will love and sing thee, my wife elect! All those names, eminent as they were, shall give place to thine, Eliza. Tell me, in answer to this, that you approve and honour the proposal, and that you would (like the Spectator's mistress) have more joy in putting on an old man's slipper, than associating with the gay, the voluptuous, and the young. Adieu, my Simplicia!

Yours,

TRISTRAM.

LETTER X

MY DEAR ELIZA!

I have been within the verge of the gates of death. I was ill the last time I wrote to you, and apprehensive of what would be the consequence. My fears were but too well founded; for, in ten minutes after I dispatched my letter, this poor, fine-spun frame of Yorick's gave way, and I broke a vessel in my breast, and could not stop the loss of blood till four this morning. I have filled all thy India handkerchiefs with it. It came, I think, from my heart! I fell asleep through weakness. At six I awoke, with the bosom of my shirt steeped in tears. I dreamt I was sitting under the canopy of Indolence, and that thou camest into the room, with a shaul in thy hand, and told me, my spirit had flown to thee in the Downs, with tidings of my fate; and that you were come to administer what consolation filial affection could bestow, and to receive my parting breath and blessing. With that you folded the shaul about my waist, and, kneeling, supplicated my attention. I awoke; but in what a frame! O my God! "But thou wilt number my tears and put them all into thy bottle." Dear girl! I see thee, thou art for ever present to my fancy,—embracing my feeble knees, and raising thy fine eyes to bid me be of comfort: and when I talk to Lydia, the words of Esau, as uttered by thee, perpetually ring in my ears, "Bless *me* even also, my father!" Blessing attend thee, thou child of my heart!

My bleeding is quite stopped, and I feel the principle of life strong within me; so be not alarmed, Eliza. I know I shall do well. I have eat my breakfast with hunger; and I write to thee with a pleasure arising from that prophetic impression in my imagination, that "all will terminate to our heart's content." Comfort thyself eternally with this persuasion, "that the best of beings (as thou hast sweetly expressed it) could not, by a combination of accidents, produce such a chain of events, merely to be the source of misery to the leading person engaged in them." The observation was very applicable, very good, and very elegantly expressed. I wish my memory did justice to the wording of it. Who taught you the art of writing so sweetly, Eliza? You have absolutely exalted it to a science! When I am in want of ready cash, and ill health will not permit my genius to exert itself, I shall print your letters, as finished essays, "by an unfortunate Indian lady." The style is new; and would almost be a sufficient recommendation for their selling well, without merit—but their sense, natural ease, and spirit, is not to be equalled, I believe, in this section of the globe; nor, I will answer

for it, by any of your country-women in yours. I have
shown your letter to Mrs. B——, and to half the literati
in town. You shall not be angry with me for it, because
I meant to do you honour by it. You cannot imagine
how many admirers your epistolary productions have
gained you, that never viewed your external merits.
I only wonder where thou could'st acquire thy graces,
thy goodness, thy accomplishments—so connected! so
educated! Nature has surely studied to make thee her
peculiar care, for thou art (and not in my eyes alone)
the best and fairest of all her works.

And so this is the last letter thou art to receive from
me; because the Earl of Chatham [1] (I read in the papers)
is got to the Downs; and the wind, I find, is fair. If so,
blessed woman! take my last, last farewell! Cherish the
remembrance of me; think how I esteem, nay how
affectionately I love thee, and what a price I set upon
thee! Adieu, adieu! and with my adieu let me give thee
one straight rule of conduct, that thou hast heard
from my lips in a thousand forms, but I concenter it
in one word,

REVERENCE THYSELF.

Adieu, once more, Eliza! May no anguish of heart
plant a wrinkle upon thy face, till I behold it again!
May no doubt or misgivings disturb the serenity of
thy mind, or awaken a painful thought about thy
children—for they are Yorick's—and Yorick is thy
friend for ever! Adieu, adieu, adieu!

P.S. Remember, that Hope shortens all journies, by
sweetening them, so sing my little stanza on the subject,
with the devotion of an hymn, every morning when

---

[1] By the newspapers of the times it appears that the *Earl of
Chatham* East-Indiaman sailed from Deal, 3 April, 1767.

thou arisest, and thou wilt eat thy breakfast with more comfort for it.

Blessings, rest, and Hygeia go with thee! May'st thou soon return, in peace and affluence, to illume my night! I am, and shall be, the last to deplore thy loss, and will be the first to congratulate and hail thy return.

FARE THEE WELL!

FINIS

EVERYMAN'S LIBRARY: A Selected List

BIOGRAPHY

ESSAYS AND CRITICISM

FICTION

4

HISTORY

LEGENDS AND SAGAS

POETRY AND DRAMA

Pope, Alexander (1688-1744). COLLECTED POEMS. Edited (1956) by *Prof. Bonamy Dobrée*, O.B.E., M.A. 760
Restoration Plays. 604
Rossetti, Dante Gabriel (1828-82). POEMS. 627
Shakespeare, William (1564-1616). A Complete Edition. Cambridge Text. Glossary. 3 vols. Comedies, 153; Histories, Poems and Sonnets, 154; Tragedies, 155
Shelley, Percy Bysshe (1792-1822). POETICAL WORKS. 2 vols. 257-8
Sheridan, Richard Brinsley (1751-1816). COMPLETE PLAYS. 95
Silver Poets of the Sixteenth Century. Edited by *Gerald Bullett*. 985
Spenser, Edmund (1552-99). THE FAERIE QUEENE. Glossary. 2 vols. 443-4. THE SHEPHERD'S CALENDAR, 1579; and OTHER POEMS. 879
Sophocles (496 ?-406 B.C.). DRAMAS. This volume contains the seven surviving dramas. 114
Stevenson, Robert Louis (1850-94). POEMS. A CHILD'S GARDEN OF VERSES, 1885; UNDERWOODS, 1887; SONGS OF TRAVEL, 1896; and BALLADS, 1890. 768
Swinburne, Algernon Charles (1837-1909). POEMS AND PROSE. A selection, edited with an Intro. by *Richard Church*. 961
Synge, J. M. (1871-1909). PLAYS, POEMS AND PROSE. 968
Tchekhov, Anton (1860-1904). PLAYS AND STORIES. 941
Tennyson, Alfred, Lord (1809-92). POEMS. 2 vols. 44, 626
Twenty-four One-Act Plays. 947
Virgil (70-19 B.C.). AENEID. Verse translation by *Michael Oakley*. 161. ECLOGUES AND GEORGICS. Verse translation by *T. F. Royds*. 222
Webster, John (1580 ?-1625 ?), and Ford, John (1586-1639). SELECTED PLAYS. 899
Whitman, Walt (1819-92). LEAVES OF GRASS, 1855-92. New edition (1947). 573
Wilde, Oscar (1854-1900). PLAYS, PROSE WRITINGS AND POEMS. 858
Wordsworth, William (1770-1850). POEMS. Ed. *Philip Wayne*, M.A. 3 vols. 203, 311, 998

REFERENCE

Reader's Guide to Everyman's Library. Compiled by *A. J. Hoppé*. This volume is a new compilation and gives in one alphabetical sequence the names of all the authors, titles and subjects in Everyman's Library. (An Everyman Paperback, 1889). *Many volumes formerly included in Everyman's Library reference section are now included in Everyman's Reference Library and are bound in larger format.*

RELIGION AND PHILOSOPHY

Aristotle (384-322 B.C.). POLITICS, etc. Edited and translated by *John Warrington*. 605
METAPHYSICS. Edited and translated by *John Warrington*. 1000
Bacon, Francis (1561-1626). THE ADVANCEMENT OF LEARNING, 1605. 719
Berkeley, George (1685-1753). A NEW THEORY OF VISION, 1709. 483
Browne, Sir Thomas (1605-82). RELIGIO MEDICI, 1642. 92
Bunyan, John (1628-88). GRACE ABOUNDING, 1666; and THE LIFE AND DEATH OF MR BADMAN, 1658. 815
Burton, Robert (1577-1640). THE ANATOMY OF MELANCHOLY, 1621. 3 vols. 886-8
Chinese Philosophy in Classical Times. Covering the period 1500 B.C.-A.D. 100. 973
Cicero, Marcus Tullius (106-43 B.C.). THE OFFICES (translated by *Thomas Cockman*, 1699); LAELIUS, ON FRIENDSHIP; CATO, ON OLD AGE; AND SELECT LETTERS (translated by *W. Melmoth*, 1753). With Note on Cicero's Character by De Quincey. Introduction by *John Warrington*. 345
Descartes, René (1596-1650). A DISCOURSE ON METHOD, 1637; MEDITATIONS ON THE FIRST PHILOSOPHY, 1641; and PRINCIPLES OF PHILOSOPHY, 1644. Translated by *Prof. J. Veitch*. 570
Ellis, Havelock (1859-1939). SELECTED ESSAYS. Sixteen essays. 930
Epictetus (*b. c.* A.D. 60). MORAL DISCOURSES, etc. Translated by *Elizabeth Carter*. 404
Gore, Charles (1853-1932). THE PHILOSOPHY OF THE GOOD LIFE, 1930. 924
Hindu Scriptures. Edited by *Nicol Macnicol*, M.A., D.LITT., D.D. 944
Hobbes, Thomas (1588-1679). LEVIATHAN, 1651. 691
Hooker, Richard (1554-1600). OF THE LAWS OF ECCLESIASTICAL POLITY, 1597. 2 vols. 201-2
Hume, David (1711-76). A TREATISE OF HUMAN NATURE, 1739. 2 vols. 548-9
James, William (1842-1910). PAPERS ON PHILOSOPHY. 739
Kant, Immanuel (1724-1804). CRITIQUE OF PURE REASON, 1781. Translated by *J. M. D. Meiklejohn*. 909
King Edward VI (1537-53). THE FIRST (1549) AND SECOND (1552) PRAYER BOOKS. 448
Koran, The. Rodwell's Translation, 1861. 380
Law, William (1686-1761). A SERIOUS CALL TO A DEVOUT AND HOLY LIFE, 1728. 91
Leibniz, Gottfried Wilhelm (1646-1716). PHILOSOPHICAL WRITINGS. Selected and translated by *Mary Morris*. 905
Locke, John (1632-1704). TWO TREATISES OF CIVIL GOVERNMENT, 1690. 751
Malthus, Thomas Robert (1766-1834). AN ESSAY ON THE PRINCIPLE OF POPULATION, 1798. 2 vols. 692-3

SCIENCE

TRAVEL AND TOPOGRAPHY